T-BONE

SATAN'S FURY MC-MEMPHIS

L. WILDER

D1501734

T-Bone

Satan's Fury MC-Memphis

Copyright 2020

L. Wilder- All rights reserved.

Be sure to stay connected with L. Wilder-

Sign up for L. Wilder's Newsletter: http://bit.ly/1RGsREL

Social media Links:

Facebook: https://www.facebook.com/AuthorLeslieWilder

Twitter: https://twitter.com/wilder_leslie

Instagram: http://instagram.com/LWilderbooks

Amazon: http://www.amazon.com/L-Wilder/e/B00NDKCCMI/

Bookbub: https://www.bookbub.com/authors/l-wilder

Cover Design: Mayhem Cover Creations
www.facebook.com/MayhemCoverCreations

Editor: Lisa Cullinan

Proofreader- Rose Holub @ReadbyRose

Proofreader: Honey Palomino

Personal Assistant: Natalie Weston PA

Catch up with the entire Satan's Fury MC Series today!
All books are FREE with Kindle Unlimited!

Summer Storm (Satan's Fury MC Novella)

Maverick (Satan's Fury MC #1)

Stitch (Satan's Fury MC #2)

Cotton (Satan's Fury MC #3)

Clutch (Satan's Fury MC #4)

Smokey (Satan's Fury MC #5)

Big (Satan's Fury #6)

Two Bit (Satan's Fury #7)

Diesel (Satan's Fury #8)

Blaze (Satan's Fury MC- Memphis Book 1)

Shadow (Satan's Fury MC- Memphis Book 2)

Riggs (Satan's Fury MC- Memphis Book 3)

Murphy (Satan's Fury MC- Memphis Book 4)

Gunner (Satan's Fury MC- Memphis Book 5)

Gus (Satan's Fury MC- Memphis Book 6)

Rider (Satan's Fury MC- Memphis Book 7)

Prospect (Satan's Fury MC-Memphis Book 8)

Ties that Bind (Ruthless Sinners MC)

Day Three (What Bad Boys Do Book 1)

Damaged Goods- (The Redemption Series Book 1- Nitro)

Max's Redemption (The Redemption Series Book 2- Max)

Inferno (Devil Chasers #1)

Smolder (Devil Chaser #2)

Ignite (Devil Chasers #3)

Consumed (Devil Chasers #4)

Combust (Devil Chasers #5)

My Temptation (The Happy Endings Collection #1)

Bring the Heat (The Happy Endings Collection #2)

His Promise (The Happy Endings Collection #3)

❀ Created with Vellum

PROLOGUE

NOT EVERYONE FINDS THAT ONE *THING* THAT DRIVES THEM to get up in the morning or makes their life worth living, but I'd been one of the lucky ones. I'd found that and more when I became a brother of Satan's Fury. I'd only been a member of the Washington chapter for a couple of months when my president, Saul, came to me with the opportunity to help Gus, a fellow brother, start up a new charter in Memphis, Tennessee. I was just a kid and didn't have a clue about much of anything, let alone how to get a club off the ground, but even back then, I knew there was something extraordinary about my future president. As our sergeant-at-arms, Gus had shown that he was a natural leader, so after agreeing to tag along, I'd done everything I could to help him and my other brothers make Satan's Fury the club it is today.

I'd never regretted that choice—not once. In fact, I believe it was the best decision I'd ever made. For the past twenty-five years, I'd had everything a man could want: money, women, adventure, and peril, all while having my brothers at my side. There was just one thing I was missing—an ol' lady. Sure, I'd had plenty of women over the years. Hell, there's been more than I could count, but try as I might, none of them lasted.

I wasn't giving up, though. I knew that sooner or later, the right woman would come along. I just never dreamed that woman would be Hyde's sister and that she'd be broken in ways I couldn't imagine.

1

T-BONE

THE BROTHERS OF FURY KNEW HOW TO THROW A HELL OF A party. It didn't matter what we were celebrating; there was always plenty of booze, loud music, and hot women. However, nothing compared to the parties when a prospect patched into the club. Those were always the best—not just for our new brother, but for all the club members. For us, it meant Satan's Fury was growing, prospering the way Gus and the rest of us had always hoped it would, and for a prospect, it meant all his hard work had finally paid off.

Being a prospect was never easy. It was a year or more of busting his ass and doing whatever it took—from a late-night rescue to a clean up after a club party—just to prove himself worthy of wearing the club's colors on his back. It wasn't for anyone who lacked courage, especially when prospecting for Satan's Fury, but just as Gus knew he would, Hyde had proven time and time again that he could handle whatever we threw his way.

I'll admit, at first I had my doubts that he'd actually

pull it off. The kid had been all kinds of green when he first showed up at the clubhouse's doorstep. Even though his uncle, Viper, was the president of the Ruthless Sinners in Nashville, he didn't know much about what went into prospecting or working in a garage, but I had to give it to him, he was determined. Hyde never once gave up and even managed to complete his final task as a prospect without so much as a snag.

There was no doubt that he'd get the job done, so we called everyone to the clubhouse to celebrate his success. I was sitting at the bar with Blaze and Riggs, two of my fellow brothers, and we all watched in silence as Gus presented him with his Satan's Fury cut. As Hyde slipped it on, a proud smile crossed his face. Blaze looked over to me and said, "You remember the day you were patched in?"

"Hell, yeah. Might've been twenty-five years ago, but I remember it like it was yesterday. You?"

"The same. No better feeling than putting on that cut for the first time."

"No doubt."

Blaze glanced over at Hyde. "I would've given anything to see his face when he walked into his garage and found his bike like that."

"Had to be one hell of a surprise." Riggs snickered. "Don't know what I'd think if I found my Harley completely disassembled like that."

"Still don't know how they didn't hear us, especially with Duchess around."

Hyde's dog, Duchess, was a Rottweiler-Great Dane mix that his ol' lady, Landry, accidentally hit with her car on the way home from work. He and Landry had actually met when Hyde stopped to help her get the dog to the vet. Even though she was normally a well-behaved, easy-going dog, I'd worried about her barking while we were working on Hyde's bike, so I brought along some preventative measures. I turned to Blaze and smiled. "Like all women, she just needed the right distraction."

"Yeah." Blaze chuckled. "Guess you were right about bringing those rib bones along."

"What can I say?" I shrugged. "I know how to please the ladies."

"You know how to please a mutt. Not sure I'd say the same for the rest of the female population," Blaze poked. "Otherwise, you wouldn't be sitting here without an ol' lady by your side."

"Fuck you, man." I glanced around the room at the crowd. The place was fucking packed with all the brothers and their women. Even Hyde's uncle, Viper, and several of his Ruthless Sinners' brothers were there to join the celebration. "I can get a chick anytime I want."

"Oh, yeah?" Blaze cocked his eyebrow with skepticism. "Prove it."

"All right then, I will, and when I do, I won't be hooking up with some skank twat that's been passed around more than a bottle of fucking Crown. I'm gonna find me a real classy chick who knows a good man when she sees him." He didn't reply. Instead, he just sat there staring at me with that fucking cocked eyebrow. "What?"

"Just wondering what the fuck you're waiting for." He motioned his hand out to the crowd. "You know what they say ... there's no time like the present."

I knew he was just fucking around, but he'd laid down a challenge and there was no way I could pass it up. I picked up my beer and quickly finished it off before I stood up and said, "Fine, I'll show your ass what's what."

"Mm-hmm, I'm sure you will."

Ignoring his last jab, I started walking towards the thick of people. I hadn't gotten far when I noticed Hyde talking to his mom and younger sister, Alyssa. They were both busy congratulating him on getting his cut when I noticed Alyssa looking in my direction. As soon as Hyde noticed that she was looking at me, a menacing look crossed his face. His reaction gave me a thought, and I found myself smiling as I continued walking towards them. Hyde was a good guy, too good at times, and that made it way too easy to fuck with him. I figured there was no better way than to let him believe I was making a play for his sister.

I'd just made my way over to them when I overheard Clay growling at Alyssa, "That's not going to happen."

Throwing his words back at him, I asked, "What's 'not gonna happen'?"

There was something about the surprised look on my brother's face that made me wonder if he'd been talking about me when he said those words to his sister. Feeling the tension radiating off her brother, Alyssa's eyes dropped to the floor. In almost a whisper, she replied, "Nothing. Clay is just being Clay."

Hyde gave her a disapproving look. "Oh, really?"

I could tell by his expression that my suspicions were correct. I knew he'd never admit it, but there was no doubt he'd been talking about me. Alyssa reminded me of a young Rachel McAdams with her delicious curves and long blonde hair. She had dark soulful eyes that made me wonder what secrets she was hiding beneath them. It didn't matter. It was obvious just by looking at her, the girl was out of my league. She was young and beautiful with the world at her fingertips, and I found it doubtful that she'd give me—a bald-headed biker, more than twice her age and three times her size—a second thought. That was fine with me. I had no intention of actually making a play for her, but Hyde didn't know that. "Why don't you let me get you a drink, and you can tell me all about it?"

Her eyes skirted over to me, and with a bashful smile, she simply answered, "Okay."

She gave Hyde a quick shrug, then followed me back over to the bar. We sat down on two empty stools at the end of the counter, and I motioned over to Jasmine, the bartender for the night, to grab us both a couple of beers. After she brought them over, I offered one to Alyssa and asked, "You having a good time?"

"I am ... much better than I expected."

"You weren't expecting to have a good time?"

"Not really." Concern crossed her face as she said, "Don't get me wrong. I'm glad Clay is happy and I wanted to be here for him, but parties really aren't my thing."

"Oh, really? Why's that?"

Alyssa took a long drink of her beer before answering, "I just have my reasons."

"Maybe you can share those reasons with me someday."

"Maybe." A slight smile slowly crept over her face as

7

she looked at me for a moment, then quickly glanced over her shoulder at a couple of the brothers playing pool. "You been a member for long?"

"Yeah, you could say that."

The tiny freckles across her nose crinkled as she studied her brother. After several moments, she turned her attention back to me. "You like it here?"

"I wouldn't be here if I didn't," I said, then continued. "Becoming a brother was the best decision I ever made, and if I had to guess, I'd bet your brother would say the same."

"I think you're right. I can't remember the last time I'd seen him look so happy."

"He's found his place. Not many out there can say that." Alyssa's dark eyes met mine when I asked, "What about you?"

"I'm working on it." She gave me a small shrug. "I'm actually moving here in a couple of weeks."

"Here ... as in *Memphis*?"

"Yeah. I applied for a culinary internship at Chez Philippe at the Peabody. I never dreamed that they'd actually consider taking me on, but I was accepted into their program."

"Culinary? You a chef or something?"

"I'm aspiring to be—someday anyway." I could hear the hope in her voice as she added, "If this internship goes well, they might offer me a permanent position."

"That's awesome. I'm sure you'll do great."

"I hope so. I've dreamed of being a chef since I was a little kid." Her face lit up as she went on, "Growing up, I was always making up all these wild concoctions for Mom and Clay to try."

"That must have been awesome. I'm sure they loved seeing what you'd come up with."

"I don't know about that. Some of them were pretty awful, but others weren't so bad."

"Maybe once you're here and settled, you could let me try out one of your concoctions. I could be your test critic for new recipes or something."

"I'd like that." She let out a heavy sigh. "I've just got to get moved first. I'm supposed to start working in two weeks, and I haven't even found a place yet."

"What kind of place are you looking for?"

"I'm not really picky." She shrugged. "Maybe an apartment or a small house that's in a safe neighborhood."

"I might be able to help you out with that."

"Really?"

"Yeah. I'll make a few calls and see what I can come up with."

"That would be incredible. Thank you so much."

"No problem."

We continued on with our small talk, and I was surprised that Alyssa was so easy to get along with. It felt like we were old friends, sharing stories about this and that, and I genuinely enjoyed getting to know her better. That was the very reason why I suggested that we go outside and continue our conversation without having to shout over the loud music. When she agreed, I grabbed us another round of drinks, and then she followed me out to one of the picnic tables next to the bonfire.

We'd been talking for a while when a smile crossed Alyssa's face. "So, tell me, what's your story, T-Bone?"

"My story?" I scoffed. "I don't know. Not much to say ... Besides, I doubt you'd be interested."

"I'm sure there's plenty." When Alyssa smiled, it got me right in the gut. Her full pink lips curled into a bashful smile as she looked me right in the eye. "Anyway, I wouldn't have asked if I wasn't interested in hearing it."

"In hopes of keeping you from dozing off, I'll give ya the basics." I took a drink of my beer as I settled into my seat. "I was raised in Washington with my folks and younger brother. Pretty simple life growing up, but it was a good one. Had two parents who did what they could to give my brother and me a roof over our heads and food on the table. When I turned eighteen, I ventured out to make a life of my own, and that's when I met Saul and some of the other brothers of Satan's Fury."

I went on to explain how I ended up prospecting for the Washington chapter only to end up coming to Memphis with Gus to set up the club here. I didn't go into any great detail. Just gave her enough to understand that a lot of work went into getting things the way they are today. When I was done, she took a moment to mull over everything, then said, "You never mentioned a girlfriend or a wife."

"That's because I don't have one." I wasn't sure if she was just curious about my relationship status or because she was actually interested in me. As I sat there gazing at her, I had no doubt that I could fall head-over-fucking-heels for her. Hell, any man would. Alyssa was smart, beautiful, and easy to talk to, but there were simply too many variables that stood in our way. Not only was she Hyde's sister, she was simply too young. Even so, I was enjoying my time with her and wasn't ready for it to end. I smiled at her and said, "Don't get me wrong, there've been plenty of women in my life, but none who really made a lasting impression."

"I see."

"What about you? You got a boyfriend?"

Her brows furrowed as she shook her head. "No, not since high school, and even then, I'm not sure I'd call him a boyfriend."

"Seriously? I figured a beauty like you would have guys crawling all over ya."

"It's not that there aren't guys who are interested. I've just ..." Alyssa's expression quickly grew troubled as her voice trailed off, and I could tell there was something big weighing on her mind. I gave her some time, hoping she'd bring it to light, but after several moments of silence, she simply said, "I really haven't had the time to invest in a relationship."

"I understand." I knew there was more to the story but decided not to push. Perhaps, in time, she'd realize I was someone she could trust. "Maybe that'll all change when you get moved and start your new job."

"Maybe?"

We were both so engrossed in our conversation that neither of us noticed Hyde had walked up. "Hey ... Is everything all right?"

"Yes, why wouldn't it be?" Alyssa asked.

"You tell me," Hyde scolded. "You're the one who disappeared on me."

"What's the big deal? We were just out here taking a break for a minute!"

"A minute?" Clay argued. "You two have been out here for hours."

Alyssa sighed in frustration. "This is your party, Clay. You should be celebrating, not keeping tabs on my every move."

"Just looking out for you, Lyssa."

"And I appreciate it, but I'm not sixteen anymore. I can take care of myself."

"Not sure I agree." Just as she was about to rear back at him, Hyde announced, "Mom's wiped. I think she's ready to call it a night."

"Okay, I'll take her back to the hotel."

"No." Hyde glanced down at the beer in her hand and said, "You've been drinking. I'll get one of the prospects to drive you."

"Fine." Alyssa stood, then looked over to me. "It was really nice meeting you. I hope we can do this again sometime."

"Definitely."

With that, she turned and followed Hyde back into the clubhouse. Moments later, she and her mother were on their way back to the hotel. I considered going back inside to join the party but decided against it. The only person I was interested in spending time with was no longer there. I walked out to the parking lot, got on my bike, and as I started heading towards my place, I thought back to my conversation with Alyssa.

Most women I'd met were only interested in the whole bad-boy biker bullshit and cared very little about getting to know me as a man, but it wasn't like that with Alyssa. I felt no pressure to try and impress her, yet she seemed interested in everything I had to say. That wasn't something I was accustomed to, and I liked it. I liked it a lot. I had to keep myself focused on the fact that the chick was too young, too beautiful and innocent, for a man like me. Sadly, that would be something easier said than done.

2

ALYSSA

WHEN MY UNCLE VIPER HAD COME TO THE HOUSE, TELLING us about Clay earning his Satan's Fury patch and the upcoming celebration at their clubhouse, it left me more than a little apprehensive. I wasn't one to do the whole party thing, especially after what'd happened on Homecoming night.

I was just sixteen at the time—a sophomore with a with a head full of fairytales and schoolgirl dreams. When Lucas Brant, the star football player and one of the most popular guys at school, had asked me to the Homecoming dance, I couldn't have been more excited. I'd thought I found my prince charming, but instead, I found a monster who stole my innocence. I blamed myself for what happened. I was careless and so caught up in the moment that I hadn't realized I'd put myself in a precarious situation. By the time I'd figured it out, it was too late. The damage had been done.

I should've gone to the police and told them what Lucas Brant had done to me but decided against it. I'd convinced myself that if the residents of my small town ever found out that the "star quarterback" had raped me, they would've turned against me and blamed me for tempting him ... or called me crazy for not wanting to be with him in the first place. So I kept my terrifying ordeal a secret—only sharing the details with my brother.

Clay hadn't understood why I wouldn't tell anyone else about what happened and ended up taking matters into his own hands. He'd gone to the party, found Lucas and then beat the hell out of him. I'd like to say that it helped knowing that Lucas paid some small penance for his crime, but it didn't. Every time I saw his stupid face, I'd find myself thinking about that night—the way he'd held me down and how I fought him as he inched my dress up over my thighs—but most of all, it was what he'd said to me. I'd just gotten off the bed and was fixing my clothes when he came over to me and shoved his hand between my legs, gripping me tightly as he taunted, *"Damn fine pussy you got there, Lyssa girl. I gotta tell ya, popping that fucking cherry of yours was the icing on the cake. Hell, I can't wait to come back for seconds. If you're lucky, I might even come back for thirds."*

And just like that, all the feelings of fear and helplessness would come rushing back, making it difficult to breathe. I'd hoped that over time it would get better, and in some ways it did, but I was never able to truly put that night behind me. I couldn't let myself trust anyone, so I didn't have a lot of friends—just my roommate, Nicole, and Hannah, my best friend from high school. I never really dated, at least not of my own free will. Nicole and Hannah were constantly trying to fix me up with guys they knew, but it didn't take long for them to lose interest, especially when they realized I wasn't going to jump into bed with them. The same held true for guys I'd met at parties. I would cringe at their touch, and they'd quickly figure out that I wasn't an easy lay and move on to their next target. It wasn't their fault. It was me who was damaged. I was the one who was unable to make a personal connection in fear of being hurt again.

I decided I was done letting Lucas Brant take from me. I wanted a normal life, and even though it meant facing all my fears head on, I was going to have it. Determined to take life by the horns, I couldn't think of a better way to do that than to go to a party at an MC clubhouse. Besides, the party was for Clay, and after all he'd done for me, I owed it to him to be there.

Mom and I rode down to Memphis with Viper and a few of his brothers. Viper was my father's brother, and after my dad died, he'd taken it upon himself to keep an eye on us, doing whatever he could to keep our family going. It was actually his idea for Clay to go to Memphis to prospect for Satan's Fury, and there was no missing the proud look on his face as we drove through the main gates of their clubhouse. As he glanced around at all the cars and motorcycles, he smiled and said, "Looks like one hell of a turnout."

"I didn't realize that there'd be so many people here."

While Viper never found out about what'd happened to me, he could tell from the tone of my voice that I was feeling somewhat uneasy by the large crowd. He glanced over his shoulder and looked me in the eye as he tried to reassure me. "These are good guys, Lyssa. I can *almost* guarantee that you'll have a good time, and if not, I'll get one of the boys to take you over to the hotel."

"Okay. Thanks, Viper."

Mom gave me a little pat on the leg and said, "It's going to mean a lot to Clay that we're here."

"I know. I'm really looking forward to seeing him."

"Me too. It's been so long." Her expression grew solemn when she added, "Now that you've gotten that internship at Chez Philippe, I'll have both of my kids living in Memphis. I don't know what I'll do with the two of you gone."

"You can come visit anytime you want, and you know, you could move down here with us. There's nothing keeping you in Nashville."

"True, but I don't want to be one of those mothers who isn't able to let go and smothers her kids."

"You would never smother us, Mom."

Mischief crossed her face as she asked, "So, you'd be okay with me moving in with you?"

"Umm ... I don't know if I'd go that far"—I giggled —"but it would be nice to have you close by."

"Well, it's definitely something to think about it."

Our conversation had distracted me momentarily, but as soon as we'd parked and started inside the clubhouse, my anxiety quickly returned. I knew the second I stepped through the door this wasn't going to be like any party I'd ever been to before.

The bar was packed full of burly bikers and scantily dressed women, drinking and talking as the loud music roared in the background. The room was filled with tables and chairs along with several pool tables and a long wooden counter with stools in the side corner. Most of the seats were already taken, but after stopping several times to speak to some of the men he knew, Viper managed to find a few empty spots for us to sit. As soon as we were settled, the girl behind the bar took our drink order, then brought them over several minutes later. I was looking around, taking in my surroundings, when Mom leaned over to Viper and said, "Everyone seems so friendly. They're nicer than I expected."

"I doubt Fury's members would consider themselves nice." He chuckled. "But they are good men. I wouldn't have sent our boy down here if they weren't."

"You're right. I guess I'm just a little surprised. I would've thought they'd be more ferocious or something, especially with a name like Satan's Fury."

"No different than the Sinners. We know how to play nice when we need to," Viper cocked his eyebrow as he continued, "but that doesn't mean we take any shit. You fuck with us, you pay the price."

"Someone would have to be pretty crazy to mess with you and your boys."

"You're right about that." Viper took a sip of his beer, then added, "Clay's going to have a good life here with these boys. You'll see."

Before she could respond, the front door opened and Clay appeared in the doorway. I'd never seen my brother look more proud as his brothers surrounding him, congratulating him with hugs and pats on the shoulder. We all watched in awe as Gus, the large and very intimi-dating looking president of Fury, presented him with a leather vest that had been embroidered with the Satan's

Fury logo. My heart melted as I watched Clay put on that vest like it was his most prized possession. My brother looked so utterly happy that it brought tears to my eyes to watch his new brothers share the moment with him. We gave him a few minutes to speak with everyone. When his brothers started to disperse, Landry approached him and gave him a big hug. After they talked for a few minutes, Viper motioned over to me that it was time for us to head over to him. When Clay saw Mom and me walking towards him with Viper, his eyes immediately lit up. "You came."

"Of course, we did," Mom answered. "We wouldn't miss it for the world."

Viper crossed his arms as he looked at Clay and asked, "Well, you gonna say it?"

"Say what?" Clay questioned with a smirk.

"You know damn well what." Viper narrowed his eyes. "Come on. You know I'm not gonna let it go until you say it."

"Fine." Clay chuckled as he replied, "You were right."

"Damn right," Viper boasted. "Always am."

"I don't know about that," my mother scoffed before turning her attention to Clay. A bright smile crossed her face. "You look good, Clay. I wish your father was here. He would've been so proud."

I could tell by her tone that she was about to tear up, so I slipped my arm around her, giving her a tight squeeze. "He is here, Mom. There's no way he'd miss this."

"She's right. He's definitely here." Clay reached over and hugged us both. "Damn, it's good to see you."

Landry slipped up beside him and smiled. "Hey, honey. Congratulations. That cut looks great on you."

Clay grabbed her around the waist, pulling her towards him, then planted a kiss on her lips. "Thanks, babe."

We were all standing in a circle, catching up, when one of his brothers caught my attention. I'm not sure exactly what it was about him, but there was something about the burly, bald-headed biker covered in tattoos that had me intrigued—which surprised the hell out of me. Normally, a man of his size and intimidating physique would completely terrify me, and I'd do whatever it took to steer clear. Unsettled by my interest in him, I quickly turned my attention back to my conversation with my mother, Landry, and Clay. I tried to keep my focus on what they were saying, but after only a few seconds, I found myself glancing over my shoulder for another peek at the handsome biker. He was tall and broad shouldered with dark brown eyes, and there was a kindness to his smile that one wouldn't expect from such a fierce-looking man. I watched as he started laughing at something one of his brothers said, and a strange warmth rushed through me. I dug deep and gathered all the courage I could muster, then turned to Clay and asked, "Who's he?"

Typical Clay, I thought, when he searched around the room and asked way too loudly, "Who?"

"Him." Trying not to draw any more attention to the situation, I motioned my head to the back of the room. "The bald guy in the corner?"

When he realized who I was talking about, he quickly

looked back at me with a stunned expression. "You gotta be fucking kidding me."

"What?" Clay had always been protective of me, even more so after what had happened with Lucas, and while it was sweet of him to look out for me, it was time he learned that I could take care of myself. Besides, if I could gather the nerve to talk to a big, tough biker, then I could do anything. I knew my brother would never understand, and as I stood there studying his horrified expression, I couldn't stop myself from teasing him a little. With a mischievous grin, I shrugged innocently and goaded, "He's hot—"

"Lyssa, no," he warned.

"Well, I happen to think he—"

"Nope! Not gonna happen, Lyssa."

Landry and I were so caught up in giving Clay a hard time, I hadn't noticed that the man had come up behind us until I heard him ask, "What's 'not gonna happen'?"

When I glanced up and saw the smirk on his face, I couldn't help but smile. As he stood there towering over me, I didn't feel threatened by him—not in the least. Instead, I found a warmth in his eyes that I didn't expect. "Nothing. Clay is just being Clay."

"Oh, really?"

It was clear from Clay's expression that he wasn't pleased I'd blown off his warning, and his disapproving expression only grew more intense when the man smiled down at me and asked, "Why don't you let me get you a drink, and you can tell me all about it?"

"Okay."

Before Clay had a chance to talk me out of going with

him, I gave my overprotective brother a quick wave, then followed the stranger back to the bar. After I sat down next to him, he quickly introduced himself and ordered us both a drink. As I sat there waiting on the bartender, I was feeling quite proud of myself. I was actually sitting next to a man who belonged to one of the most notorious MCs in the South, and I wasn't freaking out. Instead, I did my best to remain cool, calm, and collected. To my surprise, it was much easier than I thought. Then again, T-Bone made it easy. The entire time we talked, he didn't put on any airs and try to impress me. He simply treated me as though I were an old friend, and we were just taking some time to catch up.

I'd just started telling him about my upcoming move to Memphis when he leaned towards me and said, "The music is a little loud in here. You want to continue this outside?"

I couldn't remember a time when I'd enjoyed a man's company so much and didn't hesitate when I answered, "Sure."

Once we'd found a spot at one of the picnic tables, T-Bone looked over to me and asked, "Is it just me, or is this your first time being at a clubhouse party?"

"What makes you say that?"

"I don't know. Just a hunch."

"Well, your hunch is right. It's my first time."

Looking surprised, he asked, "You never went to a Sinners' party?"

"No, Viper wasn't too keen on the idea. Clay went to a couple, and it always seemed like he'd had a good time." I shrugged. "I guess I missed out on all the fun."

"So, now that you've finally made it to a club party, what do you think of it?"

"It's not exactly what I expected."

"What exactly were you expecting?"

"Honestly ... I figured it would be a little rowdier." I should've thought before I spoke, especially considering that T-Bone was one of the very guys I was talking about, but for some reason, I didn't feel the need to hold back. "Guys cussin', fightin', and chuggin' back beers ... You know, basically a frat party with big and scary badass bikers who'd just as soon kill you than buy you a beer."

T-Bone didn't immediately respond. Instead, he just sat there staring at me with a blank expression, making me worried that I'd said too much, but then his lips slowly curled into a smile. When he started to roar in laughter, I did right along with him. "Scary badass bikers, huh?"

"Well, you all are pretty badass, but I've come to see that you all aren't as scary as I thought you'd be, especially you." My eyes skirted to the ground as I admitted, "When I first saw you, I was a little intimidated, especially when you asked me to have a drink, but after talking to you, I see that I had nothing to worry about."

"Well, I'm glad you took a chance."

"Me too."

He looked over to me, and suddenly an awkward silence settled between us. I wasn't sure what he had on his mind, but it was clear from his expression that he was deep in thought. After several moments, he finally said, "You mentioned earlier that you got that culinary internship at the Peabody, so that's gotta mean you graduated from college or something, right?"

"I did."

"So, you're what ... twenty-three ... twenty-four?"

"No." I chuckled as I told him, "The culinary program was just two years, so I'm twenty-one. I'll be twenty-two next month."

"Damn. Never would've guessed you were that young."

"Oh, really? Why's that?"

"It's hard to say." He studied me for a moment before he continued, "You know that saying, 'wise beyond your years'?" I nodded. "Well, it's partly that. You seem to have a good head on your shoulders, knowin' where you've been and where you wanna go, but there's more to it than that."

"How so?"

"Well, if I didn't know better, I'd say you'd been dealt a hard hand, a really hard hand, but you haven't let it beat ya. Instead, you're doing what you gotta do to play that hand as best you can."

"You've known me all of what ... an hour or so, and you've managed to come up with all that?"

"What can I say?" A smile crossed his face as he leaned towards me. "You make a hell of a first impression."

I giggled, then said, "I'm not sure if that's a compliment or not."

"It's definitely a compliment. Nothing better than a girl who's willing to fight for what she wants."

"Well, thank you. I'm glad you think so."

My time with T-Bone came to an abrupt end when Clay came outside to tell me that Mom was ready to go to the hotel. I was certain that it was just an excuse to get me away from his brother, but I knew better than to argue. Besides, I had a feeling I'd be seeing T-Bone again. I just didn't realize that it would be sooner than later. The next afternoon, Viper was driving us all back to Nashville when I got a text message from a number I didn't recognize. I opened it up, and as soon as I read it, a big smile swept across my face.

T-Bone:

I think I've found you a place to live.

Me:

Seriously? That was fast.

T-Bone:

Nothing to it. Just made a few calls. I've actually got a couple for you to check out.

Me:

That's awesome. When can I see them?

T-Bone:

That's up to you. When will you be back in town?

. . .

ME:

I was actually planning to come down on Tuesday. Would that work?

T-Bone:

Absolutely. I'll see you then.

3

T-BONE

"Why do you need her number?" Hyde asked, sounding troubled by the thought.

"Aww, damn." Blaze chuckled as he looked across the kitchen table and said, "T-Bone's got a thing for Hyde's baby sister."

"You might be moving a little fast there, brother," Riggs warned. "You just met the girl last night."

I watched as Hyde's back stiffened and his jaw locked. It was then that I knew without a doubt that Hyde wasn't exactly keen on the idea of me hooking up with his sister. I couldn't blame him. I already knew all the reasons why it wouldn't be a good idea myself. I'd admit, it stung a little. I liked Alyssa, and if the situation was different, I might've taken a chance with her—even if I was too old and had a terrible track record with women. Who knows? Maybe things would've worked out. Regardless, I wasn't going to take that chance—not with so much laying on the line. I could've eased Hyde's mind, let him and the rest of the guys know that I had no intention of pursuing her, but I decided to give my new brother a little hell. "What can I say? There's no speed limit on the highway to love."

As soon as the words left my mouth, everyone at the table started laughing—everyone except Hyde. When the roar of laughter started to die down, Hyde turned to me and growled, "You didn't answer my question."

"Come on, Hyde. You're a smart guy. If you had to guess, why do you think I'd want her number?" A smirk crossed my face when I added, "I'm sure you can figure this one out."

"Fuck you, smartass." He crossed his arms and glared at me. "You know damn well that's not what I was asking."

I could've fucked with him even more, really made him think I was going to make a play for his sister, but I figured he'd had enough. "Brother, you've got nothing to worry about when it comes to your sister and me. I'm not going to make a play for her. Don't get me wrong, she's fucking hot and any guy would be lucky to have her, but I know better than to go down that road."

"Um-hmm. So, what's with wanting her number?"

"She mentioned last night that she was looking for a place here, so I made a few calls."

"And?"

"I think I might've found her a couple in Midtown that she might wanna check out."

"Really?" he asked with surprise. "That's awesome, brother. Thanks."

"Just trying to do what I can to help out." I waited a

moment, then asked, "So, are you gonna to give me her number or what?"

"Yeah, hold on." He reached into his pocket for his phone, and after he texted me the number, he said, "She's already on her way back to Nashville, but I think she's planning on coming back early next week to look around and see if she can find something."

"Good deal. I'll message her and let her know I have a few places to check out while she's here."

"Thanks again, brother." Hyde thought for a moment, then said, "Hey ... Make sure Lyssa picks something nice. One that's safe and she can be proud of. I don't care what it costs. I'll pay whatever she can't."

"You got it."

After we'd finished lunch, I messaged Alyssa about the rentals I'd found, then followed Blaze and Murphy over to the garage. We usually didn't go in to work on the weekends, but Blaze hoped it would give us the time we needed to finish the 1958 Chevy NAPCO 4x4 we'd been working on. It was in pretty rough shape when it arrived, covered in rust with torn, worn-out seats and an engine that was non-existent. We'd been at it for over a week, and there was still a shit-ton of stuff that needed to be completed by the end of the week. Blaze was in charge of running things at the garage, managing the orders on remodels and all the various repairs, and he took his job seriously. We all did. With so many different orders coming in and out, it provided us with the means to launder the money we'd made from gun trafficking without any unwanted suspicion. Considering how much money we were moving, it was important for us to maintain our reputation as being the best restoration garage in the area.

When we pulled up, I wasn't surprised to see that Rider and Darcy were already there. Darcy was our custom painter, and damn, the chick was a real go-getter —blowing us away with each and every job she completed. I had no doubt the same would hold true for the Chevy. As soon as we were inside, I went over and started sandblasting the passenger side door while Murphy and Blaze worked with Rider to get the engine up and going. I hadn't been working long when Blaze walked over to me with a curious expression. "So, Big T, what's really up with you and the little sister?"

"Already told ya. Just trying to help her out."

"Mm-hmm. I saw you two together last night." He crossed his arms and leaned back against the frame of the truck. "You can't tell me you weren't interested."

"Didn't say I wasn't." I turned to look at him. "I like her ... Hell, I like her way more than I should, but come on, brother, we both know it could never work."

"Never say never." Blaze chuckled. "Hyde might not be thrilled about the idea, but he knows you're a good man. Eventually, he'd come around."

"Maybe, but I've done complicated before. It never once worked out in my favor."

"Who knows? This chick might just surprise you."

"Maybe, but ..." I shrugged. "Best to keep things simple. I'll show her around, help her find a place, and leave it at that."

"Well, if you're sure that's the way you wanna play it, I won't try and talk you out of it." He shook his head as he started back towards his office. "But just so you know, I think you're fucking up."

As I went back to work, I thought about what Blaze had said. He might've been right. I might've been fucking up by not pursuing Alyssa, but my gut told me differently. Besides, there was too much shit going on with the club for me to be distracted with a girl I could never have. With a newfound resolve, I turned my attention back to my work and kept that focus over the next few days. I was doing pretty good until the day Alyssa came back to town to look at apartments. I was just wrapping up an engine install when she texted that she was waiting for me over at Hyde's place. I quickly finished up and drove over to meet up with her.

The second I knocked on the door Duchess started barking, and I could hear Landry trying to wrangle her in. Once the dog was settled, she opened the door with a big smile. "Hey, T-Bone. How's it going?"

"I can't complain." As I stepped inside, I asked, "What about you?"

"I'm great. I was just about to head into the office. I've got a new case to investigate." Landry worked with child services, and living in Memphis, she had a hell of a job on her hands. "But I wanted to make sure you and Lyssa were all set before I left."

"Well, I'm here and ready whenever she is." Just as the words left my mouth, Alyssa appeared in the entryway with a bright smile. The sight of her nearly took my breath away. I'd gone there with the mindset that I was just helping out a friend, but seeing her in that little denim miniskirt and fitted yellow t-shirt had me

31

wondering if I'd been wrong in thinking I could keep things simple. Knowing I had no other choice, I inhaled a deep breath, then smiled and said, "Hey there, freckles."

"Hey, T-Bone." I didn't miss the excitement in her voice when she said, "I'm really looking forward to today. I can't wait to see what you've found."

"Well, let's get to it then."

"Great."

She grabbed her purse and followed me out to my truck. Once we were both settled inside, I started towards our first destination. "I've got four places for you to check out. I just need to know which one you want to see first— the one I think will be your favorite, or the one I think will be your least favorite?"

"Hmm." Her brows furrowed as she thought for a moment. "Let's go with the one you think I'll like least."

"You got it."

We headed towards downtown, and I couldn't help but notice the way Alyssa was fidgeting with the strap of her purse. She was nervous—really fucking nervous. I wanted to set her mind at ease, let her know she didn't have anything to be nervous about, but I had no idea how to do that. Hoping to put an end to the awkwardness that was settling between us, I turned to her and asked, "Have you ever been downtown to the Pyramid?"

"No, but I've heard the Bass Pro Shop they just put in is incredible."

"It is. You'll have to check it out sometime."

She glanced over to look at me and said, "Maybe you could take me sometime ... You know, after I get moved and everything."

"Yeah, I could definitely do that." If I hadn't known better, I might've thought she was actually asking me out, but I let that thought quickly skirt away as I pulled into the parking lot of our first destination. Once we were parked in front of the apartment complex, I motioned my hand towards the building and said, "This is it."

"It's incredible!" She leaned forward to get a better look at the large pond that was centered in the middle of the various apartments. I had to admit, the place did look pretty good, especially with all the crepe myrtles in full bloom and the colorful flowers they'd planted around each sidewalk. Alyssa's eyes were wide with excitement. "This is the place I'm supposed to like least?"

"Yeah. You'll have to check out the others to see why." I smiled as I opened my door and said, "Hold tight. I've gotta run in and get the keys."

"Sure."

Alyssa got out to look around while I went into the main office and picked up the keys from the manager. Once I had them, I walked back out and motioned for her to follow me over to the apartment. Like a kid about to open a Christmas present, she rushed over to me with a bright smile on her face. Hell, she was practically bursting at the seams as she waited for me to unlock the door. We finally stepped inside and I told her, "It's a two bedroom with a bath and a half—"

"It's amazing!" She gasped, cutting me off before I could finish describing all the amenities. Not that it mattered. In two seconds flat, she'd scoped out the entire place and was checking out the master's closet when I asked, "What do you think?"

"I think it's great." Her expression quickly grew somber. "But I could never afford a place like this."

"It's not as bad as you might think, besides, Hyde's already said that he wants you to have a nice place."

"I want something nice, too, but it has to be something that I can actually afford."

"You don't have to worry about the money, Alyssa. Your brother wants you to have the place that *you* want, no matter the cost."

"Well, that's easy for him to say. He's not the one paying for it."

"Actually ... he will be. At least, some of it."

"What?"

"He'll pay for whatever you can't." I could tell from her expression that she didn't like the idea of her brother taking up her slack, so I tried to smooth things over by adding, "He's just looking out for his little sister. I'd do the same if I were in his shoes."

"That's just it. Clay has been looking out for me since I was kid, even more so after our dad died. I don't want him thinking that he's gotta take care of me." She let out a frustrated sigh. "I want to be able to fend for myself."

"And you will. It's just gonna take a little time for you to get on your feet." I had the feeling that she wasn't convinced though. "How about this ... Let's look at the other places, then you can decide what you want to do from there."

"Okay." A look of relief crossed her face. "Thanks, T-Bone."

"No problem."

After she took another quick survey around, we

headed over to the second apartment complex. I tried to keep my focus on the road, but every so often my eyes would drift over to her long tan legs, and I'd find myself wishing that miniskirt was a little shorter. I knew I needed to get a fucking grip, but damn, I was just a man, and having a woman as beautiful as Alyssa sitting just a couple of feet from me was just too tempting. Thankfully, she was so focused on figuring out her apartment situation that she didn't seem to notice my struggle.

When we pulled up to the next complex, I again ran into the manager's office to get the keys, then took her for a quick tour of the grounds. I thought she'd like the fact that it was a little bigger and had a full fitness center and swimming pool, but she didn't seem all that enthused as she followed me inside the apartment. She didn't say a word as she strolled through the two different bedrooms and the living room with a large fireplace. Confused by her silence, I asked, "You don't like it?"

"Are you kidding?" she scoffed. "It's even more incredible than the last place."

"So, what's the problem?"

"I'm just worried."

"About?"

"Clay." She walked into the kitchen and opened the pantry. "He's starting his new life with Landry, and they've got their own bills to pay. I don't want to burden him with—"

Before she could finish her sentence, I said, "Hold on, Alyssa. If you're worried about Hyde being able to afford it, you don't have to. He can pay for this place and more."

"But how? He's a mechanic at the garage."

"He's more than a mechanic, and the garage does damn well, so you can rest easy there. Besides, you might be able to afford it on your own."

"Maybe"—she glanced around the apartment and smiled—"but if I can't, I could always pay him back when I start making more."

"Doubt he'd let ya, but yeah, you could." I walked into the kitchen and leaned against the counter. "So, what do you think of the place?"

"I love it."

"Good. I thought you would." I gave her a quick wink. "You ready to go see the others?"

"Absolutely."

She followed me back to the main office, and after I'd returned the keys, we drove over to our next stop—a small rental house with a fenced-in back yard. As I'd hoped, she really liked it, even better than the two apartments, which made her very excited about seeing the last place I had to show her. As soon as we got back in the truck, Alyssa turned to me and said, "I really appreciate you doing this for me. I don't know how I'll ever thank you."

"I can think of a way."

"Oh, really?"

I could tell by her tone that she thought I had something inappropriate in mind, and even though it was tempting to play along, I decided against it. "Once you're all moved into your new place, you can fix me one of those fancy dishes of yours."

"Oh ... Yeah, I could definitely do that."

"Great. I'll look forward to it."

We were getting close to the final house I wanted to show her when she turned to me with an odd expression. "Hey, can I ask you something?"

"Sure. Whatcha got on your mind?"

"You told me that your road name is T-Bone, but you never told me your real name."

"It's Beckett. Beckett Walker."

"Hmmm ... I get why the guys call you T-Bone and all. There's not many people who can eat a steak that big and win dinner for the entire group, but Beckett is a great name."

"Thanks, glad you think so."

"Do you mind if I call you Beckett instead of T-Bone?"

"Baby, you can call me whatever you want."

Before she could respond, I pulled up into the driveway and parked. When she saw the quaint yellow house centered in the middle of the historical district, she gasped. "Oh my ... Is this it?"

"Yep."

"Seriously?"

"Do you want to see inside or what?"

"Are you kidding me? Of course I want to see inside!"

We got out of the truck and climbed up the front porch steps. Excitement was radiating off of Alyssa as she watched me reach into the mailbox and pull out the key then unlock the door. When we stepped inside, I was impressed to see that it looked even better than I'd expected. As she started to walk through the living room, I said, "They just renovated the kitchen. It has all new granite countertops, new cabinets, and tile floor. There are hardwood floors throughout with two bedrooms and—"

I stopped talking when Alyssa started to giggle. "You sound like a realtor."

"Is that right?"

"Um-hmm. But you don't look like any realtor I've ever seen."

"What exactly are you trying to say?"

Her brows furrowed. "Nothing ... I, uh ..."

"You don't think I could do the whole snub-nosed, suit-wearing sales-guy thing?"

"W-wait a minute. I didn't mean it like that," she stammered. The freckles that dappled her nose crinkled as her brows furrowed with worry. It was clear that she thought she'd actually offended me. "I just—"

"Don't sweat it." I chuckled. "I was just messing with ya."

"Seriously?" She raked her teeth across her bottom lip, then smiled and shook her head. "That's just wrong."

"Sorry, couldn't help myself." I laughed as I headed into the kitchen. "So, what do you think of the place?"

"You were right. This is definitely my favorite, but how much is the rent? It has to be insanely high."

"Actually, it's fifty a month less than the first place I showed you."

"Really?"

"Yep. There's a fenced-in backyard and a full security system, but you gotta keep in mind, there's no pool and no fitness center."

"Yeah, but this place is incredible. It feels like home."

"Well then, it's yours."

A bright smile crossed her face. "Thank you, thank you, thank you!"

Before I had a chance to prepare, she rushed over and wrapped her arms around me, hugging me tightly. I couldn't deny how good she felt in my arms, too fucking good; she felt even better when I was hugging her back. Damn, this *just being friends* thing was gonna be harder than I thought.

4

ALYSSA

When I'd agreed to have a drink with Beckett at Clay's party, it was like some task I needed to complete for myself—a way to prove that I could face my fears. I never dreamed it would lead into anything more than just a brief conversation, but the big muscular biker with the intense eyes surprised me. Not only was Beckett easy to talk to, he was charming and funny, and in a matter of minutes, I'd all but forgotten that I was at a party with a room full of bikers.

It was the same way today when we went to look at apartments. Without even trying, he helped set my mind at ease, and now I was actually looking forward to moving. I absolutely adored the house he'd found for me, and I couldn't wait to get moved in and start my new life in Memphis—and maybe, just maybe, spend a little more time getting to know Beckett.

Hoping to prolong our day together, I turned to him and asked, "Would you like to come in for a bit? Maybe grab a bite to eat or something?"

"I wish I could, but I've gotta get back to the garage." He opened the door to his truck, then walked me up to the front door. "I'll get the realtor to send the rental papers over later today."

"Okay." Trying to hide my disappointment, I smiled at him and said, "Thank you for all your help. I can't tell you how much it means to me."

"Glad to do it." I watched as he walked down the steps and back to his truck. Before he got inside, he gave me a quick wave. "See ya around, freckles."

"Bye, Beckett."

Once he was gone, I went into the house and was surprised to find Clay waiting in the kitchen for me. He reminded me of our father as he stood there, leaning against the counter in his work clothes. They were covered in grease and grime, but he didn't seem to mind. He was too focused on devouring his peanut butter and jelly sandwich to even care. When Duchess came racing towards me, Clay looked over and asked, "Well? How'd it go?"

"I found a place."

"Really?"

"Yep." I knelt down to rub Duchess's head. "I think you'll agree that it's pretty great."

"Glad to hear that." His brows furrowed. "Things go okay with T?"

"Actually, they did. He was a perfect gentleman" I gave Duchess one last rub, then stood up and stepped over to the fridge for a soda. "I really enjoyed being with him."

"You did?" There was a mix of surprise and concern in his voice.

"Yes, Clay, I did, but don't worry"—I feigned a smile —"we're just friends."

I felt a twinge of disappointment as the words left my mouth but forced myself to keep smiling in hopes that he wouldn't push the matter. Thankfully, he didn't. Instead, he said, "Well, tell me about your new place."

"It's really something, Clay."

I went on to describe everything about the house and the area surrounding it, and when I was done, I walked over and wrapped my arms around him. "Thank you."

Clay hugged me back and asked, "For?"

"T-Bone told me you offered to help pay for my place." I took a step back. "I'm going to try to do it on my own, but if I can't manage it, I'll let you know."

"I don't want you worrying about money, Sis."

"I know, and I really appreciate it, but I think I can afford it, especially if I get a part-time job and—"

"What? You're not getting a part-time job, Lyssa," Clay argued. "You've finally gotten your chance to try this cooking thing, and you need to focus on that, not busting your ass to pay the fucking rent."

"But—"

"No buts, Lyssa. I'm gonna help you pay for the rental house, and I don't wanna hear anymore about it."

"Okay, but once I start making money, I'm gonna pay you back."

"We'll figure that out later, but for now, let's focus on getting you moved." He took a drink of his sweet tea, then said, "I'll talk to the brothers and see if they can give us a hand."

"That would be great." I glanced down at his half-eaten sandwich and asked, "You mind if I make myself one of those?"

"You don't have to ask, Sis." He pushed the jar of peanut butter towards me. "What's mine is yours."

"Thanks, Clay."

"I've gotta head back to the garage, but I'll be done early."

"Okay, I'll just hang out here until you get back."

"Good deal." As he started towards the door, he looked over to me and said, "Make yourself comfortable. Landry should be home soon."

"Sounds good."

Once I finished my sandwich, Duchess and I went into the living room; she settled down on the floor while I sprawled out on the sofa. Nestled into the cushions, I thought back to the moment I found out I'd gotten my internship at Chez Philippe and how I had immediately envisioned myself fulfilling all my childhood dreams. Sadly, it didn't take long for reality set in. I had years of hard work ahead of me, and not only that, I had to move to a big city where I really didn't know anyone—except my brother. I was feeling completely overwhelmed by it all, but then Beckett came into the picture. I couldn't help but smile as I lay there thinking about our morning together.

I was lost in my thoughts when Duchess suddenly got up and bolted towards the kitchen. Seconds later, Landry walked through the door. Duchess started pacing back and forth, waiting eagerly for Landry to pet her. "Hey there, sweetie. Have you been a good girl?"

"She's been a very good girl"—I sat up on the sofa —"and great company all afternoon."

"I'm glad to hear that." Landry dropped her things down on the counter, then walked into the living room. "Clay told me that you found a place to live."

"I did, and it's perfect. I can't wait to get moved in."

"We'll have to plan a moving party ... Get all the guys and their ol' ladies to help."

"Do you think they'd be up for that?"

"Absolutely." She giggled. "They'll use any excuse to have a get together."

"That would be awesome, but I really don't have all that much to move. I barely have any furniture."

"I've got some things in storage that you might be able to use." Landry sat down on the sofa next to me. "They're just a few odds and ends from my old apartment, and if I had to guess, I bet there'll be others who have some things for you to borrow."

"That would be incredible. I don't know how to thank everyone for helping me." I could feel the warmth building inside. "It means so much to me."

"You mean a lot to Clay, Alyssa. There's nothing he wouldn't do for you."

"I know. He's a great big brother, and I'm so happy that he's found you and his brothers."

"You and me both." She smiled as she stood up and started towards the kitchen. "I was thinking about making some dinner. Are you hungry?"

"Starving." I joined her in the kitchen and asked, "What can I do to help?"

"How about we cook spaghetti? You could brown the

hamburger?"

"Sure thing."

The days that followed went by in a blur. It was as if everything in my life shot into high gear the second I signed my rental agreement. One minute, I was signing on the dotted line, and the next thing I knew, I was standing in my new house, completely decorated with all this amazing furniture. It was absolutely perfect, and I owed it all to Clay and his brothers. With their ol' ladies' help, they turned my place into a home, and I was ready to start my new life in Memphis. I was standing in the living room, looking at the pictures we'd just hung on the wall, when Clay came up behind me and asked, "Well ... What do you think?"

"Oh, Clay. I love it. Thank you so much for doing all this."

"You gotta stop thanking me, Alyssa. I wanted to do it. Besides, the girls did most of the work."

"They've been amazing." I looked around my living room, noting the sofa Murphy and Riley had given me along with the oversized chair Darcy and Rider contributed, and smiled. "I can't believe they were willing to give me all their old furniture like this."

"It's not like they were using it anymore. Most of it was locked away in storage."

"Maybe so, but it was still very sweet of them."

He nodded. "The burgers are ready, and the beer ain't gonna get any colder."

"Well then, we best get to it."

I followed Clay into the backyard where everyone had gathered to make their plates. While the entire club hadn't come, there was enough of them there that they were all enjoying themselves, especially my brother. When Viper had first suggested that Clay come to Memphis to prospect for Satan's Fury, I had my doubts that it was the right move for him, but as I looked around at Clay's brothers sitting around, talking and eating like they were family, it couldn't have been more clear that it was. I hoped the same would hold true for me and my new life in Memphis.

I reached into the cooler for a beer, and I'd just popped it open when Beckett came walking up. He was wearing a fitted t-shirt with the sleeves cut off and a pair of jeans, and I couldn't help but stare at his enormous biceps covered in tattoos. The man looked like some kind of Greek god, and I found myself wanting to reach out and touch him. Thankfully, he pulled me from my inappropriate thoughts by asking, "Mind grabbing one of those for me?"

"Oh, uh ... yeah, sure," I stammered, then quickly pulled out a cold beer and handed it to him. "Can I get you anything else?"

"I was about to grab a burger. You want one?"

"Sure."

I followed him over to the table, and we each made ourselves a plate. We carried our food towards a couple of empty lawn chairs and had just sat down when Rider and Darcy came over to sit with us. A big smile crossed Darcy's face as she said, "You've got a great place here, Alyssa."

"Thank you." I hadn't gotten a chance to get to know many of the ol' ladies, but the ones I'd met had been very sweet, including Darcy. She was so creative and had a great eye for design. "I really appreciate you helping me decorate today. It looks even better than I imagined."

"I'm glad I was able to help." Darcy took a bite of her burger before continuing, "I think you'll really like living in Memphis. There's so much to do here."

"I know. I can't wait to check out the Pyramid and maybe Mud Island and the zoo."

"Those are all awesome. It's been a while since I've been to the Pyramid. Maybe we could all go one day."

"I would love that."

"So, when do you start your internship?"

"Thursday will be my first day, and while I'm excited to get started, I'm actually pretty nervous about it. I haven't had much experience with cooking French cuisine before."

Rider's brows narrowed. "Not sure I've ever eaten any French food before."

"You probably have and just didn't know it—for example fondue, meringues, crème brûlées, mousses, and crepes. And a good roux has become an American staple."

"What the fuck is a *roux*?"

"It's a fat and flour base that cooks use to season their dishes." I could tell by his expression that he had no idea what I was talking about, so I added, "You know ... like what you use for a good gumbo or a gravy."

"Or a chicken pot pie," August added.

"Exactly."

"Damn." Murphy complained. "I just ate, but hearing y'all talking about all this food has got me hungry again."

I looked up at the club's sergeant-at-arms and smiled. "Well, thanks to you, there's plenty of food. Go back for another round or take some with you when you go. I'll never be able to eat all that."

"Don't mind if I do."

Several of them followed Murphy back over to the table for another helping, but even after they'd each made another full plate, there were enough leftovers for an army. I was staring over at all the mounds of burgers, chips, and beans when August, Gunner's ol' lady, leaned over to me and whispered, "Don't worry. By the time the guys finish grazing, most of this will be gone, and whatever's left, we can always carry back over to the clubhouse."

"Well, that's a relief. I had no idea where I was going to put all this."

"Just leave it for now, and come have another drink. We're celebrating, after all."

"That we are."

I followed her back over to the cooler, and after we each grabbed a beer, we headed over to the others. Clay had started us a fire in the small fire-pit that one of his brothers had given me. While it was nothing like the big bonfire they had at the clubhouse, it was cozy, especially with all the little white lights we'd put up around the trellis. I sat down next to Clay and Landry and sipped on my beer. We hadn't been talking long when August announced, "I think we need to take a trip somewhere."

"I would love that," Darcy agreed. "Where should we go?"

"I have no idea." August shrugged. "The weather has been great, so maybe we could do something outdoorsy?"

"Have you ever floated the Buffalo?" I asked. "I've heard it's a lot of fun."

"Yes! That's a great idea," August replied. "We could take a cooler with food and drinks and spend the entire day on the water. What do you think, Darcy?"

"I could definitely go for that," Darcy answered. "I haven't been since I was a kid, but I had a blast."

With a hopeful look in her eye, August turned to Gunner and asked, "Hey, babe, would you and the guys take us to float the Buffalo next weekend?"

"Umm ... I don't know about that," Gunner answered, sounding less than enthused. "We have a lot going on down at the garage."

"Come on. It would be fun," August pushed. "Besides, it's the weekend. You guys could use a break."

Gunner nudged Rider. "You hearing this?"

"Mm-hmm ... I'm with you." Rider's eyes skirted over to Darcy as he said, "We've gotta a lot of work to do."

"You both know I work at the garage too," Darcy fussed. "I know we aren't that busy. If you don't wanna go, just say so."

"Canoeing isn't my kind of thing," Rider told her.

"That's all you had to say." Not giving up so easily, Darcy turned her attention to Beckett. "Hey, T-Bone ...What about you? Would you take us to float the Buffalo next weekend?"

A mischievous smirk crossed his face as he replied, "A canoe full of hot women in bikinis? Are you kidding me? Hell yeah, I'll take you wherever you wanna go."

"Oh, hell no," Gunner argued. "No way that's gonna happen."

"What?" August fussed. "You don't want to go, so what's wrong with—"

"August, this isn't up for discussion," Gunner cut her off.

"But—"

"But nothing. If my ol' lady is going somewhere, I'll be the one taking her."

A hopeful smile crossed August's face. "Does that mean you'll take us to float the river?"

"Nope." Gunner smiled. "But I'll take you anywhere else you wanna go."

"Oh, good grief." She gave him a silly look. "Just forget it. We'll figure something else out."

"I'm sure you will."

While I was a little disappointed that the trip to the river wasn't going to pan out, it was fun talking to the girls about our other options. By the time everyone was ready to call it a night, we'd come up with several good options, but before any final decisions were made, they decided to check with the other ol' ladies to see if they'd like to come along. Even though it was because of my being Clay's sister, it still meant a lot that they'd even think of including me. When it came time to pack up and leave, I gave the girls each an armful of leftovers and thanked them once again for all their help.

After I watched them back out of my driveway, I headed inside to finish cleaning up. I was about to start washing dishes when I heard a commotion in the backyard. I went to see what was up and found Beckett picking up empty bottles and trash and tossing it all into the garbage can.

"Hey, I thought you'd already gone."

"I wanted to help you clean up a bit first."

"Thanks, but I can do that."

He continued on with what he was doing like I hadn't said anything. "You got any more trash bags?"

"Yeah, let me grab one from the kitchen." I rushed inside and pulled out a couple, then took them back out to Beckett. "Here ya go."

I grabbed some empty bottles and tossed them inside the bag. As we continued on, he asked, "You have a good time tonight?"

"I had a blast. What about you?"

"Yeah, I had a good time."

He threw some more trash into the bag, then looked over to me when I said, "We didn't get much time to talk."

"No, we didn't."

A smile crept across my face. "Maybe we can rectify that."

"Oh yeah? What do you have in mind?"

"Well, we could have a drink now, or you could come back one night next week, and I could fix you dinner or something. Let you try out my cooking."

When he didn't immediately answer, I thought he was going to turn me down, but then he surprised me by saying, "How about both?"

"Both would be great." I walked over to the cooler and grabbed a couple of beers, then walked back over to Beckett. As I offered him one, I told him, "Just leave that. I'll get it in the morning."

"You sure?"

"Yeah. Besides, you've already gotten most of it."

Beckett followed me over to the lawn chairs the guys had brought, and we sat down. Like the times before, our conversation came easy. We talked about everything from what he was working on down at the garage to how nervous I was about starting my internship. I found it strange how much I enjoyed being with him, but no matter how strange it might've seemed, he had a way of setting my mind at ease and making me feel safe in a way no man ever had. That thought made me want to get to know him a little better.

"Okay ... So, I've got a question for you." I took a sip of my beer and smiled. "Actually, I have a few questions—if you're up for it."

"I'm up for it." He opened his beer and took a drink. "Whatcha got on your mind?"

"Just a couple random questions, but as one friend to another, I'll warn ya—think before you answer." Beckett's brows furrowed as he considered what I said, and I knew I had him. With a big smile, I crossed my legs and leaned towards him. "Are you ready?"

"Bring it, friend."

"What's your favorite movie?"

"Seriously?"

"You said you were up for it," I pushed.

"Well, I'm going to need you to be a little more specific." He cocked his eyebrow, and I felt a little chill rush down my spine. "Are we talking about a recent movie or an old one? Specific genre or whatever?"

"You're overthinking it."

"Well, you told me to think before I answered, *sooo* ..."

"Touché. Let's just say your all-time favorite. Any genre. Any timeframe."

"Okay, then I'd say *Rio Bravo*."

"Hmm ... John Wayne. My dad loved his movies. How about your favorite band?"

"That depends. Are we talking about—"

"Beckett," I fussed.

"Okay. When I'm out riding, it's Metallica all the way. If not, then I'm pretty much an 80s guy."

"'Enter Sandman.'" I smiled.

"So, you know them?"

"A little. Clay used to listen to them when we were growing up."

He nodded. "'The Unforgiven' is one of my favorites, but 'Enter Sandman' is a close second."

"Good to know. And one last question ... How old were you when you got your first kiss?"

"Eleven or twelve." He shook his head with a snicker. "Damn, that was a really long fucking time ago."

"You got yourself an early start." I took a sip of my beer hoping it would help ease the sinking feeling that was growing in the pit of my stomach. "I was fifteen before I had my first kiss, and it wasn't all that great."

"Oh? Why's that?"

"I don't know. Maybe it was just the fact that I didn't know what I was doing or maybe it was because the guy had braces. Either way, it was pretty terrible."

"Nothing worse than a mouth full of metal." He chuckled as he said, "Well, I hope your other firsts weren't as bad."

That feeling in the pit of my stomach plummeted,

making me regret ever bringing up the "first kiss" question. I'd enjoyed our light-hearted conversation, and the last thing I wanted to do was dampen it by delving any deeper into the *firsts* conversation. Even though I wasn't ready for the night to end, I figured it was best to keep things on a light note, so I yawned and stretched. "As much as I'm enjoying this, it's getting kind of late."

"Yeah, it is." Beckett stood and took my empty bottle from my hand, tossing it into the trash. "You need help with anything else before I go?"

"No, thanks. You've already done enough."

He nodded, then paused as he studied me for a moment. I would've given anything to know what was going through his head at that moment, but I was left completely in the dark as he turned towards the back gate. "I'll see you around, freckles."

"Hey, wait a minute." I rushed over to him. "What about dinner?"

"You don't have to go to any trouble."

"But I want to ... you know, as a way to thank you for everything, and maybe you could give me your thoughts on a new French recipe I've been putting together for work."

Beckett thought for a moment, then nodded. "Sure, I'd be up for that. Just name the day and time, and I'll be there."

"How about tomorrow night around six?"

"I'll be here."

"Great, I'll see you then." Once he was gone, I finished cleaning up and went to bed.

The next morning I woke up late, fighting a fog, when

I suddenly remembered that I'd invited Beckett over for dinner. I sat up in the bed and started to panic. Damn, I wasn't the least bit prepared. I had no idea what I was going to cook; I didn't have any groceries, and I wasn't even sure if I had enough pots and pans. That thought had me jumping out of bed and rushing into the kitchen. I rummaged through all the cabinets, and the second I found my grandmother's old cast iron stew pot, I knew exactly what I'd make for Beckett. My Louisiana French-Creole recipe was a family favorite, and with all the craw-fish, shrimp, sausage, and corn, I hoped Beckett would love it just as much as they did.

I pulled out the pots and pans I'd need, then made a grocery list. Once I had everything planned out, I raced back to the bedroom, threw on some clothes, then headed to store. Since I didn't have any of the basics, it took me a while to gather all the items, and by the time I got back to the house and put the groceries away it was already after three.

I knew once I started cooking it would be hard to stop, so I decided to get my shower out of the way. Choosing to keep it simple, I wore a pair of shorts and a t-shirt with my hair pulled up. I put on a little makeup, then rushed into the kitchen to start the creole.

The roux was the most complicated and essential step to my gumbo, so using my grandmother's pot, I added the butter and flour and got to work. I'd just started getting the roux to where I wanted when there was a knock at the door. I glanced over at the clock and groaned, noticing it was almost six; then I pulled the pot off the burner and went to answer the door. Beckett was standing on my front porch, looking hot as molasses in his black t-shirt and jeans.

"Hey, Beckett. Come on in." I smiled at him.

He nodded, then followed me into the kitchen and placed a bottle of wine on the counter. "I brought wine."

"I see that. Thanks." I motioned my hand at the huge mess. "I'm sorry. I'm running a little behind."

"Anything I can do to help?"

"Would you mind dicing up some onion, a red pepper, and the celery?"

"Sure." He went over to the sink and washed his hands, then opened a couple of cabinets until he found the cutting board. I started working on the stock while he got busy dicing. After several minutes, he asked, "So, what are we making?"

"Gumbo."

"Seriously?" he asked, sounding pleasantly surprised. "I haven't had gumbo in months."

"So you like it?"

Beckett chuckled as he stuck his belly out and ran his hand over it. "Can't you tell? There aren't many things I don't like."

"Hush. You look great."

"If you say so." I continued to stir the stock as he asked, "You mentioned that you've been cooking since you were a kid, right?"

"Yeah, or maybe I should say that I started *trying* when I was just a kid. It took some time before I was any good at it." I glanced over my shoulder and smiled. "What about you? Do you like to cook?"

"I guess you could say I know my way around the

kitchen, but I don't really cook all that often." He shrugged. "Just don't have the time."

"So, what do you do with your free time?"

"I don't get much of that, but when I do, I usually take the bike out. Do a little riding with a couple of the brothers. Usually head down to the lake or just spend the day checking out the back roads."

"Sounds like fun."

"You should come with us sometime," Beckett offered.

"I would really like that." I gathered the vegetables Beckett had diced, then added them to the pot. As I stirred them into the roux, I continued, "I rode a couple of times with Viper, but that's been ages ago."

"We'll have to rectify that." He walked over to the stove, and as he peered over his shoulder, he said, "It smells great."

"Oh, we're just getting started." I motioned my hand over to the sausage and asked, "Would you mind cutting those for me?"

"Sure, no problem." He placed the sausage on a cutting board and got busy once again. "So, did you girls ever decide on what trip you wanted to take?"

"No, they were kind of all over the place."

"They usually are." He joked. "But they definitely keep things interesting."

"I'm sure they do." I added the garlic to the roux and then slowly poured in the stock. "I bet you all have a great time over at the clubhouse."

"We do." He nodded. "Some greater than others."

"I can still remember the times my dad took me over to see my uncle, Viper, at his clubhouse. There was always music playing in the bar, and the guys were either acting all goofy and silly, or they were deadly serious, making me scared to even be in the same room with them."

"I get that. I'm sure the girls would say the same was true about us." Beckett started prepping the corn and other vegetables as he said, "Guess you could say there's a time and place for everything."

"Viper would definitely agree with you there." I collected the rest of the vegetables from Beckett. "Thanks for helping. I'm really sorry I didn't have it all ready when you got here."

"Don't be. I'm enjoying watching the fancy French chef do her thing."

"Ha! I'm far from fancy, and I'm still learning the ins and outs of French cuisine."

"You're a smart girl. I'm sure it won't take you long to figure it out."

Beckett and I continued to banter back and forth as we put together the best gumbo I'd had in years. We ate outside under the stars, and I couldn't remember a night when I'd enjoyed someone's company as much as I had his. I hated for the night to end, but it was getting late and Beckett had an early morning. On his way out the door, he gave me a quick hug and thanked me for dinner. I stood in the doorway and watched as he walked over and got on his motorcycle. Damn, I'd never seen a sexier sight than that man on his black Harley motorcycle. Just looking at him had my hormones raging to life. I closed the door, and as I headed to bed, I knew I was going to have all kinds of good dreams.

5

T-BONE

"GOTTA BE THERE BEFORE TEN." WE WERE ALL SITTING around the conference table, listening as Gus went over the plan for our upcoming run. We'd been doing the pipeline with five of our other chapters for the last couple of years, each clubhouse contributing to make one big take. I had to admit that things have been going very well. We all made a fuck-load of money and had every intention of continuing our success. "That's earlier than usual, so we'll need to head out around four in the morning instead of seven," Gus continued.

Clearly concerned, Moose's eyes narrowed as he asked, "What's with the change?"

Moose was the club's VP, and just like Gus, he was always careful, wanting to make sure that nothing put the club at risk. Knowing Moose like he did, Gus didn't seem surprised by his question. Instead, he simply answered, "Ronin said there was an issue at the dock last week ... Something to do with the water quality or some shit around the inlet we've been using, and they've got the

Coast Guard monitoring the number of boats coming in and out."

"How the hell are we supposed to get around that shit?" Murphy asked.

"Ronin assured me that he's got it covered, and he's never given me reason to think that he doesn't." Ronin was our main distributor and an invaluable asset to the club and our pipeline. Once we received the shipments from our other chapters, it was up to us to deliver the goods to him, then he would distribute them to our buyers. Even when times got tough, Ronin had always pulled through for us, so it was no surprise that Gus had such faith in him. After a brief pause, Gus looked out at us and said, "I still want you boys to take every precaution; be certain you do your part to make sure this run goes off without a hitch."

"You know we will," Murphy assured him.

"That's what I wanted to hear." He stood as he said, "You know what needs to be done to get things ready for the morning. Make sure it gets done."

"Understood."

As soon as Gus left the table, church was over. Each of us left the conference room and headed to prepare for the run. It was the same every time—inspect the weapons and ammunition, check the contents of each crate, and prep the trailers we'd use to haul the load. We all did our part in getting everything sorted for each and every run. Murphy and I had just finished checking all the munitions with Hyde when Shadow, the club's enforcer, came over to us.

"Everything set?"

"Yeah, we're all good here."

"All right. I'll let Gus know." A smirk crossed Shadow's face as he asked, "How'd it go with the move the other day?"

"I think it went pretty well." It'd been almost a week since the party, but I could still remember the smile on her face when she talked about her place. "She seems happy with it."

"She's more than happy," Clay added. "Hell, I haven't seen her that excited since she was a kid."

"Glad to hear it. Sorry we couldn't help out. Alex had a big shipment come into the bookstore, so we were pretty wrapped up."

"Don't worry about it. We managed just fine." Clay gave him a pat on the shoulder. "You missed some good eatin' though. Murphy made us one hell of a burger."

"Hate I missed it."

"We'll do it again soon. Landry has been wanting have everyone over at our place."

"Sounds good."

As Clay turned to leave, he said, "I'll see you boys in the morning."

"Have a good one." Once he'd left, Shadow turned his attention back to me, and I could tell by his expression that he had something on his mind. "So, what's Clay think about you and Alyssa?"

"What about me and Alyssa?"

He cocked his eyebrow. "You know."

"Nah, man. There's nothing going on between us."

"I don't know, brother. From what I'm hearing, she was all about the Bone the other night at the party."

I knew he was just fucking with me, so I shook my head and said, "Bullshit. You and I both know better than that."

"I don't have any idea. I wasn't there." He studied me for a moment, then asked, "Have you seen her since?"

"Yeah, she made me dinner." It seemed all my brothers had it in their head that something was up with Alyssa and me, and to my surprise, none had seemed to have an issue with it. That was something I didn't quite understand. I would've thought they'd have told me to steer clear; instead, they seemed to be encouraging it. I could see the wheels turning in his head, so I quickly added, "It was no big deal. She just wanted to do something to thank me for helping her find a place."

"Mm-hmm. Sure," he scoffed. "Whatever you say, boss."

He gave me a brotherly slap on the back, then turned and walked away, leaving me wondering if I'd been wrong about this whole dinner. It was a thought that stuck with me as I headed home for the night. I won't deny that I was intrigued by the idea of there being something more going on between us, but I'd already gone over it a million fucking times. There was no way in hell it would ever work, so I wasn't going to waste any more time thinking about it. Besides, I didn't have time for distractions. I needed to be focused on the run and nothing else. I held that resolve as I made it to the house and went straight to bed. It felt like I'd just gone to sleep when the time came for me to get up and head back to the clubhouse. Not wanting to be late, I forced myself out of bed, grabbed some coffee, and minutes later, I was on my way.

When I pulled through the gate, I saw that Murphy was already busy checking the trailers. I parked, then walked over to give him a hand. "Hey, brother. What do you need me to do?"

"You can start bringing the crates over so we can get them loaded." He motioned his hand towards the clubhouse garage. "Shadow and Riggs are already inside."

"Will do."

I walked over to the garage, and when I stepped inside, I found Riggs and Shadow stacking the crates onto the dollies. "Murphy is ready to start loading."

"Good timing." Shadow glanced over his shoulder as he said, "Give us a hand with the rest."

I nodded, then walked over and got to work. In no time, all the crates were loaded into the hidden compartments of the horse trailers. Once everything was secured, Rider and Hyde led the horses inside the trailers. We'd brought them over from Gus's place, and like all the times before, we used them to conceal the hidden compartments even more than they already were. As soon as they were settled inside, we were set to roll out right on time. Gus came over, and after he checked everything one last time, he gave the nod. "All right, boys. Looks good. Remember to keep your head in the game and no fuck ups."

"You got it, Prez."

Murphy motioned over to the rest of us, and we started loading up. I got in the SUV with him and Shadow, while Gauge, Blaze, and Hyde drove with Riggs.

With both trailers hitched behind us, we started towards Mobile to meet up with Ronin. It was still hours before sunrise, so it was no surprise that the ride there was quiet. It took some time for us to shake that early morning haze, but by the time we arrived at the dock, we were ready to get the job done. After we parked, Murphy got out of the SUV to check in with Ronin. It was then that I noticed all the Coast Guard boats monitoring the port. I looked over to Shadow. "You seeing this shit?"

"Hard to fucking miss. What the hell is Ronin thinking?"

"No way we're going to be able to get this shit loaded without someone seeing us."

Shadow opened his door. "We need to see what the fuck is going on."

I followed him over to Murphy and Ronin. Shadow wasn't a man who fucked around, especially when it came to matters of the club, so I wasn't surprised when he charged up to Ronin and pointed out to the water. "What the fuck, man? Thought you were gonna handle this shit."

"Like I was telling Murphy, I've got it taken care of."

"Oh really?" I knew it was Murphy's job, as sergeant-at-arms, to deal with Ronin and the exchange, but the situation was making it difficult for me to get a grip on my frustration. "'Cause from where I'm standing, I don't see you handling a damn thing!"

"You'll see."

"What the fuck? You need to get to talking and tell us what the fuck is going on, or there's gonna be all kinds of hell to pay."

"I get that you're pissed about all this, and I am too," Ronin tried to explain, "but right now you're all just gonna have to trust me. I need you to get back in your trucks and hold tight for a minute."

"Fine," Murphy bit out, then glanced back over his shoulder as we headed towards the SUVs. "You've got five minutes."

Once we'd gotten back in the truck, Shadow looked over to Murphy and said, "I don't know about this, Murph. Last thing we need is the fucking Coast Guard on our ass."

Just as Murphy was about to respond, a thunderous roar shook the SUV, and our attention was quickly drawn out to the water. About a mile and a half out, there was a massive ball of flames engulfing a boat. I was completely blown away as I watched the smoke billow into the sky. "What the fuck was that?"

"That would be Ronin."

"He blew up a fucking boat?"

"Apparently so."

I looked back over to the water and watched the Coast Guard immediately change course and head towards the fire and wreckage. Once they were mostly out of sight, Ronin motioned over to us, and we knew it was time to move. Murphy got out first, and as soon as he was certain all was clear, he gave us the nod. We immediately rushed to the trailers. I could hear the others talking about the explosion as we waited for Rider and Hyde to move the horses out of the trailers. After they'd gotten them sorted, Shadow barked, "Move it, boys. We don't have much time on our hands."

Without hesitating, I went into the first trailer and unlocked the hidden compartment. Once we had them all unloaded and the crates stacked on the dollies, we moved to the second trailer. I was busy unlocking the main compartment when I heard Gauge say, "It's official. Ronin is my fucking hero."

"I gotta admit"—Gunner chuckled—"that was pretty fucking smart."

"Yeah, but wouldn't it have been easier to just change ports?" Riggs asked, sounding concerned.

I put the lock in my pocket, and when I stepped out of the way, Gauge reached in and started pulling out the crates. A smirk crossed his face as he looked over to Riggs and said, "Maybe, but what's the fun in that."

"None of this shit is about being fun, brother," Blaze barked. "He can't blow up a goddamn boat every time we need to make an exchange."

"He's aware," Murphy told him.

"Good. Now, let's get this shit done."

Not wasting any time, we stacked the remainder of the crates and pushed the dollies down to Ronin's boat, a souped-up seventy-foot yacht, and took them below deck, hiding them beneath the storage compartments. Once they were all loaded, we got the horses back in the trailers, and in no time, we were on our way back to Memphis. We hadn't been riding long when Murphy announced, "We need to stop to fuel up and grab something to eat."

"Usual spot?"

"Yeah, sounds good."

I nodded, then sent a message to Gauge, letting them

know that we'd be taking the next exit. Not long after, we were pulling up to the diner where we'd stopped many times before and parked. As we headed towards the entrance, I heard Rider say, "I still can't believe he blew up a fucking boat."

"You're just jealous that you didn't think of it." Gauge taunted him.

"Maybe just a little."

They continued back and forth into the diner. Once we were seated, they carried on with their banter even as we placed our orders. While waiting for the server to return, we talked about everything from the run to work in the garage. Our food had just been brought over to the table when I overheard Murphy say, "Yeah, we gotta be careful when we get them together. You never know what those women will come up with."

"You got that right." Rider shook his head. "I still can't believe they actually wanted to float the fucking Buffalo."

"It had to be the beer talking," Gunner replied with a chuckle. "Once one of them saw a fucking water moccasin, it would've been all over."

"Yeah, that or a fucking tree in the river. Nothing worse than getting caught up in one of those damn things," Rider grumbled.

"I don't know," I told them both as I took a bite of my burger. "The right day with a cooler full of beer, some good tunes, and sweet lookin' women in bikinis, and a man could have a damn good time."

Blaze glanced over at me with a smile. "The man's got a point."

"Maybe, but he'd need to find him an ol' lady before that can happen." Hyde snickered.

"He'll find one soon enough." Blaze gave me a wink. "Maybe sooner than you think."

Hyde's smile quickly faded as he asked, "What the hell's that supposed to mean?"

"Nothing, brother." Blaze smirked as he picked up his burger. "Nothing at all."

"Can I get you guys anything else?" the waitress asked, bringing an end to Blaze and Hyde's conversation.

"Nope. We're all good."

After we finished eating, Shadow paid the check, and everyone headed back out to the trucks. After we checked the horses and fueled up, we started back towards Memphis. We were following behind Riggs and had just crossed the state line into Mississippi when one of the back tires on their trailer blew, causing it to sway dangerously across the white line. Murphy followed behind Riggs as he eased over to the shoulder and stopped. We all got out to lend a hand and to check on the horses while Shadow pulled out the spare and jack. Just as Shadow started to crank the jack, our attention was drawn to the flashing lights behind us. Dread washed over me as I watched the state trooper get out of his car and start over to us. "You boys okay?"

"Yes, sir. Just trying to get this flat changed so we can be on our way," Blaze answered.

"Hmmm." The cop clicked his tongue as he glanced around the trailer. Maybe it was his snarled-up nose or the hillbilly sideburns he was sporting, but there something about the guy that gave me an uneasy feeling. I knew we didn't have anything to worry about. We'd already unloaded the weapons, but I still didn't like the fact that he was snooping around our shit. If their expressions were any indication, I'd say my brothers felt the same way. "You boys been down to a rodeo or something?"

"No, sir. No rodeo this time." Blaze motioned over to the horses as he told him, "We just bought these beauties for the ranch."

"That right?" Clearly suspicious, the cop stepped over to Blaze and asked, "You got a bill of sale for 'em?"

"Yes, sir. We sure do," Riggs nodded as he started towards the front of the truck. "I'll grab them for you."

Riggs had just opened the door when the cop said, "That's all right, son. Don't worry about it."

"You sure?"

"Yeah, It's fine." He glanced down at Shadow as he asked, "You need a hand with that?"

"I'm good, thanks."

"Well, all right then. I'll let you boys get to it. I'm gonna stay until you get the flat taken care of." The officer gave us a quick wave, then walked over to his patrol car and sat there with his flashers on. Knowing he couldn't hear me, I looked over to Riggs and asked, "You actually got a bill of sale for the horses?"

"Fuck no. I was just calling his bluff." Riggs shook his head. "That guy was a real fucking asshole."

"Don't disagree with you there." I shook my head. "But then, most cops are."

As soon as the flat was replaced, the cop pulled off, and then we got back on the road. We were all relieved when we finally pulled through the gates of the clubhouse.

Everyone was busy unloading when Alyssa pulled up to the gate. She spoke to the prospect on guard, then sped over to us. The second she got out of the car, I knew something was wrong. She was still wearing her work clothes, and even in the dark, I could tell that her eyes were puffy from crying. My chest tightened as I listened to her voice tremble when she called out to Hyde. "Clay!"

"Alyssa?" He rushed over her as he asked, "What's wrong?"

"I saw him," she cried. "He's here."

6

ALYSSA

"What the fuck are you talking about, Lyssa?"

I couldn't say the words. I was too upset, crying too hard. I hated that Lucas could still get to me after all these years, but there was little I could do to stop it. No matter how hard I tried, I couldn't seem to pull myself together. My hands were shaking as I struggled to breathe.

"Are you sure it was him?"

"Yes, it was ... h-him," I stammered, biting back my tears. "I'm sure of it."

The vein in his neck started to pulse and his face grew red as he growled, "Tell me what happened!"

I wasn't surprised by his reaction. Since we were kids, Clay had always had a short fuse, especially when it came to me. He did his best to look after me and my mother, and since my father died, he'd become even more protective. I didn't want to rattle him any more than I already had, so I inhaled a deep breath and let it out slowly. Once

I'd gathered myself a little, I explained, "I was leaving work ... about to get in my car, and that's when I saw him."

"Where was he?"

"In the parking lot." I thought back to the moment I'd recognized Lucas's smug face and how he was laughing while he talked to the man and woman walking next to him. He seemed like he didn't have a care in the world, whereas I felt like the rug had been pulled out from under my feet. "He was going into the Peabody with some other people."

"And you're sure it was him?"

"Yes. There's no doubt in my mind." I wiped the tears from my face. "That guy's face has been burned into my memory. There's no way I would ever mistake him for someone else."

"Goddamn it." I could almost feel the anger radiating off him as he paced back and forth. "I thought you were done with this motherfucker."

In hopes of calming him down, I stepped over to Clay and said, "Maybe tonight was just a one-time thing. Maybe he was just visiting friends or something, and he'll be leaving soon."

"Goddamn it!" He raised his fist and slammed it into my car, denting the hood. "I should've killed him when I had the fucking chance!"

"Clay ... Stop!" I threw my hands up in the air. "This isn't helping anything."

"What do you want from me here?"

"Not this!" I motioned my hand towards the huge dent in my hood. "This isn't helping anything."

"I just got carried away."

I opened the door and got inside, then snapped, "I shouldn't have come."

"Wait, Lyssa. I'm sorry. I'll fix your hood first thing tomorrow."

"Just forget it."

I don't know why I'd gotten so angry with my brother. He was just trying to look out for me and had let his emotions get the best of him. I should've accepted his apology, but I was just too worked up. I slammed the car door shut, then sped out of the clubhouse parking lot. By the time I got to my house, my anger at Clay had dissipated; instead, my fear had returned. Once I was inside, I locked all the doors, then turned on every light in the house. Deep down, I knew I was being crazy. Lucas didn't know where I lived, and it was doubtful he had any idea that I was even in the city limits, but seeing him tonight in that parking lot rattled me, bringing back all those feelings of helplessness I'd tried so hard to overcome. I went into the kitchen and took out a bottle of wine from the fridge. After I poured myself a large glass, I went to my room and changed into my sleep shorts and an oversized hoodie. I'd just crawled on top of my bed when my phone chimed with a text message.

BECKETT:

Are you okay?

ME:

No, not really.

. . .

BECKETT:

I'll be there in ten.

I SHOULD'VE TOLD him not to come. I was a complete mess and hated the idea of him seeing me this way, but I didn't want to be alone. I picked up my glass of wine and finished it off, then went to the kitchen for another—and then another. I was just starting to feel the effects when I heard a knock at the door. Beckett was standing on my porch wearing a pair of worn jeans and a dark t-shirt along with his cut. He hadn't shaved in a couple of days and his eyes looked tired, which made the fact that he'd come to see me at such a late hour even more thoughtful. I could hear the concern in his voice as he said, "Hey, how ya making it?"

"I've been better."

"I see that." As soon as he stepped inside and took a quick glance around, the concerned expression on his face only grew more intense when he noticed that every light in my house was on. Once I'd locked the door, he turned to me and said, "I heard you talking to Clay."

"Yeah." I walked over and sat down on the sofa. "I figured that's why you messaged me."

"You wanna tell me about what happened?"

"No." I took big sip of my wine. "I'd really rather not talk about it."

"Then we won't."

He took off his cut, then sat down next to me and

didn't say anything more. For the first time since I'd seen Lucas in the parking lot of the Peabody, I felt like I could actually breathe. Almost an hour had passed when I looked over to him and said, "Thank you, Beckett."

"You don't have to thank me. I'm exactly where I want to be."

I didn't know what it was about him that made me feel so safe. This big, badass biker guy lived in a world that I'd never truly understood, but his strength and calm nature made me feel protected, like nothing—not even Lucas Brant—could hurt me. I curled up next to him, and it wasn't long before I dozed off. I had no idea how long I'd been sleeping when I felt myself being lifted up and carried down the hall to my room. Beckett carefully lowered me down onto the bed, and as he pulled the covers over me, I looked up at him and said, "Please don't go."

"I'm not going anywhere, Lyssa. I'll be on the sofa if you need me."

"Okay."

He turned out the lights, and I watched as he walked out into the hallway. Knowing that he was just in the next room, I was able to fall right back to sleep. Unfortunately, it wasn't enough to keep me asleep. It was almost three when I woke up in a panic. There was no way I'd be able to go back to sleep, so I got out of bed and started towards the kitchen to make myself something to eat. I noticed that the TV was on in the living room and figured Beckett had nodded off until I heard him ask, "You okay?"

"Yeah." I leaned into the room. "I was just going to grab a bite to eat. Can I get you anything?"

"No." He held up a bag of chips. "I'm good."

"Okay." I pulled out a bag of Oreos and poured myself a glass of milk, then went back into the living room. "Mind if I join you?"

"Not at all." He moved his feet, giving me a spot to sit, and once I was settled, he asked, "You gonna share?"

"Of course." I grabbed a couple of cookies, then handed him the rest of the package. "Have you been up long?"

"Haven't been to sleep yet." He motioned his head towards the TV. "I got caught up in the movie."

I looked over to the black and white movie playing on the screen, and it didn't take me long to recognize it. "*True Grit*?"

"Yeah. Seen it a million times, but never get tired of watching it."

"You sound like my dad."

"I remember you saying he liked John Wayne movies. My ol' man did too." Beckett took an Oreo and shoved it in his mouth. "He's probably the reason I like them the way I do. Seemed like he was always quoting some line from one of his movies."

"Mine did that too. He did the same with Clint Eastwood movies."

"Yep, he's another great one." Beckett looked over to me and asked, "Were you and your dad close?"

Yeah, I was pretty much a daddy's girl. I was always so excited when he'd come home from a long haul on his truck. He was a really great guy. He had such a good heart. Sweet. Thoughtful. Always there when you needed him." I smiled as I said, "You know ... you remind me a lot of him."

"Aw, come on, now. You can't be saying shit like that." He chuckled as he said, "You'll have me thinking you've got daddy issues or something."

"Beckett!" I gave him a playful slap on the arm. "I can't believe you said that."

"I'm just saying." He teased.

"I'll have you know that I'm not one of those girls with 'daddy issues.'"

"Mm-hmm. That's what someone with daddy issues would say."

"Are you being serious right now?"

A smirk crossed his face. "No, I'm just messing with you."

"You're a mess."

"Yeah, but I got you to smile. That has to count for something."

"It most certainly does."

I settled back and continued to munch on my Oreos as we watched the rest of the movie. When it was over, I looked over to Beckett and found him sound asleep. Being careful not to wake him, I eased up off the sofa and headed back to my room. As I got into bed, I was feeling much better and even slept a little. When I woke up the next morning, I felt fairly decent. That didn't mean I wasn't still rattled over seeing Lucas. I remembered how much better Beckett had made me feel the night before and went into the living room to find him. To my disappointment, there was no sign of him—only a note saying that he had to get back to the clubhouse. I was just about to go get my phone to text him when I noticed the time. It was already almost nine, and having to be at work in half an hour, I raced to the bathroom and took the quickest shower of my life. I was so afraid that I was going to be late, but after moving around like a speed demon to get ready, I somehow managed to get there just in time. As soon as I walked into the employee locker room, I ran into Jack, one of the restaurant's busboys.

"Cutting it kind of close, aren't ya?"

"Yeah, I, uh ... overslept."

"Long night?"

"You could say that." I opened my locker, placed my things inside, and reached for my apron. As I slipped it on, I asked, "What about you? Did you have a good night?"

"It wasn't too bad. After you left, it got a little busy until the end of the dinner rush, then things were pretty chill."

Jack was a couple of years younger than me, tall with red hair and green eyes, and like me, he was relatively new to Chez Philippe. Even so, he'd done what he could to help me get my bearings on my first day, and I appreciated it more than he could ever know. "Glad to hear it. I guess I better get going. I don't want to be late."

"Good luck in there."

"Thanks. With the way my morning has been going, I need all the luck I can get."

I didn't know just how true that statement was until I entered the kitchen. As soon as I walked in, Alexandre Bisset, the most arrogant sous chef I'd ever met, came storming over to me. Sounding like an overbearing drill sergeant from hell, he growled, "If you can't be on time, then don't bother coming in at all."

I knew I wasn't late but I wasn't exactly early either, so I just nodded. "Sorry, Chef Bisset. I won't let it happen again."

"You best see to it that you don't." He motioned his hand towards the crate of potatoes. "They aren't going to peel themselves."

I rushed over to the crate and got busy. I knew that I'd have to start at the bottom. It was just the way things worked, so I never complained. I just did the work that was assigned to me the best I could and hoped that in time I'd be able to work my way up the food chain. I spent over an hour peeling all those potatoes, and when I finished, I moved on to the other vegetables, dicing and prepping them for the upcoming lunch crowd. As I worked, I watched in awe as lead chef, Antoine Boucher, and his crew moved through the kitchen. To an outsider, it might've looked like utter chaos, but to me, it was simply magical. It was as if they were all dancing to a tune that only they could hear—each of their movements were fluid, precise, and completely in sync with one another.

As the day turned into night, I kept observing, making notes of how things worked, especially where Chef Bisset was concerned. I needed to know what he expected from each member of his team. While it wasn't easy to keep up with everything going on, I loved every minute of it. Being there, in all the craziness, helped distract me from thinking about Lucas—at least temporarily. When my shift was over and it was time to leave, I started to get anxious, fearing I might see him again. I'd gotten my things together and headed towards the back, but when I reached the door I froze. No matter how hard I tried, I couldn't make myself step outside and into the dark. The thought of Lucas being out there again terrified me and I couldn't move.

Thankfully, Jack walked up behind me and asked, "Hey, everything okay?"

"Yeah." I glanced over at him and noticed that he was carrying two large bags of garbage. "Everything's fine."

"You heading out?"

I nodded. "I was about to."

"You want me to walk you to your car?"

"Would you mind?"

"Not at all." He pushed the door open with his hip. "Just let me take care of these first."

I nodded, then followed Jack over to the dumpster. After he'd tossed the garbage inside, we turned and started towards the parking lot. When we reached my car, he waited for me to unlock the doors and get inside. Before I closed the door, I said, "Thank you, Jack."

"Anytime." He turned to go back into the restaurant and waved. "See ya tomorrow."

I started the car and while easing out of the parking lot, I found myself looking for any sign of Lucas. Thankfully, I didn't see him or anyone who looked remotely like him. Feeling only slightly relieved, I headed home. When I pulled up, Clay was waiting for me in the driveway. Curious to see why he'd come, I got out of my car and walked over to him. "What are you doing here?"

"I wanted to talk to you."

"It's late, Clay." I walked past him with a huff and headed up the stairs. "You should be home with Landry."

"Look, Lyssa. I get it. You're pissed about last night and the way I handled things, and I'm sorry about blowing up, but—"

"It's okay." I unlocked the door, then walked inside. "I know you were upset and I was, too, but I think we're just gonna have to let it go. Lucas was probably just there to see some friends or something."

"Well, about that." I knew my brother well enough that he was about to drop a bomb on me, but I wasn't expecting him to say, "I looked into Lucas, and it turns out that you were right. He is living here."

"What?"

"He moved here a year ago." My stomach twisted into a knot as he continued, "He's been working with a couple of his buddies from back home at some heating and cooling place."

"You're kidding me, right?"

"Sorry, Sis. I'm not." He stepped towards me with a pained expression. "I know this isn't the news you were wanting, but things are different now. He's married now ... even has a kid on the way."

"Is that supposed to make me feel better"—I clenched my fists at my sides as I bit back my tears—"because it doesn't. Not at all."

"Look, I know this is tough, but it's gonna be okay."

"How can you be so sure?"

"Because I'm here"—he wrapped his arms around to hug me tightly—"and if he even thinks about coming close to you, I'll fucking kill him."

"Thank you for looking out for me." I hugged him back before pulling away. "I really do appreciate it, but it's late. You should get back to Landry."

"Landry is fine. She's—"

Even though I wasn't thrilled about the idea of being alone, I pushed, "Clay, I'll be okay. Just go home."

"You sure?"

I nodded. "I'm wiped. I'm just going to change my clothes and go to bed."

"Okay. Do what you need to do." Before I closed the door, he said, "I'll give you a call tomorrow."

"Sounds good. Be sure and tell Landry I said hey."

"Will do." Just as he turned to leave, he added, "Make sure you lock up."

I watched Clay walk towards his bike, then I closed the door and locked it. I could hear the rumble of his Harley as he backed out of the driveway. I'd done my best to keep it together when Clay told me about Lucas, but the second he was gone, I lost it—not because I was afraid, but because I was angry. I'd moved to Memphis thinking I was getting a fresh start, that I was leaving Lucas and my past behind, and it infuriated me that I was wrong—that he really wasn't out of my life. I threw my bag down on the table, and with tears streaming down my face, I screamed at the top of my lungs. I shouted a stream of curses as I grabbed the throw pillows off my sofa and tossed them across the room, then did the same with some magazines I had laying on the coffee table. I was in the midst of a total, raging meltdown when I heard a knock on the door. I figured it was Clay coming back to make sure I was okay, so as I opened the door, I sassed, "I thought I told you to go home."

The words had already left my mouth before I realized it was actually Beckett. I didn't even give him a chance to speak before I stepped out on the porch and threw my arms around his neck, clinging to him tightly. I felt his arms wind around my waist, and as he pulled me close, my body melted into his. After several minutes of holding me, he said, "Let's get you inside."

"Okay."

Beckett followed me back into the house, and when he saw all the pillows and magazines strewn all over my living room, he didn't say a word. Instead, he just walked over and started picking things up and putting them back where they belonged. As he placed the pillows back on the sofa, he looked over to me with concern in his eyes. "I'm guessing things aren't going so great."

"They've definitely been better."

"You sure you don't wanna tell me what's going on?" When he saw the expression on my face, he shook his head and sighed. "*Okaaay.* Have it your way."

"I'm just not ready to get into it."

"I understand." He studied me for a moment, like he was trying to make sense of what was going on with me, then said, "It's late ... I best get going. I probably shouldn't have come in the first place, but for some reason, I couldn't seem to go home without coming by to see if you were okay."

"I'm glad you did. Do you really need to go?"

"I can stay as long as you need me to." He motioned

his head towards my sofa. "I'll be right here if you need me."

"Thank you, Beckett."

I did as he said. I went to my room, took a shower, put on my pajamas, and crawled into bed. As I rested my head on the pillow, I thought about everything Clay had told me about Lucas. Since he was married now and expecting a baby, I wanted to believe that Lucas had changed, but when I thought about the night he raped me, I knew better. It was that wild look in his eye. I knew then that my fear was exciting him, and dominating me gave him a thrill. It sickened me to even think about it, but I knew the monster that lurked deep inside him wouldn't just disappear completely. At first, it had me tossing and turning, but with Beckett in the next room, I was eventually able to fall asleep.

Over the next few weeks, I'd had good days and bad days. I went to work, tried to face the day with a positive outlook, but it wasn't easy. I never knew when the panic would rise up inside of me, crippling me like it had when Lucas first raped me, and while Clay had done what he could to support me, it was Beckett who'd helped me the most.

Every night, he'd come by to see how I was doing. If I was having a good day, he'd go home, but if not, he'd come in and do whatever he could to ease my mind. We'd talk, watch movies, and on some nights, Beckett would take me out for a ride on his Harley. Those nights were my favorite. I'd ridden some with Viper when I was younger, but it felt nothing like it did when I was with Beckett. I felt so free, so alive. I couldn't have been more pleased the night he showed up at my door with a helmet in his hand. A smile crossed his face as he asked, "You wanna get out of here for a while?"

"Sure. Where we going?"

"No idea. Guess we'll figure it out when we get there."

"Sounds good to me. Just let me grab my jacket."

Beckett waited in the doorway while I went to get my things, and once I was ready, he led me out to his bike. As soon as I had my helmet on, he backed out of the driveway and sped off into the night. Since it was late, there wasn't much traffic, and we were able to move from street to street without any cars getting in our way. The lights of the city seemed so much brighter on the back of his bike, and with the wind whipping around us, I almost felt like I was flying. All thoughts of Lucas and work were gone. It was just Beckett and me, soaring through the night without a care in the world. After riding around for almost an hour, he took us into a neighborhood in Midtown. I was just about to ask him where we were going when we pulled up to a beautiful two-story brick home. Beckett parked, but before we got off the bike, he asked, "You wanna see my place?"

"This is your house?"

"Yeah, I figured since we were close I'd show it to ya."

Beckett held out his hand and helped me keep my balance as I got off his bike, then I slipped off my helmet and he did the same. I followed him up the front porch and waited as he unlocked the door. When we stepped inside, he turned on the lights, and I was blown away at how perfect it was. There were hardwood floors throughout the entire house with furniture that looked like it came right out of one of those home-decor magazines. "It's really beautiful, Beckett."

"It's just a house."

"Well, I happen to think it's amazing." I walked into the living room, noting all the artwork on the walls and large lanterns on the end tables. It couldn't have been decorated any more tastefully. "Did you do all this yourself?"

"Pretty much. Just kind of threw it together."

"You did more than just throw this together, Beckett. A house like this takes a lot of time and effort." I looked over to him and said, "You did an incredible job with it. You should be proud."

"I'm glad you like it."

"I more than like it. I love it." I crossed my arms and cocked my eyebrow. "How come you haven't helped me more with my place?"

"Your place looks great just the way it is."

"It's nothing like this, but maybe one day."

"Something tells me one day you'll have everything you've ever wanted and more."

"What makes you say that?"

"Just a feeling." He shrugged.

Beckett took me for a tour of the rest of the house, and it was no surprise that each room was just as beautiful as the next. I loved it all, but when we got to the kitchen, I was blown away. He had a gourmet stainless steel oven with a six-burner gas cook top and an extra-large refrigerator. The pots and pans were on a hanging rack above a butcher-block island, and I could imagine myself cooking in that room for hours on end. With wonder in my eyes, I turned to him and said, "This kitchen is spectacular!"

"I'm glad you think so."

"I've always wanted a kitchen like this. It's like you read my mind."

A strange look crossed his face as he said, "You know, it's getting late. I better take you back home."

"Okay."

I knew he was right. I had to be at work the next morning, so I needed to get some sleep. When we arrived back at my place, Beckett asked, "You good tonight, or would you like me to stay?"

"I'm good, but you know you're welcome to stay."

"Appreciate that, but I'm gonna head on home. I'll check in with you tomorrow."

"Okay." When he turned to leave, I called out to him, "Hey, Beckett."

"Yeah?"

"Thank you."

"Anytime, freckles. Anytime."

He gave me a wink, then turned and walked towards his bike. I waited until he'd started the engine before I closed the door and locked it, then I headed to bed.

The next few days had gone pretty well. I was actually starting to feel like things were going to be okay, and then I saw Lucas again. While I was on the way to my car, I noticed him walking across the Peabody's parking lot with a woman. I assumed she was his wife, but I could've been wrong. It didn't matter. The fact was I'd seen him, and that was enough to put an end to my good days. That night when Beckett came to check on me, he didn't have to ask if I needed him to stay. It was written all over my face. He gave me a hug, then sent me to bed as he headed over to his spot on the sofa. My mind was reeling with thoughts of Lucas as I drifted off to sleep, so it was no wonder that I had a bad dream. Apparently, it was really bad—bad enough to wake up Beckett and have him come rushing into my bedroom. He pulled me into his arms and held me close as he whispered, "You're okay. I'm here."

"He was here, Beckett... He was in my bedroom."

"No one's here, Lyssa. It's just us." He ran his hand down my back. "It was just a dream—a really bad dream."

"It seemed so vivid. It was as if he were here, on top of me, and I couldn't breathe. I was so scared."

"You're okay. I'm right here." Beckett's voice was calm and reassuring as he whispered, "I won't let anything happen to you."

"You promise?"

"You have my word. I'll never let anyone hurt you again." He eased me back off of him so he could see my face. His expression was marked with concern. "I think it's time you told me what the hell is going on."

"I can't. If I do, it'll change everything."

"I have no idea what you mean by that."

"I know, but you're just going to have to trust me."

His dark eyes narrowed in confusion. "What exactly do you think is gonna change?"

"You." Over the past couple of weeks, Beckett had been my one true constant. He anchored me, made me feel like everything was going to be okay, and even if we were just friends, I liked the way things were between us. I was afraid if I told him what had happened with Lucas, he would treat me differently—like I was broken or damaged beyond repair. "You'll change."

"I'm sorry, freckles, but I'm not following."

"Something happened to me, Beckett. Something that was out of my control"—I lowered my head—"and if you knew what that something was, you wouldn't think the same way about me as you do now."

"Are you kidding me?" He brought his hand up to my chin, gently lifting my head, and when my eyes met his, he whispered, "I think you're an incredible woman, inside and out, and nothing you could ever tell me is gonna change that."

"You're wrong."

"Try me."

"Okay, but don't say I didn't warn you." I let out a deep breath. "I was sixteen when Lucas Brant asked me to go to Homecoming ..."

I spent the next half hour rehashing everything that had happened that night. It wasn't easy. No one knew except Clay and I hadn't spoken about it since. I swallowed back the knot that was growing in my throat, and then told him about seeing Lucas in the parking lot as I was leaving work. I tried not to cry, but the tears came just the same. Even so, I was able to tell him everything, and when I finally stopped talking, he leaned over to me and took me in his arms once again. He quietly held me until I stopped crying, and then he softly kissed me on the temple. "I'm sorry that happened to you, Alyssa, but it doesn't make me think any less of you. If anything, it makes me admire you even more."

"How can you say that?"

"Because you're a survivor. You didn't give up. You didn't let what happened to you stop you from living your life." He looked down at me with emotion in his eyes as he said, "You're a fighter, Alyssa."

"Look at me, Beckett. I'm a wreck." I don't know what came over me. Maybe it was the fact that I knew I could trust him. He'd been there for me in so many ways, and I hoped that he'd be there for me when it counted the most. I reached out, placed my hands on his face, and as his eyes met mine, I whispered, "I'm so tired. I just want to have a normal life. I want to stop being so afraid. Please help me. Help me stop being so afraid."

"What do you need me to do?"

I inched forward as I whispered, "This."

I pressed my lips against his and kissed him. When his muscles grew tense, I feared he might pull away, but he didn't. Instead, he kissed me back.

7

T-BONE

Night after night, I found myself standing on Alyssa's front porch, having no clue what the fuck I was doing there. I felt this unexplainable pull to her that I simply couldn't understand. I tried to tell myself that I was just looking after a friend in need. It was easy to do, too. I'd seen how distraught she was the night she'd come to the clubhouse to talk to Clay, and the days that followed were more of the same. Hell, she'd struggled to just get through the day. It gutted me that I didn't know why. I thought I might be able to help if Alyssa would just talk to me, but anytime I brought it up, she always refused to discuss it.

I figured she just needed time, and I was doing my best to give it to her. It wasn't easy. Seeing her hurting got to me, so much so, I'd even considered going to talk to Hyde. I'd seen the way he'd lost it the night she came to the clubhouse, so I had no doubt that he knew why. But I just couldn't do it. I wanted Alyssa to be the one to come to me, and now that she had—that scared look in her eyes, the crying herself to sleep, and even her lack of relationships with other men—it all made sense. I finally understood why she was so broken, and even though I knew I was going down a rabbit hole, I couldn't walk away—especially after that kiss.

Damn. It was the last thing I'd expected her to do, but holy hell, having her mouth on mine felt better than I could've imagined, and yes—I'd imagined it many times since the day I first laid eyes on her. Alyssa's gaze never left mine as she reached for the hem of my shirt, eased it over my head, and tossed it onto the floor. Sensing my apprehension, she placed the palm of her hand on my bare chest and said, "I know you're worried about the fact that I'm Hyde's sister and all that it entails, but this has nothing to do with him or the club. Here … in this house, it's just you and me."

"It's not that simple."

"If you're going to say that you're too old for me, you're wrong. You being older is one of the reasons I want to do this with you." Her brows furrowed. "Don't you get it? I know I can trust you to do this right. I know I'm asking a lot, but I need this. I need you, Beckett."

She slowly lifted her t-shirt over her head, exposing her flawless skin and perfectly round breasts. It was then that I realized her scars weren't in plain sight. They were hidden deep within where they took longer to heal, which made me wonder if following through with her request was the right thing to do. Alyssa, on the other hand, didn't have the same doubt. "I want it to be you … *only you.*"

The second the words slipped from her mouth every

ounce of resistance I had left in me vanished, leaving me completely helpless to fight the urge to have her. I reached up, slipped my hand around the back of her neck, and pulled her close as I pressed my mouth against hers. Her lips were warm and soft, and each swirl of her tongue made the blood rush straight to my cock. I knew I needed to take it slow. After what she'd been through, the last thing I wanted was to scare her or push her, but it wasn't going to be easy.

I hadn't wanted to admit it, not to myself or anyone else, but Alyssa got to me in a way that no woman ever had—maybe it was the fact that she was so incredibly beautiful or maybe it was simply the way she made me feel whenever I was with her. I'd intended to keep things simple, but the second her lips met mine, I knew everything between us was going to change, yet it didn't stop me from lowering my mouth to her ear. "I want to erase all those bad memories...every damn one of them."

I ran my lips leisurely from the curve of her jaw down to her shoulder as she rasped, "Yes."

She felt so damn good in my arms. I continued trailing kisses past her collarbone as her arms reached for me, pulling me towards her as I lowered my mouth to her breast. Heavy breaths and low moans filled the room as I raked my tongue against her nipple. Her head fell back, leaving no doubt that she liked having my mouth on her. With her eyes closed, she mumbled, "You have no idea how good that feels."

Goosebumps prickled across her skin as my fingers worked their way across her abdomen, through the waistband of her sleep pants. A small whimper escaped her throat as my fingers trailed further down between her legs; she was just as turned on as I was. But when I grazed across Alyssa's center and her entire body tensed, I knew then that I was taking things too fast. Hoping to assure her, I lowered my mouth to her ear as I whispered, "I'd never hurt you."

"I know. I'm okay."

"You can trust me ... Let me make you feel good."

I kissed her, long and hard, taking pleasure from the sounds of all her little whimpers and moans. When I felt her body start to relax, I slid my fingertips inside her and had just begun to stroke her when she moaned, "Oh god, Beckett."

I could feel my need for her building, burning deep inside my gut. Fuck, it was more than I could take. I wanted to be inside her, but first I needed to make sure she was ready for me. I sat up and reached for the waistband of her pink satin panties. Her eyes widened, not with fear but anticipation, as I started to ease them down her long slender legs. That spark of anticipation quickly faded as I settled back on the bed with my head between her legs. "Wait ... What are you—"

"You gotta trust me, Alyssa."

She nodded, then silently watched as I slid my hands under her ass and pulled her towards me. A light hiss slipped through her teeth and her head fell back when I started to kiss along her inner thigh. Alyssa's fingers dug into the sheets and her back arched off of the bed as I pressed the flat of my tongue against her sensitive flesh. "Yes!"

Her eyes clamped shut as I continued to nip and suck,

teasing her clit with my mouth. It wasn't long before her legs started to tremble. I realized then that she was letting go, giving in to the moment and even relishing in it. I increased the pressure, and her breath quickened. I knew she was getting close when she started to writhe and gasp for air. The feeling was foreign to her and she tried to resist, but no matter how hard she tried to fight it, she couldn't stop the inevitable torment of her building orgasm. "That's it, baby. Come for me."

Seconds later, her head fell back as her entire body jolted with her release. Still in a haze, Alyssa looked up with wonder in her eyes. Damn, I'd never in my life seen a more gorgeous sight. Unable to wait any longer to have her, I stood up and started to remove my jeans. "Do you ... um ... have protection?"

I didn't answer. I simply reached into my back pocket and took the condom out of my wallet; as soon as I'd rolled it on, I lowered myself back onto the bed. My breath became strained as I hovered over her. She looked so damn beautiful lying there beneath me, and I couldn't imagine wanting her more than I did at that moment.

"You sure about this?"

"Yes," she whispered as she brought her hands up to my face. She pulled me towards her, pressing her mouth against mine, kissing me. I knew she was ready, and I gently slid deep inside her. She inhaled a deep breath, holding for a moment as she adjusted to my size. I stilled, listening as she exhaled slowly, and after tilting her hips forward, she was ready for more. I started to rock against her body, slow and steady. Fuck, she felt so damn good—so tight and warm and wet. I had to pause for several breaths just to get a grip on myself before I exploded right there on the spot. "You're incredible, Alyssa—every fucking inch of you."

"Beckett," she whispered.

The longing in her voice as she said my name spurred me on. I started to move once again, driving into her until I found steady pace. I watched her every move, listened to every moan and whimper, making sure that I was giving her exactly what she needed.

The muscles in her body grew rigid, her chest stilled as she held her breath, and I knew she was close again. I increased my pace, just enough to push her over the edge, and soon after, her fingernails dug into my back as her entire body grew taut. Seconds later, I heard the sound of air rushing from her lungs as she fell limp in my arms.

I continued to drive into her, the tight grip of her body bringing me closer to climax with every thrust until I finally came inside her. I took a moment to catch my breath, then lowered myself down on the bed and pulled her over to me. The room stilled as she nestled into my side and rested her head on my shoulder.

Our breaths started to slow, and just as the lustful haze began to fade, Alyssa looked up at me with tears in her eyes as she said, "I didn't know it could be like that."

"What's with the water works? You okay?"

"I'm more than okay." A soft smile crossed her face. "In fact, I've never been better."

A sense of peace washed over me as she laid her head back down on my shoulder and curled up next to me. Feeling better than I had in weeks, I closed my eyes and listened to the soothing sound of her breathing, and it wasn't long before we both drifted off to sleep. It was early when I woke up that next morning, and a smile crossed my face when I found Alyssa still nestled up against me. She looked so damn sweet lying there, and I hated the idea of leaving her, but I didn't have a choice. If I was going to talk to Riggs before work, I needed to get moving. Doing my best not to wake her, I eased her off of me and onto the pillow before slipping out of the bed. I gathered my clothes from the floor and quickly got dressed. I stepped back over to the bed and kissed Alyssa on the forehead, then turned to walk out the door. I hadn't gotten very far before I heard her say, "Sneaking off so soon?"

"Not sneaking off, babe. I've gotta get to the garage and didn't want to wake you."

"Oh, okay."

I walked over and sat down on the edge of the bed next to her. "I want you to know that what happened last night is going to stay between us. I won't say a word about it."

"I know, Beckett. I wouldn't have asked you to ... you know, if I wasn't sure that I could trust you." A strange look crossed her face as she sat up in the bed. "Do you regret it?"

"Regret what?"

"You know ... being with me. Did you do it because you wanted to or because you felt sorry for me."

"You're kidding me, right?" Seeing the doubt in her eyes gutted me. It got to me even more that I was the reason it was there. I'd never been good with the romantic shit. I always seemed to say the wrong things, do the wrong things, and in the past, it never really mattered. Deep down, I knew the women I'd pursued were just a flash in the pan, but Alyssa was different. I actually cared about her, and I didn't want to fuck things up any more than I already had. I reached out and brushed a loose strand of hair from her face. "I'm not a man who does things I don't want to do."

"But—"

"No buts, Alyssa. I've been coming here every night because I wanted to, and I was with you last night because I wanted to be with you. Hell, I've never wanted anything more."

"Good ... So, I didn't mess things up between us?"

"Not a chance." I leaned down and kissed her on the forehead. "Now go back to sleep, and I'll check in with you later."

"Okay." As I stood to leave, she smiled and said, "Have a good day, Beckett."

"You too, beautiful."

On my way out, I locked the door, then headed out to my bike. On the way to the clubhouse, I thought about everything Alyssa had told me about the night of Home-coming. I thought about the anguish in her voice as she talked about that asshole forcing himself on her, the tears that fell as she told me how helpless she'd felt when she couldn't stop him, and how she'd never told anyone except Clay about what'd happened to her. She also mentioned how Clay had gone and beat the living hell out of the guy, but it did little to suppress my need to seek my own revenge on him. That overwhelming need is what drove me to go find Riggs. When I got to the club-house, it was still pretty early and I was worried that he might not have made it in yet, but as luck would have it, he was in his room working on something for Gus. As soon as he saw me entering the room, his brows furrowed.

"Something wrong, brother?"

"I need you to do something for me." I sat down next to him as I continued, "I need all the information you can find on a guy named Lucas Brant."

"What is it with this guy? Hyde was just asking about him the other day." He pushed his chair back from his desk and turned to face me. "Does he have something going on with his sister?"

"I can't get into it right now, brother. I just need to get all the information I can on this guy."

I hadn't realized that Gus had come into the room until I heard him ask, "And what exactly are you planning to do with this information?"

"Don't know just yet."

"Hyde know you're looking into this fella?"

"No." I knew he didn't like my response. It was written all over his face. Before he could try to talk me out of pursuing this guy, I told him, "This doesn't have anything to do with him."

"If it involves his sister, then I'd say it has plenty to do with him."

"Hyde had his chance to fix this thing with Lucas, Prez." I stood up and took a step towards him. "You know me well enough that I wouldn't be doing this if I didn't think it was the right thing."

99

"Going behind Hyde's back isn't the way to go about this."

"How about this? I won't do anything with Lucas before talking to him."

"I have your word on that?"

"You know you do." As soon as the words left my mouth, I turned my attention back to Riggs. "I'm gonna need everything you gave Hyde."

After a few strokes of the keys, his printer started shooting out page after page. When it was done, Riggs grabbed the stack of papers and offered it to me. "This is everything I've got."

I took a moment to flip through the pages, then said, "I'm gonna need you to track his phone and credit cards. I want to know every move this motherfucker makes."

"You got it."

"Appreciate it, brother." Before leaving, I turned to Gus and asked, "You got a minute?"

"Yeah, let's go down to my office."

I followed him down the hall, and once we'd made it to his office, he closed the door behind us. "This about the girl?"

"It is." I waited for him to sit down, then said, "Things just got really fucking complicated, and I've got no one to blame but myself."

"You want to tell me what the hell you mean by that?"

I sat down and sighed. "I let myself get too close ... Crossed a line that shouldn't have been crossed."

"All right, so what are you gonna do about it?"

"That's just it. I don't have a fucking clue."

Gus leaned back in his chair and studied me for a

moment. We'd been friends for a long time. He knew me better than anyone, so I had no doubt that I could trust him to lead me in the right direction—even if it was a direction I didn't want to go. I took a deep breath and tried to prepare myself for a reprimand, but instead he said, "You're a good man, Bone. I trust you to do the right thing by her and the club."

"But what if I—"

"I trust you." Gus leaned forward, resting his elbows on his desk, and looked me dead in the eye. "Now it's time for you to do the same."

"Damn, brother. As much as I appreciate you saying that, you're not giving me anything here," I complained. "I came to you for advice on what to do."

"You didn't need my advice before you crossed that line you said you shouldn't have," he scoffed. "But if I had any advice to give you, it would be to take things slow. Keep it as simple as you can for as long as you can."

"And Hyde?"

"He'll come around when the time is right. Like the rest of us, he knows you're a good man." His expression grew hard as he warned, "Just don't give him a reason to think otherwise."

"I won't. You have my word on that."

"Best be getting to work. I'm sure Darcy is already there waiting on you now."

"No doubt." As I started to leave, I said, "Thanks, Prez."

After I left his office, I headed out to the parking lot. Once I'd made it to my bike, I stowed the papers that Riggs had given me into my saddlebags and headed to the garage. As much as I wanted to stop and look through everything, it would have to wait. I had to finish breaking down the 1969 Camaro I'd been working on for the past couple of days. Darcy had already started painting and was waiting on me to finish sandblasting the rear end. She wasn't exactly patient, so I wasn't surprised to find her waiting for me when I pulled up to the garage. She was standing at the front door in her paint suit with her hand planted on her hip. "Well, look who finally decided to show up."

"What the hell, Darc? It's not even eight o'clock yet."

"You know I have to finish priming today."

"I'm well aware of that." I lumbered past her as I started inside. "That's why I got here early."

"Well, clearly your idea of early and mine are very different."

I could've shot back at her. Hell, under any other circumstance, I would have, but I knew she was just eager to get the job finished and finished right. Darcy might've been a chick, but damn—she worked as hard as any man I'd ever met, and I respected her for it. We all did. She followed close behind while I walked over to my station and picked up the sandblaster. "I'm on it. It'll be ready for you in thirty."

"Okay." Her expression softened as she said, "Thanks, Bone. I knew I could count on you."

"Um-hmm. Sure, ya did," I scoffed. "That's why you were waiting at the door to bust my balls."

"Well, they're still intact, aren't they?"

I reached down, cupped my balls in my hand, and

held them for a minute. "Yeah, they're just fine. Thank you very much."

"Such an asshat."

"Yeah, but you love me. You know you do."

"Shut up and get to work, Bone." Darcy turned and started to walk away. "The clock's a ticking."

I shook my head as I watched her go back into her paint room. As promised, I finished the rear end in less than a half hour, and after Gauge and I carried it to her room, we got busy on the engine. The entire time we were working, I was thinking about Brant and all the intel on him that was waiting for me in my saddlebag. Sensing that something was bugging me, Gauge nudged me and asked, "What's with you today?"

"Just got some things on my mind."

"I see that. You wanna talk about it?"

Gauge was a good guy. I knew without a doubt that I could trust him with anything, but I'd made a promise to Alyssa and I intended to keep it. "Thanks, man, but I've gotta handle this one myself."

I turned my focus back to the task at hand, and together, Gauge and I busted our asses to get it done. When we finally wrapped things up, I cleaned up my station and headed out to my bike. I wasted no time getting on road and to my place. Once I pulled up, I grabbed the papers out of the saddlebag and went inside; then I sat down at the kitchen table and read through every page, line by fucking line. It didn't take me long to pick up on the fact that the guy had married up with Hillary *Livingston* Brant. Not only was Hillary's family loaded, she was a nurse practitioner, making enough money to support them both. At first glance, Brant seemed like an average Joe who'd played his cards right, but then I came across his police record. It seemed that Alyssa wasn't the only woman he'd raped. While the charges were either dropped or never formally made, there were at least five other women who'd accused Brant of rape, and just like he had with Alyssa, the motherfucker had gotten away with it—well, that shit was about to fucking change.

8

ALYSSA

"WHAT'S UP WITH YOU?" JACK TEASED AS HE CARRIED A load of dishes to the sink. "All smiles like all is good in the world. You must've had one hell of a night last night."

"I did." I smiled. "That doesn't mean I'm gonna tell you about it."

"Seriously?" He turned on the water and let it run over the dirty dishes. "You're really gonna hold out on me?"

"Sorry, dude." I could've told him about my night with Beckett, but I found it doubtful that he'd understand how much it had meant to me. I couldn't put into words how after being with Beckett, I felt like a weight had been lifted off me. I couldn't remember the last time I felt so alive, so free and happy—really happy. I grabbed my crate of potatoes and gave him a wink. "This one I'm keeping to myself."

"I'm gonna remember that! Next time I've got tea to spill, I'm keeping that shit to myself."

"Mm-hmm. Sure you will." Over the past few weeks,

Jack and I had become pretty close friends. He made it easy. He was always goofing around, doing his best to lighten the mood whenever things got tense in the kitchen, and he was a great listener. It also helped to know that he wasn't the least bit interested in me. He'd let it be known early on that he was involved with someone —someone who just happened to be named Tony. They'd been dating for over a year, and from the way Jack spoke, they were very happy together. I looked back over my shoulder as I smiled at him and said, "As soon as Tony does something sweet for you, you'll be itching to tell me all about it."

"Yeah, you're probably right."

I walked over to the cutting board laying on the counter and started peeling my second crate of potatoes. I'd been at it for almost an hour when Bisset came over to me. He stood silently watching as I continued on with my task, and after several moments, he cleared his voice. I looked over to him and listened as he said, "I'm moving you to plating."

"Oh, okay," I answered, unable to hold back my excitement. I'd only been there a few weeks, and to be moved so quickly was a big deal. As much as I wanted to reach up and hug him, I simply gave him a nod and said, "Thank you for the opportunity."

"I'll be watching. One screw up and you're back to the potatoes."

"Understood."

Bisset then turned and made his way over to Jack. I watched as they spoke for a couple of minutes, and seconds later, he went back to his regular routine of barking out orders to the rest of the crew. Jack was smiling ear to ear as he made his way over to me and said, "Looks like I'm finally moving up."

"Really?"

"Yep. I'm moving to the line," he answered proudly. "I'm gonna be taking your place with the vegetables and salad."

"That's awesome. Congratulations!"

"Thank you very much."

"I didn't realize you were interested in becoming a chef."

"Ain't like I'm gonna bus dishes for the rest of my life." He lifted his head and placed his hands on his hips as he rocked them back and forth. "I'm working my way up in the world, sunshine. You just wait and see."

"I have no doubt that you'll do great." I motioned my hand towards the crate of potatoes. "You best get busy."

"Right back at ya."

I was walking on cloud nine as I headed over to the main cooking station, but the second I got into position, my nerves kicked in. I knew Bisset would be watching my every move, and he'd be expecting me to keep up with the line's fast pace without making any mistakes. While there were plenty, none of them were too major, and I made it through the night without a single plate being returned to the kitchen. That in itself was enough to have me smiling as I headed into the locker room at the end of the night. I was about to gather my things when Jack walked in. "How'd it go?"

"Could've been better." I shrugged and gave him a slight smile. "Could've been worse. How about you?"

"Peeling potatoes isn't an ideal job, but it sure as hell beats washing dishes."

"Yes, it does." I took my purse and umbrella out of my locker as I asked, "You about to head out?"

"Yeah. You want me to walk you out to your car?"

"That would be great."

Eager to get home, I held my keys in my hand and followed him towards the door. When we reached my car, I thanked him and we quickly said our goodbyes. I rushed home, wanting to be ready in case Beckett came by. He'd been stopping in every night for the past couple of weeks, but after what had taken place the night before, I wasn't sure that the same would hold true tonight. I hoped we could remain friends and keep things simple, but deep down I knew that wasn't possible. There was no way things between us wouldn't change after the night we shared, but I at least hoped the change would be a positive one. After taking a shower and changing clothes, I went into the kitchen to search the fridge for something to make for dinner. It had been a couple of days since I'd been to the grocery store, so I was down to just the basics. I pulled out a carton of eggs, some bacon, and a can of biscuits.

I was just about to turn on the stove when I heard a knock at the door. A big smile crossed my face when I opened it and found Beckett standing on the porch. "Hey, I wasn't sure if you were going to come by."

"Me neither." He gave me a small smile. "But I wanted to make sure you were okay."

"I'm good. I was actually just about to make myself something to eat if you'd like to come in and join me."

"You sure?"

"Yes, I'm sure." I reached out and grabbed his arm, tugging him inside. "Now, get in here and help me cook."

"Bacon?"

"Yeah, I'm making breakfast for dinner." As we walked into the kitchen, I told him, "I haven't been to the grocery in a few days, so my options are kind of limited to bacon and eggs."

"Sounds good to me. Just tell me what I can do to help, chef."

"How 'bout you cook the bacon, and I'll start the biscuits?"

"You got it."

Beckett took the bacon off the counter and went over to the stove while I pulled out my cast iron skillet for the biscuits. I opened the can and was just starting to arrange them in the pan when Beckett asked, "A skillet for biscuits?"

"It makes the biscuits rise better." I said while slipping them in the oven. "It's an old trick my mother taught me."

"Is that right?" A sexy smirk crossed his face as he stood there looking at me. "What other tricks did she teach you?"

"Just a few things here and there, but they were nothing like the tricks you showed me last night." I teased.

"What kind of tricks are you referring to?"

"Oh, come on, Beckett." I walked over and took a bowl from the cabinet. "You know exactly what I'm talking about."

"Can't say that I do."

I started cracking the eggs into the bowl as I shook my head. "That thing you did with your fingers, for one."

"You liked that, did ya?"

"Mm-hmm." I kept my eyes on the bowl of eggs, scrambling them with the whisk as I muttered, "Liked that kissing thing you did on my neck too."

I didn't realize he'd come up behind me until I felt the warmth of his breath on my neck. A delicious tingle shot down my spine the second his lips touched the curve of my neck. "You mean this?"

"Mm-hmm."

It felt so good and I didn't want him to stop as I tilted my head. Just as I hoped, he continued nipping and sucking down to my shoulder. Just before he stopped, he lightly clamped his teeth against my skin, giving me another jolt of pleasure. That pleasure was quickly replaced with disappointment when he abruptly stopped and walked back over to the stove, turning his focus back to the bacon he'd been cooking. It amazed me that a simple touch could have such an effect on me, but that's how it was with Beckett. He brought out feelings I never dreamed I'd have. I thought I'd always be guarded, untrusting, and cold, but he'd shown me that I was wrong. I could feel trust and passion and everything in between. It was one of the many reasons why I liked to be around him so much. I didn't have to see his face to know that he was smiling when he asked, "How those eggs coming along?"

"Such a tease," I whispered under my breath.

Beckett glanced over his shoulder, his eyes dancing

with mischief. "What was that?"

"Nothing." I walked over to the stove and dumped the bowl of eggs into the frying pan. "How much longer on the bacon?"

"It's done. Might wanna check on those biscuits."

I reached for an oven mitt, then opened the door. Good thing that I did because they were definitely ready, so I pulled them out and set them down on a hot plate. Beckett leaned over and gave the biscuits an appraising nod. "Looks like your mom was right about the skillet."

"That she was." I took the spatula and stirred the eggs, and once they were done, I carried them over to the counter. "Looks like we're set."

"Plates?"

I motioned my hand above his head. "They're right behind you in the cabinet."

Beckett pulled out two, then walked over and sat down on one of the stools next to me. We each made a plate and started eating. After he'd taken a few bites, he looked over to me and said, "You didn't finish telling me about those tricks."

"Well, I was trying to, but then you had to go and distract me before I could finish."

"Yeah, sorry about that." A smile spread across his handsome face. "Couldn't help myself."

"Mm-hmm. Sure, you couldn't."

I poked around at my eggs, then took a sip of my tea. I knew he was waiting for me to tell him about the other things he'd done that had turned me on, but as I sat there, I suddenly became embarrassed and regretted ever bringing it up. I had no idea how to explain it to him, so I just kept quiet and pretended to eat. Beckett had just finished the last of his biscuit when he leaned towards me and asked, "Why don't you stop stalling and tell me what's really on your mind?"

"I don't know. It's hard to explain"—I shrugged—"and a little embarrassing."

"You're gonna have to give me more than that."

"Let's just say ... that after last night, it's pretty clear you have a lot of experience ... experience I don't have."

"You say that like it's a bad thing."

"I don't think you get what I'm saying."

"No, I get what you're saying"—he reached out and placed his hand on mine—"and you're mistaken if you think there's anything wrong or embarrassing about the fact that you haven't had a lot of experience. I personally think it's a good thing. A very good thing."

"And why's that?"

"In time, you'll see. When you meet the right guy, you'll have those experiences with him."

As I sat there focusing on him, I thought about the night before—how safe I'd felt in his arms, how his touch had made my entire body come alive, and how he'd put my needs before his own. I never realized it was even possible for me to actually enjoy having sex, but I did. I enjoyed it a lot, and I couldn't stop myself from wanting to try it again ... and again and again. That didn't mean I was being naïve about my feelings for Beckett. Sure, there were things about him I didn't know, but I was certain of how he made me feel. "And what if I think you're the right guy?"

"I'm not." With a look of regret in his eyes, he said,

"I'm too damn old, livin' a life that isn't meant for a woman like you, and—"

"Beckett, I'm not asking you to put a ring on my finger." I stood up, reached for the hem of my t-shirt, and quickly pulled it over my head. His eyes skirted over me as I tossed it over my shoulder and said, "I'm just asking you to join me in the bedroom."

I knew it was a bold move and there was a chance he might turn me down, but for another night with him, I was willing to take a chance. I gave him a wink as I walked past him and started down the hall. Moments later, I heard his stool scrape against the tile floor as he stood up and followed me into the bedroom. When he got to the doorway, he stopped, and just stood there staring at me like he was thinking about his next move. His brows furrowed as he said, "Not sure this is a good idea."

"And why not?"

"It'll complicate things."

"They're already complicated, Beckett." I shrugged with a smile. "Don't see why we can't complicate them a little bit more."

"Look, I, ah ... I don't know about this." He seemed so torn as he said, "I'm not gonna lie. Last night was incredible, really fucking incredible, but this is entering dangerous territory. As much as I want to be with you again, I don't want to do something that might end up hurting you ... *or me* for that matter."

"Well, let's just be open and honest about things. That way neither of us will get hurt." I walked over to him. "I meant what I said last night. I didn't know sex could be like that. I really didn't. After what happened with Lucas, I've always been too scared to try, but when I was with you, something in me changed. You made me see what I was missing by letting my fears get in the way."

"You said you didn't want me to put a ring on your finger, so does that mean you want to keep this thing between us simple ... just friends or whatever."

"Yes, we'll just be friends." I reached behind me and unclasped my bra. As it fell to the floor, I gave him a sexy smile and said, "Friends with benefits."

Without any further hesitation, Beckett reached for me, pulling me close as his mouth found mine. An eager moan echoed through the room when his tongue brushed against mine. With just a simple kiss, he sent a surge of heat coursing through my body, burning me to my very core.

Needing more, I reached for his t-shirt, but he grabbed it and quickly pulled it over his head. My eyes drifted down to the colorful ink that marked his chest and I couldn't stop myself from reaching out to touch him. He watched silently as I ran the tip of my finger along the intricate lines of his tattoos. His voice was low and strained as he asked, "Like what you see?"

"Mm-hmm ... very much." I looked up, and when my eyes met his, I whispered, "You're beautiful."

"Never been called that," he scoffed. "But I gotta say ... I like it coming from you."

His hands reached for the back of my neck while his fingers tangled tightly in my hair as he took a step forward, pinning me against the wall. He lowered his mouth to mine, kissing me long and hard. My hips instinctively rocked against him, and my heart started to race when I felt him thicken against me. My desire for this man was running rampant through me, and I was losing what little control I had over my body. Any inhibitions I might have had completely washed away when he took my bare breasts in his hands, holding them firmly while brushing his calloused thumbs across the sensitive flesh. I loved the feel of his hands on my body—every touch had me longing for more.

It was at that moment a thought crossed my mind. I'd never actually touched a man, never held a cock in my hand or given a blow job. While I was too nervous to go that far, I at least wanted to feel him. I lowered my hands to his waist, quickly unbuckling his jeans. A hiss escaped his lips as I started to slip my hand into his boxers. Just before I reached for him, I asked, "Can I?"

"You can do anything you want, beautiful."

His breathing became short and strained as my fingers wrapped around his hardness. I could feel his pulse throbbing against my hand as I slowly started stroking him. I tightened my grip as I glided my fingers up and down. A feeling of satisfaction washed over me when his head fell back with a deep-seated groan, letting me know that I was giving him pleasure—the kind of pleasure he'd given me the night before. I could feel my confidence growing by the second, and it wasn't long before I found myself grasping at his jeans. I lowered them down his hips, exposing his long, hard shaft. The next thing I knew, Beckett lifted me into his arms and said, "You keep looking at me like that, and we're gonna be done before we ever get started."

The words had barely left his mouth when I was on the bed. He tugged his boots and socks off, then his jeans. With the weight of his body pressed against me, his mouth dropped to my ear, the warmth of his breath sending goosebumps down my spine as he whispered, "So damn perfect."

Beckett's hands dropped to my hips as he slowly slipped my panties down my legs. A needy moan vibrated through his chest as he gazed down upon my naked body, then a devilish grin spread across his face while he settled his hips between my legs, making my entire body tremble. Lowering his face to my neck, the bristles of his day-old beard prickled against my skin as he nipped and sucked along the contours of my body.

A part of me wanted to go slow like the night before. I wanted to be able to savor the moment, but I was too far gone and just couldn't restrain myself. I wanted him. I needed him. Spreading my legs further to accommodate his huge body, I shifted my hips up towards him as he rubbed himself against my clit. My entire body ached for him.

"You ready for me?" he asked.

Unable to even string together coherent words, I nodded, praying that he wouldn't stop. His voice was stern when he said, "Need you to say the words, Alyssa. Need you to tell me what you want."

His words caught me by surprise, but I knew he meant exactly what he'd said. Without reservation, I whispered, "I want you."

"And what do you want me to do? Need you to tell me."

"I want you to do what you did last night"—I could feel myself becoming more turned on by the second —"with your fingers."

I wound my hands around his neck, pulling him closer, and kissed him.

His hand slipped between us, and his fingers entered me. Each movement was meticulous and slow, causing me to writhe beneath him while his thumb brushed back and forth over my clit. "This ... Is this what you want?"

"Yes!" I gasped.

I was unable to control my whimpers of pleasure as he delved deeper inside me. I didn't recognize my own voice as it echoed through the room. I was completely lost in his touch, loving the feel of his calloused hands against my body. The bed creaked as I arched my back, feeling the muscles in my abdomen tighten with my impending release. My breath caught in my throat as waves of pleasure rushed through me, and just when I thought I couldn't take it a minute longer, his hand was gone. He reached for a condom, and once he'd slipped it on, Beckett was back on top of me.

His forehead rested against mine as he grazed his cock against me. His erection, hot and hard, burned against my clit before he thrust deep inside, giving me all he had in one smooth stroke. I gasped at the intrusion and he froze. "Fuck, did I hurt you?"

"No, I'm good ... better than good." I lifted my hand to his face. "Stop holding back."

I rocked my hips, begging him to continue. His hands reached up to the nape of my neck, fisting my hair as he drove into me again. Slow and demanding, he was in complete control. Every smooth slide of his cock into my body was a statement of dominance. His teeth raked over my nipples, and I cried out wanting more. I dug my nails into his back as my whole body ignited with such intense heat; it was unlike anything I'd ever experienced before.

Beckett thrust deeper inside me, and as I tightened around him, he let out a growl and then quickened his pace. His control shattered, and unable to restrain himself any longer, he drove into me in hard, steady strokes. I fought to catch my breath as I felt my climax approaching. My entire body jolted and shook as my orgasm crashed through me. I continued to tighten around his throbbing cock until he found his own release. His body collapsed on top of mine, exhausted and sweaty. I loved how Beckett felt pressed against my bare skin, buried deep inside me. He took a moment to catch his breath and then rolled over to settle next to me on the bed. Neither of us spoke. Instead, we just lay there, listening to the sounds of our breathing slow, and it wasn't long before we both drifted off to sleep.

Over the next couple of months, it was more of the same. Beckett and I would spend our days apart, living our daily lives like usual, but the night was ours. After a long day at work, I was looking forward to seeing Beckett when he showed up at my house with a mischievous expression on his face. "You wanna go somewhere?"

"Where do you have in mind?"

"It's a surprise. You in or not?"

"I'm in."

"Okay, go grab a couple of towels."

"Towels? What for?"

He cocked his eyebrow as he replied, "You said you were in."

"Okay, fine. I'll go get the towels."

I rushed to the bathroom, grabbed two of them, then followed Beckett out to his bike. He stowed the towels in the saddlebags, then we were on our way. After riding for twenty minutes or so, I realized we were headed towards Fayette County. Curious, I leaned towards him with my mouth close to his ear and asked, "You really aren't going to tell me where we're going?"

"Nope. Just gonna have to wait and see."

Thirty minutes later, we were riding down a long gravel road until we reached a beautiful horse ranch. All the lights were off, and it didn't look like anyone was around when we parked and got off the bike. "Whose place is this?"

"It belongs to Riley's dad, but they're off at some horse show. Won't be back until tomorrow."

"*Okaay* ... So, what are we doing here?"

He took the towels out of the saddlebags and started walking towards the back field. "You'll see."

I followed as he opened the gate and led me towards a field. The only light we had was the moon shining down on us, making it a little difficult to see, but Beckett kept pressing forward. After a ten-minute trek, we came up on a creek. I thought we'd stop there, but Beckett just kept walking, only stopping when we came up on an enormous pond. "We're here."

He slipped off his cut, then his shirt, and when he started to unbuckle his pants, I asked, "What are you doing?"

"Going for a swim."

"In that? What about snakes?"

"Didn't take you for a chicken, Alyssa." As he kicked off his boots, Beckett asked, "You coming or what?"

"I, ah ... I'm coming?" My answer sounded more like a question. With great reservation, I started to undress. I was down to my bra and panties when I looked over to Beckett and saw that he was completely naked. The man looked incredibly hot, and just like that, all my reservations faded away. I slipped off the rest of my clothes and started running towards the water, screaming wildly as I jumped in. Laughing, Beckett followed after me. Once he was in the water, he reached for me, pulling me towards him. "I don't know how you do it."

"Do what?"

"Make me feel like I can do anything." I wrapped my arms around his neck. "A few months ago, I wouldn't have even *considered* taking my clothes off in front of a man, and now I just ran across a field naked and jumped into a damn pond."

"Everyone has a wild side. I guess I just bring it out in you."

"Maybe so." I leaned forward and pressed my lips against his. "Whatever it is about you, I like it. I like it a lot."

From the beginning, I knew in my heart that Beckett was someone I wanted to know, that he was going to be an important part of my life, and I was right. During a time when I was struggling just to get through the day, he was my one true constant. Things with him were good—even better than I could've ever imagined.

9

T-BONE

I REMEMBERED MY OLD MAN SAYING THAT THE DEVIL doesn't come to us with a red face and horns, boasting an eternity of hellfire and brimstone; instead, he was cunningly disguised as everything you've ever wanted. I never knew just how right he was until Alyssa came into my life. I tried to keep a grip, tried to remember that we were just doing this "friend thing" and keeping it simple, but the more time I spent with her, the more I wanted her to be mine. It was inevitable. Being around a woman like her, so good, so wholesome and beautiful, was the ultimate temptation, but at the same time, I had my brothers to consider, especially Hyde. I meant it when I told him and the other brothers that I had no intention of pursuing Alyssa, or at least I thought I did. Maybe I'd known it all along. Regardless, things had changed over the course of the past couple of months, and it was time for me to come clean. I just hadn't found the right time to do it.

It seemed like all my time was spent either at the garage or Alyssa's place or watching Lucas Brant. Since the night she'd finally opened up to me about what had happened to her, I'd been keeping an eye on him, monitoring his every fucking move. At his home. At his work. When he went out with friends. Wherever I deemed it necessary. I was determined to find some indication that he was the monster I knew he was. A man like him, a man who preyed on innocent women and forced himself on them, didn't just suddenly change. I didn't give a flying-fuck that he was married and had a kid on the way. That darkness he tried to hide was still there. I knew it without a doubt, and as soon as I saw a single glimpse of it, I would end him—once and for all. It was one of the many things I'd do to keep Alyssa safe. I knew it was a mistake to let myself get wrapped up in her, but I had, nonetheless.

I was playing with fire and had no doubt there'd be consequences for my actions. I just didn't know that those consequences would come sooner than later.

After I got done at the garage, I met up with Alyssa at her place. Like most nights, we ate some dinner, and after watching some chick-flick on TV, we headed to her room. As soon as I got in the bed, she curled up next to me and said, "I had lunch with Landry today."

"Yeah? What's she been up to?"

"Work mainly." She looked up at me and smiled. "She brought up all of us going somewhere again."

"Y'all come up with any ideas?"

"We were thinking about getting a cabin up in the

mountains or maybe hot springs." She shrugged. "I don't think it really matters to her where we go. I think she's needing a break from work."

"With a job like hers, I can't really blame her for wanting to get away. Maybe we can come up with something."

"Where would you want to go?"

"I don't know. Wherever is fine with me."

"Oh, come on. It doesn't have to be with everybody." Alyssa positioned her head on my chest where she could see me. "Just a place you'd like to visit one day. You know ... like a bucket list sort of thing."

"I'd like to see the Grand Canyon one day and maybe go out to Yellowstone. What about you?"

"I'd love to see both. I haven't had many chances to travel." A soft smile crossed her face as she said, "My dad worked a lot, but we went camping some ... fished and swam. And there was this one year when we actually made it to the beach. It was one of my favorite summers."

"Can't say I've ever been to the beach."

"Maybe we could go together sometime."

"Maybe so."

She rested her head back on my shoulder, and after a few more minutes of talking, she drifted off to sleep. I was relishing the feeling of her body against mine when my burner started to ring. Knowing it was one of the brothers, I forced myself up and grabbed the phone from the pocket of my jeans. "Yeah, whatcha need?"

"We got trouble, Bone," Shadow answered, sounding shaken. "Bad fucking trouble."

L. WILDER

"You gonna tell me what the fuck is going on, or am I supposed to guess?"

"You're gonna have to come see for yourself." If I didn't know better, I'd think Shadow was on the verge of completely losing it when he said, "Get your ass down to the diner."

"On my way." I quickly stood and started putting on my clothes. As I slipped on my boots, I glanced over at Alyssa and said, "I'm sorry, but I've gotta go."

Her brows furrowed. "Is everything okay?"

"Got no idea, but I intend to find out." I put on my cut, then leaned down and kissed her on the forehead. "I'll be back when I can."

"Okay, be careful."

I knew by the way Shadow spoke that I didn't have time to waste, so after I gave Alyssa a quick nod, I hurried out to my bike and started towards the diner. I had no idea what was going on, but I did know Shadow. He was a level-headed guy who wasn't one to lose his cool. The fact that he was so shaken on the phone filled me with dread as I approached the diner and saw blue lights flashing by the front of the building. As I got closer, my stomach sank when I saw four cop cars and an ambulance parked by the entrance. We didn't do cops. There were too many questions—questions we couldn't fucking answer—and we didn't do hospitals for the same reason. Seeing those lights meant someone was hurt bad—bad enough that Mack, the club's doc, couldn't manage the injuries.

With it being dark and all the cops and bystanders lurking around, it was hard to see anything, so, as soon as I was parked, I rushed over to see what the fuck was happening. I caught sight of Blaze and Murphy and hurried over. "What the hell is going on?"

Murphy's focus was on the medics as they started rolling the stretcher towards the back of the ambulance. "Somebody fucking shot him."

"Shot who?"

Before he could answer, I got a better glimpse of exactly *who* was on the stretcher. It felt like someone had knocked the wind out of me when I realized it was my brother, my friend—*my president.* With a bullet wound to the head and another to the stomach, blood covered Gus from head to toe, and the medics were working frantically to get him inside the ambulance. A million questions raced through my mind, but I couldn't speak. I was in complete shock. I'd always thought the man was invincible, that no one could fucking touch him, yet there he lay, fighting for his life. The medics had just gotten him inside when one of them shouted, "He's coding!"

Madness ensued as two of the men started scrambling around to get the defibrillator. Seconds later, they ripped open his blood-soaked shirt before the medic shouted, "Clear."

We all watched in disbelief as the guy placed the paddles against Gus's chest, and his entire body jolted from the electric surge. I couldn't move. Hell, I could barely breathe as I stood there next to Blaze and the other brothers who'd come up. We all stood there in silence as we waited helplessly to see if they could bring him back. Even if they did, it didn't take a fucking doctor to know that Gus was in bad shape. Anyone could see that. Hell, the man had a fucking gunshot to the head and another to the gut, but he was a fighter. I tried to hold on to that thought as I watched the medic shock him for a second time. Thankfully, it worked. They were able to get his heart going again, and in a matter of seconds, they had closed the doors to the ambulance and were on their way to the hospital. As soon as they pulled off, Blaze announced, "We need to get there."

"Absolutely, but Gus would want us to handle things here first," Moose answered.

"Telling me what the fuck happened would be a good start," I snapped.

"That's just it, Bone," Moose answered. "We got no fucking clue."

"Well, you gotta know something," I pushed.

Moose turned to Blaze, waiting for him to tell us what he knew. "All I know is Gus left the clubhouse to come by here and grab dinner for him and Samantha. Next thing I know, Cyrus calls to tell me that Gus is down."

"Fuck. So, we got no idea who fucking did it?"

"Not yet, but we will." Shadow turned his attention to Riggs. "We're gonna need you to get the camera footage and see what you can find out, then we'll go from there."

"If something's there, I'll find it," Riggs assured him.

"Good, 'cause it's only gonna be a matter of time before the cops start asking to see it, and I want us to have dibs on it first."

"I'll do what I can to buy us some time with them as well."

"Do whatever you gotta do." Moose glanced over and noticed the cops questioning Cyrus while another questioned a couple of the diner's customers. "'Cause this shit is gonna get messy with them involved."

"I'll head over to the clubhouse now and get started."

"Thanks, brother."

When he turned to leave, I asked, "What about Samantha?"

Samantha was Gus's ol' lady, and I knew the second her name left my mouth that neither of them had thought of her. "I'll go by their place and bring her to the hospital with me."

"Sounds good. Y'all head on over to the hospital. I'll stick around here and make sure we don't have any trouble with the cops," Shadow replied. "Keep me posted on Gus."

"You know we will."

Dread washed over me as I hopped on my bike and started towards Gus's place. I could still remember the first time I met Samantha. We'd just started getting the Memphis chapter up and running when Gus helped her out of a precarious situation. I knew from the first moment he introduced me to Sam that he was crazy about her, but I didn't know just how much he really loved her until the day she walked out on him. The man was all fucked up over it, and I couldn't blame him. He'd never cared about anyone else like he did her. After she'd disappeared on Gus, he was left wondering what the hell happened. It wasn't until twenty-five years later when August—the daughter he never knew he had—came knocking at our clubhouse door looking for help finding her own daughter. That had been how Gus found out Samantha's folks weren't happy about the two of them being together—so much so, they blackmailed her using some video they had of Gus killing a man. While Samantha knew there were extenuating circumstances, and he was just protecting his brothers, her parents didn't see it that way and used the information to force them apart.

Once everything was out in the open, the two quickly reunited, proving that theirs was the kind of love that could withstand all obstacles. Since then, they'd spent the last year making up for lost time. As I pulled up to the house, I took a deep breath, but it did little to ease the tightness in my chest. I got off my bike and climbed up to the front porch steps. I hadn't had a chance to knock before the door swung open. Before I could say anything, a panicked expression crossed her face. "What's wrong?"

"It's Gus, Samantha. He was shot."

"What!" she cried, tears quickly filling her eyes. "When? How?"

"He was at the diner. Don't know much more than that." The blood drained from her face, and it gutted me to see her so upset. We all cared for Samantha—she was one of our own—and I wanted to help ease her worry, but I only seemed to make matters worse. "They're taking him to the hospital now and—"

Not giving me a chance to finish, she gasped, "The hospital? Oh god. Oh god. It's gotta be bad if they're taking him to the hospital, right?"

"We don't know much yet."

"Oh god." Her voice trembled as she spoke, "I can't lose him, Bone. I just can't!"

I stepped towards her, took her in my arms, and

hugged her. She clung to me, sobbing uncontrollably. "Hey, it's Gus we're talking about here. You know as well as I do, he's not going out without a hell of a fight. We just gotta have faith that he'll pull through this."

"And if he doesn't?"

"You can't think like that, Samantha. He's gonna be okay. You'll see."

"Okay." She looked up at me with tears streaming down her face. "When can I go see him?"

"Won't know that until we get to the hospital. Grab your stuff and I'll run you over there now."

She nodded, then turned and went into the house. Seconds later, she returned with her purse and keys. As we started towards my bike, she suddenly stopped. "August ... I need to—"

"Gunner's with her now, and if I know him, I'm sure they're already on their way to the hospital."

"She has to be so upset."

"No more than the rest of us." Eager to get the hospital, I motioned her towards my bike. "We better get going."

I might've offered to drive her car, but I knew we'd get there faster on my Harley. Besides, she ridden with Gus many times, so I knew she'd be good with it. I grabbed the extra helmet from my saddlebag, and after she put it on, she climbed on behind me. As soon as she was settled, I started the engine, and we were on our way. Gus and Samantha lived in Midtown, so it took some time to get to the hospital. By the time we finally arrived, most of the guys had gathered in the ER's waiting room.

Samantha followed as I walked over to Blaze and asked, "Any word?"

"Got him stabilized, and he's on his way up to surgery."

Samantha looked like she was barely holding it together. "Any idea on how long it will take?"

"No, but if I had to guess, it's gonna be awhile." Blaze placed his hand on her shoulder. "He's in good hands, Samantha."

"I wish that made me feel better." She shook her head as she tried to fight her tears. "I should've known something was wrong. It was getting so late, and he was just going by the diner to pick us up a bite to eat. I was really starting to worry when Bone showed up at our door. I just don't understand how this happened."

I wanted to tell her that we were looking into who had shot him and that we'd make them pay for what they'd done, but it wasn't the time nor the place. At that moment, the focus needed to be on Gus and him making it through surgery. With that in mind, I said, "None of us do, but we'll figure it out. For now, let's try to keep a level head and wait for him to get out of surgery."

"That's easier said than done, but I'll try." Samantha took a quick glance around the room, and when she spotted August in the corner talking to Gunner and Gauge, she said, "I'll be right back."

Once she'd walked away, I turned back to Blaze and asked, "Heard anything from Riggs?"

"Not yet, but he's at the clubhouse now going over the camera feed. He'll call as soon as he knows something."

"When we find out who's responsible, they're as good as dead."

"Agreed, but for now, we're stuck here waiting."

I'd never been a patient man, especially when it came to the club, but at this point, I had no choice. I had to find a way to keep it together until we knew more. I gave him a nod, then went to find a place to sit. I needed a minute to clear my head, so I made my way to the back of the room and sat down. I looked around at all my brothers and their ol' ladies, and my chest tightened as I thought back to the days when Gus first started building our Memphis chapter. He'd chosen every man sitting in that room. Even when no one else could see it, he saw the good in each and every one of us and brought us together as one solid unit. Studying each of them, I realized that there was no clear line between my brothers and the family I was born into. Like the blood in our veins, our feelings of brotherhood ran through us like a river, deep and wide, to our very core. That thought gave me a small ounce of solace. I knew with my brothers at my side we could get through anything—even this.

After several long, torturous hours of waiting, Kenadee appeared in the waiting room. She was the lead nurse on duty, so I knew she'd be the one with information on Gus's condition. I followed Samantha and Moose as they rushed over to speak with her. Samantha was the first to say, "Please tell me he's okay?"

"He made it through surgery," Kenadee answered calmly, "and he's holding his own right now."

"But?" Samantha pushed.

We all listened silently as she admitted, "His wounds

were extensive. He lost a lot of blood. The bullet that went through his abdomen grazed his liver and spleen. The doctor removed his spleen and stopped the internal bleeding. His head wound is a different matter. It will be days, maybe even weeks before we know the true extent of the damage the bullet caused."

"I need you to be honest with me, Kenadee." I could hear the anguish in Samantha's voice as she asked, "Does he really have a chance of coming through this?"

"I know it's hard to believe that a person could survive a gunshot wound to the head, and rightly so. The survival rate is very low because there's no room for the brain to move and the shock waves from the bullet often cause irreversible damage. But for some people, the bullet velocity is high and there is no side-to-side movement or wobble. In these cases, the bullet is able to pass through non-critical parts of the brain and less damage occurs, making survival possible. The doctors believe this is the case with Gus."

"Why do they think that?"

"Since there was an exit wound, they're hoping that the bullet only damaged a small portion of his brain," Kenadee replied. "And if they're right, Gus is a very lucky man."

"And it will be awhile before we know for certain?"

"Yes," Kenadee replied. "The next twenty-four hours are critical. If his stats remain the way they are now, his chances will be much better. But Samantha, I need you to understand ... if Gus pulls through, it'll be just the beginning. He'll have a long road ahead of him. We all love him, you know we do, but the man is strong-willed and stubborn. He's going to need you to stay strong and help see him through this."

"I'll do whatever needs to be done."

"We all will," I added. "Whatever he needs, we'll see that he has it."

"I know you will." Kenadee glanced over to Blaze as she said, "I better get back. I'm sure they're wondering where I am."

"Thank you, Kenadee." Samantha reached over and hugged her. "It means so much to me that you're looking out for him."

"Of course." Kenadee hugged her back, then turned and started down the hall. "The doctor should have some more information soon. I'll be back to fill you in when he does."

As soon as she left, the others came over to see what all was said. After she gave them the run down, Samantha said, "I really appreciate you all being here and I'm sure Gus would, too, but it's late. You should all go home and get some rest. I'll let you know if anything changes."

"I'm not leaving until we're certain he's going to pull through," August argued.

"Honey, I know you're worried. We all are," Samantha glanced over to Harper who was sound asleep in Gunner's arms, "but you need to get Harper home and in her own bed. You can come back first thing tomorrow. That goes for all of you. I know you all have families of your own, and that you're exhausted. Please, go get some rest."

"And what about you?" August fussed. "We're just supposed to leave you here alone?"

"I'll stay with her," I volunteered. "You go on home like she said, and we'll call if anything changes."

"Okay, but please call the second you hear anything. I don't care what time it is."

"We will, sweetheart. I promise."

August gave Samantha a hug, then said her goodbyes. As she and Gunner left, several of the others followed suit. Moose, Blaze, Shadow, and Murphy stayed behind, but after Samantha's insistence that they go home, they finally gave in and left, leaving the two of us alone in the waiting room. It wasn't until then that Samantha finally broke down and started to cry. Hoping to give her some small comfort, I sat down next to her, but it did little to help. Even as she leaned her head against my shoulder, her tears continued to fall. I understood her pain. Hell, I was feeling it too. Gus wasn't just my president, he was my brother. I'd spent the better part of my life at his side, and the thought of losing him was more than I could stand. I remained silent for almost an hour, giving Samantha the time she needed to collect herself. When I saw that she was still struggling to pull it together, I looked down at her and said, "He's going to make it through this, Samantha."

"How can you be so sure?"

"'Cause it's Gus." Her eyes met mine. "You know I love him ... respect the man more than anyone, but he's the most bull-headed, stubborn sonofabitch I've ever met. No way in hell he'll let some asshole with a .45 get the best of him. He'll pull through this, if for no other reason than to prove that he can."

She wiped the tears from her cheeks, then rested her head back on my shoulder. I knew I hadn't eased all her doubts, hell, I had plenty of my own, but at least I'd given her a little hope to hold on to. She'd need it if she was going to make it through this thing with Gus—we all would.

10

ALYSSA

I KNEW SOMETHING WAS WRONG. I COULD SEE IT ON Beckett's face when he went rushing out of the house. I'd hoped that he would touch base the following night and tell me what had happened, but he never showed. That's when I started to worry and tried calling Clay. When he didn't answer, I tried calling Landry, but again, no answer. It was after ten. They both should've already been home. That, and the fact that Clay always answered when I called, made me even more concerned. I knew there was a possibility that they were just busy or might've been in bed, but after the way Beckett had left the night before, I couldn't help but think something was really wrong. I was growing more concerned by the second, so I got in my car and drove over to Clay's. Just as I was pulling up, I spotted Landry getting out of her car. When she noticed that I'd parked behind her, she started walking towards me. Even in the dark, I could tell from her expression and body language that she was exhausted. I rolled down my window. "Hey, Landry."

"Hey, girl. What are you doing here so late?"

"I know I'm probably being crazy and all, but I tried calling y'all and when neither of you answered, I got worried. I thought I'd run by to make sure everything was okay."

"I'm sorry." Landry sighed. "I saw that I missed your call and I was meaning to call you back, but with everything that's going on, I forgot."

"So, there is something going on?"

"Yeah." Landry's expression grew somber as she said, "Gus was shot the other night, and we've been spending a lot of time at the hospital."

"Oh, no. Is he okay?"

"Honestly, we aren't sure." I knew how much Gus meant to both Clay and Beckett. He was like a father figure to the entire club. All the brothers loved and respected him. I could only imagine how distraught they were over him being shot. "It's pretty bad. They were afraid he wouldn't pull through, but right now, he's holding his own."

"That's awful." I didn't know much about the club life —just what I'd heard from my uncle, Viper. He was the president of the Ruthless Sinners in Nashville, and like Gus, he had a reputation for being hardcore. There weren't many who were crazy enough to mess with him, and I had no doubt that the same held true for Gus, making me wonder who would've gone after him and why. "Do they have any idea who shot him?"

"If they do, they aren't saying anything, but that's no surprise." Landry shook her head. "When it comes to the club, they're all tight-lipped. Never really know what's going on. It's just part of it."

I'd noticed that neither Clay's bike nor his truck were in the driveway, so I asked, "Is Clay at the hospital?"

"Yeah. Even though the doctors won't let them see Gus, they still want to spend as much time as they can there."

"I understand." As much as I wanted to ask her how Beckett was doing, I knew I couldn't. We'd both agreed to keep our "friendship," or whatever one wanted to call it, under wraps, so I'd just have to wait and see for myself when he finally came to see me—*if* he came to see me. I knew Landry was tired, so I put my car in reverse and said, "I'll let you get to bed. Be sure and let me know if there's anything I can do to help."

"I will, and I'll be sure to have Clay give you a call tomorrow."

"Thanks, Landry. I'll talk to you soon."

I pulled out of her driveway and headed back home. When I walked in, I couldn't believe how empty and hollow the house felt without Beckett there. I missed him. I missed him even more as I got into bed and rested my head on the pillow. My heart ached as I reached over and ran my hand across the spot where he usually slept. It seemed strange that a man could have such an effect on me after such a short time; nonetheless, he had. I knew how much he cared for Gus, how worried he must've been, and it pained me to know that I wasn't there for him. He'd been so sweet and supportive when I needed someone the most, and I wanted to be able to do the same for him. Sadly, I couldn't do that unless he'd let me.

It was late and I had to work the following morning, so I tried to force the thoughts about Beckett from my mind in order to fall asleep. I was just starting to drift off when I heard a knock at my door. Hoping it might be him, I tossed the covers back and rushed into the living room. When I opened it, relief washed over me when I found Beckett standing on the porch. He was wearing the same clothes he had on when he left, and with the dark circles under his eyes and his day-old beard, he looked completely exhausted. "I'm sorry it's so late."

"Don't be." I stepped towards Beckett, wrapped my arms around him, and held him tight. "I'm so glad you came."

His voice was strained as he whispered, "Gus—"

"I know. Landry told me. I'm so sorry this happened." I hugged him even tighter as I said, "How's he doing?"

"It's hard to tell, but he seems to be hanging in there. It's gonna take some time before we know for sure." His eyes were filled with worry as he let out a deep breath. "I'm sorry I didn't call or come by sooner. I've just been kind of fucked up about this whole thing. Couldn't leave and wouldn't have if Samantha hadn't insisted."

"I totally understand, Beckett. You were exactly where you needed to be."

"It's really good to see you." He looked down at me as he asked, "Everything okay with you?"

"I was worried there for a bit, but I'm much better now that I know you're okay." I reached up and placed my hands on his face. "You look exhausted."

"That's because I am."

I took his hand in mine, then led him into the house.

Without any resistance, he followed me into the bathroom and watched as I turned on the shower. He could barely keep his eyes open when I reached for the hem of his shirt and as he bent forward for me, I pulled it over his head. He kicked off his boots, then removed his jeans, socks, and briefs. Damn. The man was unbelievably hot. Under any other circumstance, I might've joined him in the shower, but at that moment, I was only interested in taking care of him. I was busy gathering his clothes, when he asked, "Mind handing me my toothbrush?"

"Sure." I grabbed it, and as I handed it over to him, I said, "I'll go put these in the wash while you take a shower."

He nodded, then stepped under the stream of hot water and closed his eyes as he let it run down his head and shoulders. His eyes were still closed when he muttered, "Thank you, Alyssa. I really needed this."

"Don't mention it."

I finished collecting his things, then took everything to the laundry room. After I emptied all his pockets, I tossed his clothes into the washing machine. Thinking it might help to get some real food in his stomach, I went into the kitchen to fix him something to eat. I had some leftover meatloaf and mashed potatoes from the night before, so I warmed it up and poured him a glass of sweet tea. As soon as it was ready, I carried it all into the bedroom, but when I walked in, the lights were off and he was already sound asleep. Beckett looked so peaceful, so content, like he was exactly where he was meant to be. I stood there just watching him for several minutes, then returned the tray of food to the kitchen. The washer was still running, so I decided to use the time to clean the dishes and pick things up around the house. When the clothes were finally done, I put them in the dryer and headed back to the bedroom

Being careful not to wake him, I crawled in bed next to Beckett. I inched in a little closer, just enough to feel his body next to mine, and it wasn't long before he'd rolled towards me, laying his arm over my waist. For the first time since he'd left, I was able to relax. I knew then I was falling for him. It wasn't something I'd planned. We'd agreed from the start to keep this thing between us simple, promising not to complicate things by crossing that line, but it was just too hard to resist the pull I felt towards him. I knew there was a strong possibility that I was setting myself up for a disastrous fall, but for Beckett, I would take that chance. I lay there listening to the soothing sound of his breathing, and it wasn't long before I drifted off to sleep. The next morning, I woke to the heat of Beckett's breath on my neck as he whispered, "Good morning, beautiful."

"Morning."

"Did you sleep well?"

"Mm-hmm." I rolled towards him, and I was pleased to see that he looked well rested. "You feeling better?"

"Some. Thanks to you."

"I'm really glad you came last night."

"I am, too, but I've got to get going soon. I need to head over to the hospital"—he inched closer—"but first …"

I was still in a sleepy haze when he lowered his mouth down to mine, kissing me softly. Damn. The man could kiss. The second our mouths connected, my entire body came alive. Needing more, I lifted my hand up to his face, urging him closer as his tongue delved deeper into my mouth. The bristles of his beard were rough against my palm, but his lips were soft and warm, luring me in for more. His touch was tender and sweet, sending a wave of warmth rushing over me, and it was all I could do to keep myself from completely losing myself in him.

Without removing his mouth from mine, he eased on top of me, his body hovering just inches above mine. He felt so good, smelled so good, making my entire body ache for more. Like all the times before, he moved slowly and patiently, waiting for me to give him some indication that I wanted him to proceed.

Without saying a word, I lowered my hands down to my hips, slipped off my lace panties, and tossed them to the floor. After he slipped on a condom, a look of satisfaction crossed his face as he settled back between my legs. He clenched his jaw before lifting my hips and driving deep inside me, filling me completely. He slowly began to move, each thrust deliberate and powerful. When I spread my legs further for him, he growled, "Fuck, you feel so damn good."

"Beckett," I panted, tilting my hips towards him, wanting him deeper, harder. Sensing what I needed, he quickened his pace, and I soon became lost in the moment. He increased his rhythm, each thrust more demanding than the last. My body clenched around him as I felt another orgasm building inside me. "Oh God!

Don't stop!"

Beckett's pace never faltered as his body continued to crash into mine. I wanted to savor every moment ... to focus on how incredible he felt, but it was all just too much. A burst of pleasure exploded inside of me, and I shuddered around him as my orgasm took over. Wrapping my legs tighter around him, I could feel the muscles in his abdomen grow taut as he finally found his own release. He dropped down on the bed next to me, his breath heavy and strained, and said, "Don't know how you do it."

"Do what?"

"Make me forget that there's a world outside of this room."

"That's funny because you do the same thing for me."

"Really wish I could spend the entire day locked away in here with you."

"I wish you could, too, but I know you have to go."

"Yeah. I should've been out of here an hour ago"—he leaned over and kissed me on the forehead—"but someone swiped my clothes."

I smiled as I replied, "They're in the dryer."

He eased out of bed, and I couldn't help but admire his magnificent physique. Every muscle in his chest was perfectly defined, right down to the intoxicating *V*, and his back was more of the same. A smile crept across my face as I watched him saunter out of the bedroom. As he started down the hall, he announced, "If you keep looking at me like that, I'm going come back for another round."

"Promises. Promises."

"Watch yourself, woman," he warned as he disappeared into the laundry room. Moments later, he returned fully dressed. "Thanks for washing my clothes."

"No problem." I sat up on the bed as I asked, "Will I see you tonight?"

"Can't make any promises, but I'll be here if I can."

"Okay." He leaned down and kissed me briefly. "Let me know how Gus is doing."

"Will do." He gave me a quick wink. "You have a good one."

"I'm gonna try."

Once he left, I lay there thinking about what had happened with Gus. I didn't know him well, but it was clear that he'd meant a great deal to the men in his club, especially Beckett. I couldn't imagine who would want to hurt him or why. I could only assume that it had something to do with Satan's Fury. It was the only thing that made any sense. Regardless of the reasons why, I knew the brothers would be heartbroken if the worst happened and he didn't pull through. It was a thought that had me praying over and over again that he would be okay. When I noticed that I'd been lying there for longer than I thought, I quickly hopped out of bed, took a shower, and got dressed. On my way out, I grabbed a cup of coffee, then headed to work.

When I walked in, I was surprised that Jack hadn't beaten me there. He was always early, even more so now that he'd been promoted. He wanted to impress Bisset and prove that he could do the job. Concerned that something might be wrong, I went over to Miguel, one of the other line chefs, and asked, "Have you seen Jack?"

"He hasn't made it in yet." Miguel shook his head and shrugged. "Car trouble or something."

"Oh, okay. If I'd known, I would've offered to pick him up."

"Not sure you would've wanted to do that. He lives in a pretty rough neighborhood."

"I wouldn't have minded," I replied. "He would've done the same for me."

"Well, too late now." Miguel motioned his hand towards my place in the plating line. "You've got work to do."

I nodded, then went over and got to work. It was at least an hour later before Jack came rushing through the back door. I watched as Bisset went over to him and gave him the riot act. Jack took his scolding, then looking like a puppy who'd been kicked, he got busy working on peeling and dicing the large crates of vegetables. When I finally had a free moment, I made my way over to him and asked, "Everything okay?"

"Yes and no." Looking completely defeated, he explained, "The battery's dead in my car, and I can't afford to get a new one until the end of the week. Until then, I'll be stuck taking the bus, which means I'll have to leave an hour earlier just to get here on time."

"I could swing by and pick you up."

"Thanks, sweetie, but that's not necessary."

"At least let me drop you off when our shift is over," I pushed.

"You sure you don't mind?"

"Nope, not at all."

"Thanks, I really appreciate it."

At the time, I didn't know that my offer to help him out would end up turning my entire world upside down, forcing me to make a decision I never dreamed I'd make.

11

T-BONE

AFTER WAITING FOR WHAT SEEMED LIKE A LIFETIME, WE finally had a lead on who'd shot Gus. Filling his role as VP, Moose called all the brothers into church so we could figure out our next move. It seemed strange to be sitting there without Gus standing at the front of the conference table, handing out information and directing orders like he usually did, and if the expression on Moose's face was any indication, he was feeling the same way. Once everyone was seated, he looked out at us and took a deep breath.

"Never thought I'd actually be standing up here in front of you all like this, and I gotta be honest, I don't want to be here any more than you want me to be. I'd rather it be Gus, but since he can't be here, it's up to us to keep this club running. And I do mean *us*." He ran his hand through his thick gray hair and sighed. "We need to do this thing together and prove to all those mother-fuckers who thought they could come at us ... who had the balls to try and take our president down that they got another fucking thing coming. So my question is, are you with me?"

"Damn straight we are," Murphy replied.

"United we stand. United we fall," Shadow added.

I leaned forward and looked him straight in the eye. "You know we've got your back, brother. Anything you need, we'll be there."

Relief washed over Moose's face when the rest of the brothers chimed in—each of us assuring him that we would do whatever needed to be done. "Good to hear that, 'cause right now, Gus is hanging in there, but we don't know how he's gonna come through on this. No matter what happens, he's got a long road ahead of him, and when word gets out that he's out of commission, the club's gonna look vulnerable. Folks will think this is the time to come at us and take advantage while we're down. We gotta show that we're just as strong as we ever were, and while we're at it, we're gonna take care of the mother-fuckers who shot Gus and give them a taste of what Fury is all about."

"That mean you know who was behind it?"

He looked over to Riggs. "Why don't you show them what you found?"

Riggs nodded. Moose sat down as Riggs stood up and walked over to the monitor mounted on the back wall. Soon after, the security footage from that night started to play. The room fell silent as we all watched a blacked-out Dodge Charger pull up to the diner. The windows were tinted, making it impossible to see who was inside. The car remained parked with no movement whatsoever until the front door of Daisy's opened. As soon as Gus came into view, the passenger side door of the Charger opened, and a male figure wearing all black and a dark ski-mask stepped out. I could feel the tension crackling around the room as we watched the man charge towards Gus. Our president was unarmed, carrying his bags of takeout, and caught completely off guard when the man approached. Before he had a chance to react, the man fired twice, then as Gus collapsed to the ground, the guy raced back to the car. A stream of curses flowed through the room as my brothers and I watched the car speed off, leaving Gus to die on the front walkway of the diner.

Riggs paused the feed as he looked out at us and said, "I know this was tough to watch, but I wanted you all to see what kind of fucked up shit we're dealing with here. These men knew Gus was in the diner and were waiting for him to come out."

"Yeah, we got that." With fury pulsing through my veins, I growled, "Now you gonna tell us who these motherfuckers are or what?"

"In case you missed it, the Charger these assholes were driving wasn't sporting a license plate. That in itself made it tough to find these guys. Add in the fact that these damn Chargers are every-fucking-where, but after going over and over it, I finally realized I was missing the obvious." He motioned his hand towards the monitor on the wall. "Look at the hood scoop, the thin red racing stripe, and red brake lights. This isn't your run-of-the-mill Hemi. This is a 2019 Hellcat SRT limited edition. Not a lot of folks around here have that kind of ride, so I hacked into the databases of the surrounding dealers and searched their sales reports."

Growing impatient, I grumbled, "I know you worked hard on all this shit, brother, but are you getting somewhere with all this?"

"Yeah, Bone. I'm getting there. Antony Booker bought this exact model just over a year ago."

"Who the fuck is Antony Booker?"

"He's KeShawn Lewis's first cousin." Riggs walked back over to his spot at the table and sat down. "Appears that the trouble we had with Lewis and the Inner Disciples isn't quite over."

"What the fuck are you talking about?" Blaze roared. "We killed every last one of them, *and* the Red Knights."

KeShawn Lewis was the leader of the Inner Disciples. His son was shot during a drive-by, and when they took him to the hospital, Kenadee, Blaze's ol' lady, was the lead nurse on duty in the ER. The kid was in bad shape, and even though the doctors and nurses did everything they could to save him, Lewis blamed Kenadee for his son's death. He decided to seek vengeance and go after her. Needless to say, things didn't turn out the way he'd hoped. We not only took him down, we took down his entire club, and the Red Knights—a gang that decided to join him in his attempt to avenge his son's death. We thought we'd ended things there, but from the sounds of it, we were wrong.

"You're right. We did, but apparently, the two were pretty tight. Grew up together, and Lewis had saved his life or some bullshit like that. Whatever the reason, Booker is set on seeking revenge for his death."

"You sure about all this?"

"Yeah. Confirmed it all with Tyrone Davis—the

leader of the Dark Angels. His ties ended with Lewis when he didn't agree to join in on his war with us, but he still has tabs on the area. He wasn't surprised at all when he heard about the hit on Gus." Riggs changed the image on the monitor from the camera footage, to a group of men. "Over the past year, Booker has forged a new inner-city gang. He's calling them the Genocide after Lewis's son, and his numbers are growing by the minute."

"Just how many members are we talking about here?"

"Twenty ... maybe more."

"Fuck! Why in the hell are we just now finding out about this?" Shadow snapped.

"They've kept it under wraps. Nobody had a clue what they were up to until the night they shot Gus." Riggs ran his hand over his face as he mumbled curses under his breath. "And from what I'm hearing, it's just the beginning."

"What exactly are you hearing?"

A pained expression crossed Riggs's face as he replied, "They've spent the last few months collecting intel on each of us. They know our routines, where we live, who our families are, our ol' ladies, and anything else they can use to take each of us down—one by one."

"Motherfucker," I growled. "I can't believe we missed this shit."

"No way we could've known, brother."

"You're wrong. It's our job to know this shit, and we fucked up." I ran my hand over my head. "Now it's time to fix it."

"And how do you suppose we do that?" Murphy asked.

"We end them. Every fucking last one of them," I roared. "And we do it sooner than later."

"T-Bone's right. We can't wait on this. We need to act now." Murphy ran his hand over his beard. "We need a lockdown. It's the only way we can make sure these motherfuckers don't pull any more of this shit."

"Agreed," Moose replied. "We need to have everyone brought in tonight ... the morning at the latest."

"And then what? I don't want to wait on this thing with Booker." Murphy turned to Riggs as he said, "We need names and locations."

"I've got some, but I'm still working on the rest."

"Give us what you've got, and we'll start with them."

Riggs slid a folder over to Murphy as he said, "Booker bought a warehouse on the corner of Tigrett and Second. I'm working on getting surveillance for both the inside of the warehouse and the surrounding area. Booker has a security system in place, so it's going to take some time for me to get access."

"And what are we supposed to do until then?" I pushed. "Just wait for them to make their next fucking move?"

"No. I've got some thoughts on how we can show them who they're fucking with." Riggs stood up as he said, "These guys think they chopped off the head of the snake by getting to Gus, but they were wrong. They've got the rest us to contend with now, and we'll show them, and everyone else, we're a snake with a hell of a fucking bite."

"We're all ears, brother," Moose replied. "Tell us your ideas."

"With the cops involved, we're gonna have to play this thing smart and make it look like Satan's Fury wasn't involved." Since the shooting, the cops had been in and out of the hospital and the clubhouse, asking questions to not only Samantha but to several of the brothers—me included. Without the security footage from the restaurant, they hadn't managed to get any leads, and we needed to do whatever it took to keep it that way. I watched as the monitor quickly changed to a picture of Frayser, one the biggest gang-ridden areas around. "I'm thinking we stir up some trouble among the gangs ... a few gang tags painted in just the right places and maybe a drive-by or two. You know how they feel about someone encroaching on their territory. It wouldn't take much to get them fired up. I know it'll take a little work, but if we can get the talk going about the Genocide, it won't be long before the neighboring gangs will be set on taking them down."

There was no missing the concern in Shadow's voice when he shook his head and said, "I don't know, Riggs. Starting up a war between these gangs seems like a whole lot of fucking trouble just to try and keep the cops off our backs."

"We can't afford to have the cops looking into us. Hell, they've already been asking too many questions. The last thing we need is for them to start monitoring our every fucking move." Riggs shook his head. "We've already been down that damn road, and I don't know about you, but I got no desire to go down it again."

"I think Riggs is right. If we can make the cops think there's a war on the rise, they'll be more focused on that instead of us. We've just gotta make it look like another gang is responsible for bringing the Genocide down."

Blaze nodded. "If we play it right, it could work."

"Okay, then. When do we start?" I replied.

"The sooner the better," Moose replied. "We divide up. Shadow, Hyde, Bone, and Murphy will handle the drive-by, while Riggs goes with Blaze, Gauge, and Gunner to tag some walls and set a couple of fires. Just enough to get some rumors started."

"You gonna tell us who we're hitting?" Murphy asked.

"Desmond Michaels. He's one of Booker's main guys." Riggs brought his face up on the monitor. "He has a place out in Frayser. He and a couple of members are known to hang out there. Usually in the yard smoking dope and fucking with their cars. I figure they'll be a good place to start. Once we're done there, we'll hit Chris Carter's place. He's one of the Fallen." The Fallen Ones were another local gang who were known for creating mayhem in the projects. While we hadn't had any issues with them, there were plenty of others who had, so it wouldn't be a surprise that they were involved in a drive-by. Riggs slid a piece of paper over to Murphy. "Trust me when I say, this guy and his buddies have it coming. Before we do anything, I'm gonna need you, Rider, and a couple of the prospects to go pick up these two cars."

"What for?"

"We'll be using them for the drive-bys. One of them is registered to Booker's second in command, and the other is registered to the leader of the Fallen Ones. We'll use it to hit Michaels." Riggs seemed to have it all figured out. "We'll go there first, so it'll look like a counter attack when we head over to Carter's place. From what I can tell, neither of the vehicles should be hard to swipe. You'll find the Camaro parked in the back of the strip club, and the Mercedes is at one of the section-eight housing complexes."

"Got it. I'll get it taken care of."

"We gotta be able to do this shit without any innocent kids or ol' ladies getting hurt, and I want Antony Booker *alive*," Moose announced. "When Gus recovers, I want him to have the opportunity to face the man responsible for putting him in that fucking hospital bed."

"Understood." Riggs nodded. "Let's meet back here around seven. We'll sort out the rest of the plan then."

"We'll be here."

Moose stood as he said, "Consider yourselves dismissed."

When the brothers started to disperse, I walked over to Murphy and asked, "You need any help getting the cars picked up?"

"Nah, man. I got it covered."

"Okay, then I'm going over to the hospital and check in on Gus."

"Sounds good. Let me know if anything's changed."

"Will do." As I started to leave, I told him, "Give me a shout if you need a hand with anything."

"You know I will."

After leaving the conference room, I headed out to the parking lot and got on my bike. As I rode over to the hospital, I thought about everything we'd talked about in church. I had no idea if Riggs's plan would actually work, but honestly, I didn't fucking care. I was itching to take down Booker. I wanted to make him pay and pay big for what he and his fucking crew had done to Gus, and I didn't give a fuck about the consequences. Cops or not, Booker's days were numbered. When I walked into the waiting room, I found Samantha sitting in her usual spot while the two prospects we had keeping an eye on her were sitting across the room monitoring the exits. Thinking back on what Riggs had said about Booker's crew watching us, I was glad to see that they both were staying on top of things and making sure that Samantha was safe.

I knew Samantha would rather be in the room with Gus, but unfortunately, that wasn't an option. Since Gus was in the ICU, there were only certain hours she could spend with him. I walked over and sat down next to her, and she put her magazine down. "Hey, I wasn't expecting you to come by here today."

"Just wanted to see if there'd been any change."

"Not yet. I was able to stay with him a little longer this morning, but I'm not sure he even knew I was there," she replied with disappointment.

"I'm sure he did."

"I hope so." She shrugged, then asked, "How did it go with church?"

"Good." Club business wasn't discussed with anyone —not even with the president's ol' lady, but after everything she's been going through, I had to give her something. "We have a lead on who shot Gus."

"Really?" she asked, sounding hopeful. "Who is it?"

"You know I can't say." As much as I wanted to update her with what's been going on, I couldn't. It would only put her in jeopardy if I told her any more than I already had. "Just know, we're gonna take care of it."

"I don't want any of you boys getting hurt, Bone."

"You don't have to worry about that. We'll be just fine." I could see that she wasn't pleased with my response, but there was little I could do to ease her mind. "Just keep your focus on Gus, and let us worry about the rest."

"I wish it was that simple." Her eyes dropped to the floor. "You boys and that club mean so much to Gus. His whole life is wrapped up in you guys, and I don't want him to have to lose that on top of everything else."

"Gus isn't going to lose anything, Samantha. He's gonna pull through this thing, and when he does, we'll be here waiting for him to step back into his role as president."

"Thank you, T-Bone. I really appreciate you saying that."

"I said it because I meant it." I stood up and asked her, "What can I get you from the cafeteria?"

"A cup of coffee and a chicken sandwich would be good."

"You got it."

I went down and got her a bite to eat, then did my best to keep her company. When the nurse walked in the room and told her it was okay to visit with Gus, I said my goodbyes and headed back to the clubhouse. I wanted to make sure that Murphy and Rider were able to get the cars that Riggs had told them to pick up. To my surprise, both vehicles were already parked up front when I pulled through the gate. Murphy and Skillet, one of our newest prospects, were standing by their bikes when I walked up. "Looks like you got the job done."

"We did," Skillet answered proudly.

"Have any problems?"

"Not really," Murphy answered. "They were both parked with easy access, and we were able to grab them without anyone seeing us."

"Awesome." I glanced down at my phone to check the time. "It's almost seven. Anything else that needs to be done?"

"We'll need to grab some more ammo and then get Riggs to give us the exact locations of where we'll be going tonight."

"Good. Let's do it. I'm ready to get this shit done."

"You and me both, brother."

We all headed inside and started prepping for the night ahead. The plan seemed pretty cut and dry, but I'd done this sort of thing enough times to know that nothing ever goes exactly as planned. Sadly, tonight would be no different.

12

ALYSSA

"HAVE YOU TALKED TO YOUR BROTHER?" MY MOTHER ASKED. "I've been trying to call him for days, and he hasn't answered."

"He's fine, Mom. He's just busy with club stuff."

"Are you sure? It's not like him not to return my calls."

She'd called during my break, so I didn't have time to go into a lot of detail with her. "Yes, Mom. I'm sure. He'll call as soon as he gets a chance."

"Well, okay. If you say so." She paused for a moment, then asked, "What about you? How are things going at the restaurant?"

"Things are really good, actually, and if they keep going like they are, I might get promoted again in a few weeks."

"I'm not surprised. You're a natural, Lyssa. I have no doubt that you'll go far."

"Thanks, Mom. I really appreciate that."

"What about the house? Are you still liking it?"

"It's great. I can't wait for you to come down for a visit."

"Well, since you mentioned it, I was thinking I might come next weekend. If you're too busy—"

"Next weekend would be fine. I have to work, but I'll have some time to visit."

"Great. Maybe Clay and Landry will be around so I can visit with them as well."

"I'm sure they'd enjoy that." I glanced down at my screen, and when I noticed the time, I said, "I hate to rush, but my break's almost over. I better get back inside."

"Okay, I'll talk to you soon."

After I ended the call, I walked back inside, washed my hands, and returned to my spot in the serving line. Usually, we were really busy and time flew by, but for whatever reason, on this particular night we were extremely slow, making the evening seem like it was dragging on forever. When we were at a complete standstill, I turned to Miguel and asked, "What's the deal tonight? We're so dead."

"No idea. Might be a concert at the Forum or a Red Birds game. Whatever's going on, I hope things pick up soon. I'm bored out of my mind," Miguel complained.

"I can't disagree with you there." I looked over at the clock and groaned. "We've got another two hours of this."

"Yeah, and Bisset's bad mood isn't making things any better. He actually blessed me out for being distracted. What the hell is that?" he fussed. "Why does it even matter if I'm distracted when we literally have no dishes going out?"

"Don't worry about it. I'm sure he's just having a bad day."

"We all are." He shook his head with a shrug. "I'm over it. I just wanna go home."

"Me too," Jack added from across the room. "I've got shit I could be doing instead of standing around here with my thumb up my ass."

I had to hold back my chuckle as I thought of an inappropriate comeback for Jack's remark. Instead of teasing him, I simply smiled and said, "I think the same goes for everyone here."

"At least we only have a couple more hours to go."

"Very true. For now, we best get back at it before Bisset pitches a fit."

"You ain't lying." When I turned and started back to my workstation, Jack called out to me and asked, "Hey, you still gonna be able to drop me off after work?"

"Sure. Won't be a problem at all."

"Great. I really appreciate it."

"Anytime. Glad to do it."

No sooner had we returned to our positions, a large group of people came into the restaurant, and in a blink, we were back to being busy again. It was a welcomed change, making the last two hours go by much faster, but there was one drawback: the unexpected rush caused us to run a little late, and it was well after eleven before Jack and I were able to leave. After we grabbed our things, we headed out to the parking lot and got in my car. As I started the engine, Jack asked, "Do you remember where you're going?"

"I think so but keep an eye out in case I make a wrong turn."

I'd picked him up that morning on the way to work, and quickly learned that Miguel was right. Jack did live in a rough neighborhood, but it hadn't kept him from keeping his place nice. He lived in a small two-bedroom brick house with a tiny porch, and he'd planted monkey grass along the walkway, making it seem more inviting. Unlike several of the homes in the area, he'd also kept his yard freshly mowed and no litter scattered around the front yard. Seeing that he'd put such effort into making his place as nice as possible said a great deal about him. We'd only been driving for a few minutes when I turned to him and asked, "You're off for the next couple of days, right?"

"Yeah, I'll be back on Thursday."

"You have any big plans for your time off?"

"Not really." He shrugged. "I figure Tony and I will come up with something to do. I'm sure he's got some project he wants to get done around the house or some crazy place he wants to go. Hell, I never know what the man has up his sleeve, but I always just go along with whatever."

Tony was Jack's boyfriend, and from the way Jack regarded him, it was clear that he was crazy about him. I found it endearing the way the two got along, especially considering how hard life had been for them both. Jack had been on his own since he was fourteen, doing everything he could to simply survive, and Tony had grown up in foster care. He'd spent most of his teens bouncing around from family to family until he met up with Jack, and now they were forging their own life together. Even though it wasn't always easy, they worked hard to make it something they both could be proud of. I smiled as I turned my attention back to the road and said, "What kind of project?"

"He's been wanting to paint our bedroom furniture. Says we need consistency or something." He chuckled under his breath. "I don't know why he even bothers. We found all that shit sitting on the side of the damn road. It was someone's trash, but he thinks we can make it look like something he found in some magazine."

"From trash to treasure."

"Yeah." Jack chuckled as he said, "Something like that."

"I think that's really cool. I have this old antique dresser my mother gave me that really needs some love." Just thinking about the scratches on the wood and the broken handles made me groan. "I bet Tony could do wonders with it."

"I'm sure he could." He glanced over at me and said, "We could come by sometime and check it out."

"That would be great." When I came up to a red light, I asked, "I turn here, right?"

"Yeah. You'll make another right a couple of blocks down, and then the house is on the left."

"Well, how about that. I actually remembered," I replied proudly.

"Mm-hmm. Sure ya did."

It was odd how different the area seemed at night. All the gang graffiti painted on the different businesses and homes along with the various people lurking at every corner gave me an uneasy feeling. That troubled feeling only grew stronger as I continued towards Jack's house. With only a few random streetlights, his neighborhood seemed so dark and dreary, like something you might see in a movie, and although it wasn't so bad while he was in the car with me, I wasn't thrilled about the idea of driving home alone. Feeling a little apprehensive, I pulled up in his driveway and parked. After he gathered his things, he looked over to me and asked, "You gonna be okay getting out of here?"

"I think so," I answered hesitantly. "I have my GPS if I happen to get lost."

"Don't get lost. One wrong turn and you'll find yourself in some real trouble," he warned. "Use your GPS and use the shortest route to get home."

"Okay, I will. Don't worry."

"I am worried." His voice was filled with concern. "I don't like you driving alone out here, especially at night. I should've never asked you—"

"Jack, stop. It's fine." I hated that he felt bad. It wasn't his fault that he had car trouble and didn't have a way to work. I reached out and placed my hand on his shoulder as I tried to assure him, "I'll be fine. I'll even text you when I get home. How about that?"

"That would make me feel much better."

"Well, consider it done."

As he reached for the door, he said, "My car should be ready tomorrow afternoon, so you don't have to worry about coming to get me on Thursday."

"Okay." He got out of the car, and before he closed the door, I shouted, "You and Tony have fun tomorrow."

"We're gonna try!"

After he closed the door, I waited for him to unlock the door and step inside the house, then I put the car in reverse and started to back out of the driveway. I was just about to pull out onto the road when I noticed a car slowing down in front of a house with a crowd of people standing in the front yard. It looked like they were about to park when suddenly two arms extended from the windows. Even in the dark, I could tell they had guns in their hands. My heart started pounding in my chest as I watched bursts of light explode from the barrels of their weapons. Horror washed over me as the sounds of gunfire and terrified screams echoed in the darkness. I sat there completely stunned as the car sped off, leaving death in its wake.

"Oh god. Oh god," I muttered to myself, over and over again.

I simply couldn't wrap my head around what I'd seen. I couldn't comprehend it. I'd never experienced anything even remotely close to something like that and didn't know what to think or do. I was parked at the end of Jack's driveway when he and Tony came rushing out their front door. As soon as Jack noticed I was still there, he came running towards my car, but before he could reach me, I had completely backed out and was turning the wheel.

"Alyssa! Wait," he shouted. "What the hell are you doing?"

Ignoring him, I whipped my car out onto the road and raced in the direction that the car had gone. I knew it was an absolutely crazy move and that I was putting myself in danger, but I had to do something. I could hear my phone ringing in my purse, but I ignored it. I knew it was Jack. He had to be worried sick, but I didn't have time to talk to him. I had to try and get a better look at the men in the car. If I could just get the make of the car or the license plate number, I could tell the police what I'd seen.

As I drove by the house that had been hit, I spotted three men sprawled out on the ground. It was difficult to see their faces, but there was no missing the blood that soaked their clothes. I didn't even notice the color of the house or the cars in the driveway. My sole focus was on the three bodies that lay sprawled out in the tall grass. There was no mistaking that they were all dead as I watched their family members hover over them, crying hysterically as they pleaded with the heavens to heal their wounded loved ones. It was something that I might've seen in the movies, but never would've expected to see in real life. I had to do something, *anything* that might help these people in some way.

I was on the verge of tears as I continued forward, hoping to catch up to the shooters before they disappeared into the night. I never took my eyes off the car as I reached down to the floorboard and grabbed my purse. I needed to get my phone to call the police, but as I dug around, I couldn't seem to find my phone. I was still fumbling through it when I spotted them just a few blocks ahead of me. Adrenaline kicked in as I immediately slowed down and waited for an opportunity to inch closer.

Not wanting to take a chance on them seeing me, I kept my distance, doing my best to act like I wasn't actually following them. After they turned down a deserted street, I waited a couple of moments before following behind. I'd just managed to find my phone when I noticed the car slowing down. Thinking they'd arrived at their destination, I turned off my headlights and waited as they came to a complete stop a few yards ahead. I was just starting to dial 9-1-1 when the car doors opened and the men started to get out. My hands were trembling as I pressed the first two numbers, and just as I was about to press the final one, something about the men in front of me caught my attention. I stopped and leaned forward as I tried to get a better look, and that's when I noticed something oddly familiar about one of them.

I couldn't figure out what it was about him as the men grabbed a jug of gasoline from the trunk and poured it over the car. It wasn't until they lit the car on fire and the glow of the blaze revealed their faces that I realized I was looking at my brother—and not only him, but Beckett, Shadow, and Murphy. I dropped the phone in my lap as the realization hit me: they were the ones responsible for killing those men. They'd done it. It wasn't something I wanted to believe. Both Clay and Beckett meant so much to me, and it made my blood run cold to even think that they could do something so malicious. I tried to convince myself that I was wrong, that I'd made some terrible mistake, but it was impossible. I'd seen it all with my very own eyes.

As soon as the car was engulfed in flames, they rushed over to a different car that was parked directly across the street. Seconds later, they were all inside and hauling down the street. I, on the other hand, couldn't move. I was too shocked and completely distraught. It was as if the whole scene replayed itself in slow motion as I thought back to the moment I saw their car creeping down the street, the shock I felt when their hands extended through the windows, and as I sat there, I could almost smell the scent of burning gunpowder. I tried to shake the thoughts from my head, but I couldn't, no matter how hard I tried. I couldn't stop thinking about the gut-wrenching sounds of the screams and the gunfire exploding around me. It was all so surreal, and I couldn't imagine how Clay or Beckett could do something so terrible. It just didn't make any sense.

I have no idea how long I sat there on that abandoned road, crying as I watched the flames engulf that car. Hell, I probably would've still been sitting there if I hadn't heard the police sirens roaring in the distance. The last thing I wanted was to be pulled into the craziness that had unfolded before me, so I turned on my lights and started driving.

13

T-BONE

WHEN WE GOT TO DESMOND'S PLACE, IT WAS JUST LIKE Riggs had said it would be. He was out in the yard, smoking dope with a couple of the other Genocide members, and they had no clue what was about to go down. As we pulled up to the house, I could almost feel the eagerness radiating off my brothers, and rightly so. These assholes had made the mistake of thinking that they could get the best of Satan's Fury, and we were about to prove them wrong. Murphy looked over to me as he said, "Let's do this shit."

Seconds later, Murphy had pulled up to the house. Hyde and I rolled down our windows and extended our weapons, aiming directly at Desmond and the other two members. A wave of satisfaction washed over me when Desmond first noticed us pulling up to the house. His eyes grew wide with surprise as he tried to dart away, but we were too quick for him. Hyde and I started shooting, being careful not to hit any bystanders, and after only a matter of seconds, we'd annihilated them—all three of the men were dead—and there wasn't a single ounce of me that felt bad about the fact. They'd brought it on themselves.

As soon as the deed was done, we sped off and headed to the street where we'd left the second car. Once we'd parked and everyone got out, we torched the car, making sure to erase any evidence that could cause us blowback. Even though there would be little left of it, we knew the cops would still be able to use the VIN number and license plate to trace the car back to the owner, so we left it—completely engulfed in flames—as we headed to our second location.

We hadn't been driving long when Hyde said, "Is it just me, or do y'all wish there had been more of those motherfuckers?"

"Not alone there, brother."

"It pisses me the fuck off how they got Gus like that." He grumbled in frustration. "It's like—fuck, man, don't be a fucking pussy and go after the man when he's getting goddamn dinner for his family. Who does that shit?"

"Cowards do that, Hyde. Fucking cowards."

"Well, it's only a matter of time before they see just how big they fucked up."

"You got that right. These motherfuckers are going down. Each and every one of them," I growled.

"Damn straight," Murphy growled.

As we got closer to the location of the second hit, I felt a slight twinge of guilt. The club hadn't had any trouble with the Fallen, but then I remembered that the two we were about to kill were far from good guys. Riggs had done his research and had chosen Chris Carter and Johnny Hobs, two of the Fallen's worst, for us to take down. Carter was a known child sex offender who'd killed his entire family when a drug deal went bad. Hobs had a thing for getting high and robbing the elderly. He'd kill them in their sleep, then swipe anything valuable in their home. Add in the fact that they'd both kept their neighborhood up in arms with all their fucked-up antics, and suddenly I wasn't feeling the slightest bit guilty as Murphy turned to me and asked, "You ready?"

"Absolutely."

We drove by the house to make sure the two were actually outside and within range, and when we found them both sitting on the steps getting blazed, Murphy pulled us back around. As we approached the house, Hyde and I rolled down our windows and prepared to take our shot. The second I had Hobs in my line of sight, I pulled the trigger, sending a round of gunfire in his direction. Hyde did the same with Carter, and once we were certain they had both been taken out, I gave Murphy the signal, letting him know the job had been done.

As we sped down the street, Shadow said, "I'm ready for this shit to be over. Let's ditch this fucking car and get back to the clubhouse."

"You got it."

Murphy drove us to an isolated street where a prospect was waiting for us in one of the club's SUVs, and once we'd torched the Mercedes, we were on our way. We hadn't gotten far before Hyde asked, "How long are we gonna have to wait before we make our move on the Genocide?"

"Shouldn't be long," Murphy asked. "You know how things get out, especially with shit like this."

"I hope so, 'cause I'm ready to make those assholes rue the day they fucked with Fury."

"You and me both, brother."

With everything that was going on, none of us had really talked about the lockdown. I wanted to ask Hyde about Lyssa but didn't want to make him suspicious, so I was relieved when Murphy turned to Shadow and asked, "You guys ready for the lockdown?"

"Alex is there now. What about Riley? She coming tonight or waiting until morning?"

"Should be there now." Murphy turned to Hyde as he asked, "What about you? What's your plan with Landry?"

"She had to work late but should be there by the time we get back."

"What about your sister? You gonna have her come down?" Murphy asked.

"I don't know. She's got a lot going on with her new job. You really think there's a need for that?"

"It's your call, but if she were my sister, I would. I'd do whatever I could to keep her out of harm's way."

"She isn't gonna like it."

"Hell, nobody does, but at least she'd be safe."

"You have a point there." I had no idea if Booker and his boys knew about Alyssa being his sister, so I was pleased when I heard him say, "I'll go by there tonight and get her."

It was at that moment I realized that I needed to talk to Hyde and tell him about the situation with Alyssa. He had a right to know that I was spending time with his sister, but there was too much going on, too many distractions. Between Gus and taking down the Genocide, I needed to wait until we both had a clear head, so I kept my mouth shut. When we got back to the clubhouse, Riggs and the others were already back and waiting for us inside.

As soon as we walked into the conference room, they were all sitting around the table talking. The second Riggs noticed us come in, he asked, "Well?"

"It's done. Everything went as planned." I answered. "How did it go with you guys?"

"The same." Blaze chuckled as he told everyone, "I gotta tell ya, Gauge showed some real fucking talent painting those gang signs. The man's got talent."

"I wouldn't go that far, brother," Gauge argued. "Just doing what needed to be done."

"Well, he did it, and did it well." Blaze leaned back in his chair. "We made sure the Fallen's bar was empty before we torched it and did the same for Booker's liquor store. Overall, I'd say we had a successful night."

"Great." Moose stood, and there was no missing the relief in his voice as he said, "Good work tonight, boys. Really fuckin' good."

Riggs nodded. "Yeah, every gang in the city is gonna be talking about what went down tonight, and when the cops find those two torched cars, it'll only be a matter of time before they start looking into the Fallen Ones and the Genocide."

"And when that happens, we set our sights on taking down the Genocide for good," Moose added.

"So, what's the plan there?" Murphy asked. "More drive-bys and bullshit or are we gonna get a chance to give them a real taste of Fury?"

"Oh, we're gonna to give them more than just a taste. We're gonna draw them into their own warehouse and take them out one by one."

"And how exactly are we gonna draw them in?" Shadow asked.

"Still working on that."

"You said Booker has a security system at the warehouse, right?" I asked.

"Yeah, pretty damn good one too."

"Then why don't we use it to our advantage?" I leaned forward as I looked across the table at my brothers. "Booker has to know that it's only a matter of time before we start putting two and two together. I say we go on and do the drive-by, and when we're done there, we head straight to the warehouse. Make it look like we're just there to poke around and get info. Booker and his crew will come thinking he's gonna get the jump on us, but in reality, we'll be there waiting to take them down."

"It could work, but it would be risky—especially for those who are inside," Murphy replied with concern.

"Not if we play it right." I looked over to Riggs as I asked, "Have you been able to break into their security system?"

"No, but I will."

"Well, there's no point in even trying to figure this shit out until you do."

"Bone is right," Moose agreed. "Besides, it's late. We've done all we can tonight. You boys go see about your families, then try to get some rest. We can get back at it first thing in the morning."

We were all exhausted, so none of us disagreed. As we started to disperse, I noticed Hyde rushing out of the room. He was talking on his burner, so I assumed he was calling Alyssa—or so I hoped. Several of the other brothers followed him out the door, but Moose remained seated at the table. I walked over and sat down next to him. "You heard anything from Samantha?"

"She said the doctor wanted to run some tests tomorrow."

"What kind of tests?"

"Not exactly sure, but from the way she was talking, I could tell she was worried about it." Concern filled his eyes as Moose continued, "I'll go by there in the morning to see if I can find out anything more."

"Let me know when you're going, and I'll go with ya."

"Sure thing." He gave me a brotherly pat on the shoulder. "Let's plan to head over after we meet for church."

"Sounds good."

I walked out the door, and as I started down the hall, Alyssa crossed my mind. Usually by this time of night, I was already at her place. We would've had dinner and been in bed for at least a couple of hours. I hadn't had a chance to let her know I wasn't coming, but I hoped to be able to explain when Hyde brought her to the clubhouse. Wanting to make sure that he'd made it over there, I took out my phone and sent her a message.

. . .

ME:

Hey. Have you talked to Hyde?

I WAITED A FEW MINUTES, and when I didn't get an answer, I messaged her again.

ME:

You okay?

WHEN SHE STILL DIDN'T ANSWER, I tried calling her, but got no answer. Worried that something might be wrong, I left my room and started out to the parking lot. I'd just made it out to my bike when I heard Murphy call out to me. "Hey, Bone. Where you headed?"

"I was gonna go check on Alyssa."

His brows furrowed. "And why's that?"

"I just wanted to make sure she knew about the lockdown."

"Hmm. Well, Hyde's taking care of it. He's headed over to her place now."

"You sure?"

"Yeah, I just saw him leave about half an hour ago," Murphy answered. "Should be back any minute."

"Good. Glad to hear that."

"What's with you and this chick? 'Cause I got the

feeling that something more is going on with you two than what you've been lettin' on."

"It's complicated."

"I'm sure it is." He shook his head. "You gonna talk to Hyde about it?"

"Yeah, just haven't had a chance with all that's been going on."

"Well, Hyde thinks a lot of you. I'd hate for that to change, and it will if he thinks you two have been keeping shit from him," Murphy warned.

"You're right. I'll talk to him in the morning."

"Good. You won't regret it." He paused for a moment, then said, "You think this shit we did tonight is gonna play out the way we want it to?"

"Certainly hope so."

We continued talking for several minutes and were on our way back inside the clubhouse when Hyde rolled through the gate. Murphy and I stopped and watched as he pulled up to the front door and parked. The second he got off, he let out a stream of curses as he took off his helmet, making it clear that something was wrong. Curious to see what was up, we walked over to him, and before I could form the words, he grumbled, "It's official. My sister is the most stubborn woman on the planet."

"Why's that?"

"I went over there, told her that she might be in danger and that I needed her to come here for the lockdown, but she refused." He ran a hand through his hair and grumbled. "And if that's not enough, she basically told me to fuck off and give her some fucking space. Hell,

I hadn't seen or talked to her in over a week, but what-the-fuck ever. I tried."

"I don't know, Hyde. She might be a pain in the ass, but she's your sister." Concern marked Murphy's face as he asked, "We have no idea if Booker knows about her and if she's in danger, then—"

"I did everything I could, Murph. Fuck, I all but told her that we were at war, but she made it clear that she didn't want to be a part of my life or the club."

His response caught me by surprise. Alyssa had told me many times that even though her uncle, Viper, was the president of the Ruthless Sinners in Nashville, she didn't know a great deal about the MC life. In truth, she knew very little. Regardless, whenever we talked about Satan's Fury or the brothers, Lyssa always seemed generally pleased that her brother had found his place with us. She didn't seem to have any apprehensions or concerns, so the fact that she'd told Hyde that she didn't want any part of the lockdown or the club didn't make sense to me. Curious if Hyde knew what had spurred the change, I asked, "Did something happen between you two?"

"Nah, not that I know of, but that's the thing with Alyssa. Nothing really has to happen. She just gets something in her head and runs with it." He shrugged. "Anyway, it doesn't matter. I've just gotta face the fact that she's got her own life, and if she doesn't want to be a part of mine, I can't force her."

"I know you're frustrated and all, but we can't leave Alyssa as an open target. If she won't come here, then we're gonna have to send a couple of prospects over to keep an eye on her ... at least until the lockdown is over."

"Yeah, that might be a good idea."

"I'll talk to Moose, and if he's good with it, I'll send a couple of them over there tonight."

"I appreciate it, brother." He took a step towards the door and said, "I don't know about you boys, but I'm about to find my girl and call it a night."

Murphy chuckled as he replied, "Right behind ya, brother."

Once Hyde had gone inside, I looked over to him and said, "Let me know what Moose says about sending a prospect over to Alyssa's place."

"He's not gonna be happy about her not coming here, but not much Hyde can do." Murphy shook his head as he continued, "At this point, Alyssa isn't an ol' lady, and unless that changes, it's up to her to decide what she's gonna do."

"My ol' lady or not, I care about what happens to her. She needs to get her ass over here where I know she'll be safe," I argued. "Fuck this. I'm gonna go talk some sense into her."

"Hold up, now. It's after midnight. She's probably in bed, and more than likely, nothing's gonna go down tonight with the Genocide ... not with everything else that's going on. You might as well wait until tomorrow."

As much as I wanted to go over to Alyssa's place right then, I knew Murphy was right. She had work, and I needed to meet up with the brothers early the following morning. It was simply too late to go flying over there. With all the shit happening with the club, I had no idea when I'd be able to get over to her place, but like it or not, I needed to wait. "Damn, you're right again."

"I usually am," Murphy replied with a smirk. "Come on, brother. Let's call it night."

I followed him inside. He walked down to his room to be with Riley while I trudged to mine alone. As I lay down on the bed, I knew I wasn't going to get much sleep. I'd gotten used to having Alyssa by my side, but I'd soon discover that being without her was a feeling I'd have to get used to.

14

ALYSSA

IT WAS OFFICIALLY THE NIGHT FROM HELL. I JUST WANTED to go home, crawl into bed, and pretend that nothing had happened—that I hadn't actually seen my brother and Beckett kill those people. I knew it was crazy to think I could simply forget about something like that. I just didn't want to believe that either of them were capable of doing something so awful, so cold and heartless, especially when I cared so much for them both. No matter what was going on in his life or mine, Clay had always been there for me. He was the best brother and a good man. The same held true for Beckett; he had done nothing but shown me kindness and affection like no other. It broke my heart to discover that neither of the men I loved were actually who I thought they were.

I was barely keeping it together as I pulled up to the house. I'd just gotten out of my car and was walking towards the front door when my phone started to ring. I looked down at the screen and wasn't surprised to see that it was Jack. Even though I wasn't in the mood to talk to anyone, I knew I had to answer. I promised him that I'd let him know when I got home, and after what had happened, I was sure he had to be worried. With a deep sigh, I swiped the phone and answered, "Hey, Jack. I'm home, and I'm okay."

"Damn, girl. You had me scared half to death," he fussed. "I thought you were going to do something stupid like follow those guys or something. Where'd you go?"

"I was ... I was just kind of freaked out and wanted to get the hell out of there."

"Oh, good. I can't blame you for boltin'. Hell, I would've gotten the hell out of Dodge, too, if I could," he scoffed. "Seems like this shit is happening more and more around here."

A part of me felt guilty for doing it, but I had to ask, "Did you know the people who were shot?"

"I didn't know them personally, but I knew who they were. Everybody does. They made sure of that," he grumbled.

"What do you mean?"

"They're all members of the Fallen Ones. Just a local gang that's always stirring up trouble. A couple of the guys who got hit last night had just gotten out of prison a few weeks ago, and they were already back at it." Sounding hurt and resentful, he continued, "Nothing new. That's just the way it is around here."

"I've never seen anything like that."

"I didn't figure you had. It's one of the reasons why I felt so bad about having you bring me home." I could hear the anguish in his voice as he said, "You never would've seen any of that if you hadn't had to bring me home."

"It's not your fault, Jack. No way you could've known what was going to happen."

"No, but I knew it was dangerous for you to come here, and—"

"Jack, really, I'm fine," I said while opening my door and stepping inside. "Stop worrying about it."

"That's easier said than done."

"I promise it's okay."

"Well, if things keep going well at work, maybe Tony and I can find a place in a safer neighborhood."

"That would be great." I glanced over at the clock, and when I noticed the time, I said, "Look, it's really late. I've gotta work in the morning, so I better let you go."

"Okay, again, I'm sorry about tonight."

"I know. Go get some sleep."

"You do the same."

"Good night, Jack."

After I ended the call, I locked the door, dropped my keys and purse on the table, and headed to my room. I took a long, hot shower, hoping it would help to clear my head. Unfortunately, it did little. Even as I dried off and put on my pajamas, I couldn't stop thinking about it. All of it. Every second of it kept flashing through my mind as I crawled into bed. I was on the verge of crying again when I heard a knock at my door. Panic washed over me. I wasn't ready to see Beckett. I needed time to think about what I was going to do, so I just lay there, hoping that he'd get the hint and go on home. Unfortunately, there was a second knock and then a third. Realizing that he wasn't going to leave, I got out of bed and went to answer the door. To my surprise, it wasn't Beckett who was standing on my front porch; instead, it was my brother. Suffice it to say, I wasn't exactly thrilled about seeing him either.

"What are you doing here?"

"I came to get you," he answered.

"And why would you do that?"

"You need to come to the clubhouse. We're going into a lockdown."

"A lockdown?"

"Yeah. It's where all the brothers and their families come to the clubhouse," he explained. "Being under the same roof is the best way to make sure everyone is safe."

Assuming this all had something to do with what had happened earlier tonight, I asked, "Safe from what?"

"I can't get into all that. It's club business, Alyssa. That's all you need to know." His tone was hurried, like he didn't want to take the time to actually talk to me, and it was aggravating him that I was wasting time. "Now get your stuff and let's go."

"No, Clay. I'm not going.

"What the fuck, Lyssa?"

"I'm sorry. Do what you gotta do and all, but I'm not going to be a part of all that."

"Have you lost your mind?" He was getting angrier by the second, and I suddenly got why the brothers called him Hyde. My brother had a short fuse, and when things didn't go the way he thought they should, he'd struggle to keep his rage in check. Tonight was no different. It wasn't like I didn't understand why he was so angry. Clay had no idea that I'd seen what had gone down tonight, so he didn't understand why I was resisting his attempt to help me. "You're my sister. There's a chance that you might be in danger, and I'm here trying to make sure that nothing happens to you—just like I always do."

"I get that."

"Then why are you giving me fucking lip about it?"

"Because you wouldn't even be standing here if it weren't for Satan's Fury—the very club that you think will keep me safe." As I stood there staring at him, I was reminded of the moment the light from the car's blaze shined on his face. My brother, a man who I thought could do no wrong had done the unthinkable. It was easier to believe that he'd been made to do it, that someone or something had forced his hand, and it made me angry to think that the club might've put him in that position. That thought led me to say, "The whole thing is crazy. I wouldn't need to be kept safe if you weren't with *them*."

"Oh, so you suddenly got a problem with Fury?" His green eyes burned with hostility. "Now that's funny, 'cause you sure as hell didn't have a problem with them when they were getting you this house and giving you all the fucking furniture you've been using!"

"I appreciate what they've done, you know I do, but that doesn't mean I want to be pulled into whatever it is you've got going on with them." I crossed my arms and tried to keep my voice steady. "I'm trying to make a life for myself here ... a *life of my own*, and I can't do that when you're pushing your brothers and your club on me. I don't want any part of it, and honestly, I want a break from *you* for a while."

"I don't get you. Where the hell is all this even coming from?"

"It's not coming from anywhere," I lied. "I'm just telling you that I want a life without any interference from you or your brothers."

"There's something you're not telling me."

"Just go, Clay!" I shouted. "Go live your life, go do your thing, and let me do the same."

"Fine. You want space? You want a life of your own? *You got it!*" he snarled, then turned and stormed down the front porch. "I sure hope you know what you're doing, Sis, 'cause I sure as hell don't."

I didn't respond. Instead, I simply closed the door and locked it, then stood there for a moment, listening to the sound of his bike's engine roaring to life in the driveway. Once it finally faded in the distance, I turned off the front porch light and headed to my room. As soon as I crawled into bed, I pulled the covers over my head and started to cry. I couldn't remember a time when I'd cried so much. I was just so hurt, so angry, and I couldn't seem to get a grip on my emotions. I lay there sobbing until I finally ended up dozing off, only to wake the next morning tearing up again. I went into the bathroom to wash my face, and when I saw myself in the mirror, I gasped. My eyes were all puffy and blistering red, just like my cheeks and nose. I shook my head and whispered to myself, "Damn, girl. You need to pull it together."

I swallowed back the last of my tears as I placed a washcloth under some cold-running water and pressed it against my swollen eyes. I left it there for several minutes, then having no other choice, I started to get ready for work. Half an hour later, I was downing my second cup of coffee as I rushed to the restaurant, not exactly looking forward to being there. I was exhausted and depressed, and without Jack there to distract me, I feared it would be a long, dreadful night. Thankfully, that wasn't the case. From the minute I arrived, we had a steady flow of customers, so I stayed busy the entire day and night.

By the time my shift was over, I was beyond exhausted. I didn't waste any time grabbing my things out of my locker and heading out to my car. I could barely keep my eyes open as I drove home. I was so focused on taking a hot bath and slipping into bed that I hadn't thought about the possibility of seeing Beckett. I just assumed that he would've spoken to Clay, and after hearing what I'd said to him, he wouldn't come over. I was wrong.

When I pulled up in my driveway, Beckett was sitting on my front porch swing. Damn. I got out of the car, and as soon as I started walking up the front steps, he stood and met me at the front door. As luck would have it, he looked unbelievably hot in his black leather cut and faded jeans. He hadn't shaved in a couple of days, and I had to fight the urge to reach out and run my hand over the bristles of his beard. His dark eyes were filled with pain as he took a step closer. "Hey, Beckett. I, umm ... I wasn't expecting to see you tonight."

"I didn't figure you were." His eyes met mine as he said, "I talked to Clay. He told me about your conversation last night."

"If you talked to him, then why did you come?"

"I wanted to hear it from you."

"What exactly do you need to hear from me?"

"Well, for starters, you can tell me that you don't want anything more to do with me or the club."

This whole damn thing had me racked with emotion. I was mad that he was putting me on the spot, but at the same time, I wanted to cry and plead with him to make me understand why he'd done what he did to those men. Maybe there was a good reason, but I doubted it would've been enough to change my mind. I knew I couldn't tell him what I'd seen or how I really felt, so I said, "I don't have anything to do with the club, Beckett. That's your thing and Clay's, not mine. I just don't want to get pulled in any more than I already have."

"And what made you decide that our life is so bad ... that it isn't good enough for you?"

"It's not like that." I inhaled a deep breath and let it out slowly, trying to figure out the right thing to say to him. "I just need a break. I need time to figure out exactly what I want, and I can't do that unless I'm on my own."

"Didn't seem to have a problem with that the last couple of months."

"I don't know what you want me to say. We had a good run of it and all, but it's over." My chest ached as I said the words. I'd fallen for Beckett. I loved him. I'd wanted a future with him, but in just a few moments, everything had changed. "Besides, we'd agreed that we were going to keep this thing between us simple. We're just supposed to be friends, and it's become more than that."

"So, nothing happened. You just decided this without even talking to me about it?"

"There's nothing to talk about, Beckett. It is what it is."

His face grew red with anger as he snapped, "That's bullshit and you know it."

"Don't make this any harder than it already is, Beckett," I replied calmly. "You said it yourself that being with me was going to make things complicated."

"But that didn't stop me. Complicated as it was, I fell for you anyway."

I knew he cared for me, but until that moment, he'd never actually said the words out loud. I felt like my heart was being ripped from my chest, making me wonder if I was making a terrible mistake. I loved him. There was no doubt about that, but it wasn't that simple. There were things about him that he'd kept hidden from me, and now that I knew the truth, I wasn't sure how I felt anymore. "I don't want to hurt you. That's not my intention, especially after all you've done for me, but I just can't do this anymore."

"So, that's it. Just like that. We're done."

"Yeah, I think it's for the best."

"For you or for me?" His eyes dropped to the ground as he declared, "'Cause I can tell you now, it sure isn't the best thing for me."

"It is. You'll see that in time."

"Been around the block enough times to know you're wrong about that, freckles." He leaned forward, kissed me on the forehead, then said, "I'll respect your wishes. I won't come around anymore, but if you ever need me, I'm just a phone call away."

Biting back my tears, I watched him walk down my front steps and get on his bike. I had to fight every fiber of my being to keep myself from calling out and begging him to stay, knowing I had to let him go. I couldn't bear to watch him ride away, so I rushed inside and closed the door behind me, then ran to my room and lay across the bed. As the tears streamed down my face, I thought back to something my mother once told me—*"There are three things you should never break: promises, trust, or someone's heart."* Tonight, I'd broken all three.

15

T-BONE

I left Alyssa's place feeling completely defeated. I tried to get her to talk to me, to tell me what was going on in her head, but she refused. She'd had it set in her head that it was done, and there was no changing her mind. Needless to say, it didn't set well with me. In fact, it hurt like hell. It was like my fucking ribs were broken. I could barely breathe, and no one could see the pain I was feeling. The hardest part was forcing myself to let go of the dream of what could've been. As crazy as it sounds, I thought we actually had something. I sure as hell hadn't felt anything close to how I did when I was with her. Like she said, "It is what it is." I had no one else to blame. I'd let myself fall for a woman I knew I could never have, and I would have to face the consequences—starting with Hyde.

It was after eleven when I got back to the clubhouse, so I was surprised to find Hyde standing by the back door smoking a cigarette. I would've thought he'd be inside with Landry, so once I was parked, I walked over to him and asked, "Everything okay?"

"I was about to ask you the same thing." He took a drag off his cigarette, then tossed it to the ground, snubbing it out with his boot. "I went over to Alyssa's place tonight. I was gonna talk to her again about coming here for the lockdown, but to my surprise, I found you there, and I gotta tell ya, you both seemed right cozy standing up there on her porch. So, I'm wondering ... were you ever planning on telling me about what's going on between you two?"

"Yeah, actually, I've been meaning to talk to you about that for a while now, but with everything that's been going on with Gus, I haven't had the chance."

"Oh, is that right?" He shook his head with a huff. "Well, I'm here now. Let's talk about it."

"I should've come to you sooner. I get that, but honestly, even I wasn't sure what was going on with us." I shrugged. "I went over there a couple of times to check on her after she'd seen that Brant asshole, and it just kind of slipped up on me. I figured it was just me who was getting caught up in it, but I guess a part of her did too."

"So, this has been going on since the night she saw Lucas in her work parking lot."

"Pretty much, but like I said, it started off with just me checking in on her."

"And what made you feel the need to do that?"

"Got no idea. I guess I had feelings for her even then."

"You're telling me you love her?"

"I do. Not that it matters now. She pretty much squelched it all tonight."

"She ended things?"

"Yeah." I chuckled under my breath as I continued, "Pretty much kicked me to the curb."

"She give a reason why?"

I shook my head. "Something about needing time to figure out things on her own."

"Fuck, I don't know what to say, brother." Clay ran his hand through the thick of his hair and sighed. "I should be pissed about all this, but if anybody was gonna get tangled up with my sister, I'd want it to be a man like you —someone who'd be good to her and treat her the way she deserves to be treated—but at the same time, I don't like the fact you two hid all this from me."

"I understand and I'm sorry for keeping you in the dark, but I felt like I needed to be sure before I came to you."

"You think it's really done?"

"She gave me no reason to believe otherwise." My stomach twisted in a knot at the thought of never being with her again. "Probably for the best though. Alyssa deserves someone better than the likes of me."

"Nah, man. You're wrong about that." A smile crept across his face as he ribbed me. "Even if *you're old* and tired and set in your ways, I still think she'd be lucky to have you."

"I don't know if I should thank you or show you how this old man can throw a punch."

"You know I was just fucking with ya, Bone."

"Mm-hmm. Whatever you say there, brother." I gave him a pat on the shoulder. "We got a long one tomorrow. Best be getting some shut eye while we can."

"You're right about that. Hey, you happen to see Skillet over at Alyssa's place?"

"Yeah, he was there." Moose had agreed that even though she'd refused to come for the lockdown that we still needed to have one of the prospects keep an eye on her place. Through a lot of long nights and busting his ass around the clubhouse, Skillet was quickly proving himself to be a real asset to the club. "I talked to him, and he's planning to stay until Widow comes to relieve him in the morning."

"Good deal." Hyde gave me a nod, then turned and started inside. "I'll see you in the morning."

I stood there for a moment, going over everything we had said, and I had to admit, my conversation with Hyde had gone better than I'd expected. He was a man with a short temper, and I knew he had every reason to be pissed, but thankfully, he seemed to understand where I was coming from. That was the good thing about the brotherhood. We accepted each other's faults and wrong doings without holding it against one another. I was lucky to have that, and I would protect it, no matter what the cost. It was a thought that stuck with me the following morning when we all gathered in the conference room for church.

As soon as we arrived, Riggs informed us all that our plan was working just as we'd hoped it would. The cops thought all the hits were gang related and hadn't suspected that we were involved. Murphy and I had gone over to the Genocide's warehouse earlier that day, and after working his magic, Riggs was finally able to get us eyes inside the warehouse. Now that we were in, it was time to move forward with the rest of our plan.

"We're gonna need a couple of you to be inside the warehouse when they come," Riggs explained. "It'll be dangerous. These guys will be coming in on you, ready to attack, so you'll be in a compromised position."

"I'll do it," I volunteered. "Just let me know what you need me to do."

"You know I'm in," Murphy announced.

Shadow nodded. "Me too."

"I'll be there too," Rider volunteered.

"The four of you should be plenty." Moose looked over to us as he said, "We'll be counting on you boys to draw them into the warehouse. The rest of us will be waiting outside when they arrive."

"And what's the plan when they get there?"

"One of you will need to get your hands on Booker. Detain him and take him outside before we blow the place," Moose answered. "The rest of you just need to cover one another and make sure you get out of there alive."

"Understood."

"When are we heading over there?" Gunner asked.

"I was thinking tonight around nine ... hit them while the gang turmoil is still in full effect."

"We'll need to get busy gathering our ammo and—"

Before Murphy could finish, there was a knock at the conference room door. It was rare for anyone to interrupt when we were in church, so I knew it had to be something important. Rider was the closest, so he got up and opened it. To our surprise, August was standing in the doorway with an excited look on her face. "I'm sorry to intrude like this, but I thought you'd all want to know that Mom just called. Gus is awake. He's officially out of the coma, and he actually spoke to her."

The room immediately exploded with cheers of gratitude. It was the news we'd all been praying for, and I hoped beyond all hope that it wouldn't be long before he was up and out of there. I looked over to August as I said, "That's really great to hear, August. Thanks for letting us know."

"You're welcome. I'll let you know if she calls with any other news."

"Please do," Moose replied. "Be sure to tell Samantha that we'll be by there as soon as we can."

"Sure thing."

When she turned to leave, Rider closed the door and joined us back at the table. He looked over at Riggs as he said, "Let's finish this thing for Gus and give him the peace of mind knowing that it's been handled so that he won't have to worry about it while he's trying to recover."

"Agreed." Riggs opened his laptop, and seconds later, the feed from the Genocide's warehouse showed up on the monitor mounted on the wall. "As you all can see, it's a pretty standard setup. There's a small office upstairs, and other than a few stolen cars they're working to overhaul, the place is pretty barren. That can work as both an advantage and a hindrance. Depends on how this thing plays out."

"We'll make it work to our advantage," I assured him. "Just need you to keep an eye out for us, and let us know who's coming and from which direction. We'll handle the rest."

"No problem there, and if things get out of control, we'll be right outside to help take them down." The image on the monitor changed to the exterior of the building. "We'll be positioned in the woods behind the warehouse and next door at one of the abandoned industrial buildings."

"Sounds good."

Moose stood as he said, "I trust you know what needs to be done in order to prepare for tonight. Get it done and be ready to roll out of here by eight thirty."

"You got it, Moose."

We all dispersed, and while he and Shadow went to the hospital to check in on Gus, the rest of us got busy getting everything we needed loaded into the SUVs. Normally, we wouldn't fuck with bulletproof vests, but considering the fact that Shadow, Murphy, Rider, and I were going to be in such a precarious situation, I grabbed one for each of us and put them in the SUV. Once we'd gotten everything we needed, we all headed back inside. Some of the guys went to the bar for a drink, but I wasn't in the mood. I just wanted to be alone, so I went back to my room and turned on the TV. I flipped through the channels until I came across an old John Wayne movie and sat down on the bed. I tried to concentrate on the screen, but my mind was all over the place. One minute I was thinking about Alyssa, the next I was thinking about that warehouse. I couldn't seem to focus on anything, and then it hit me.

Things might not have gone the way I'd hoped with

Alyssa, but I still had my brothers and the club. It was time to focus on the good I still had in my life and to do everything in my power to make sure I didn't lose that too. As I sat there thinking about our plan of attack, there was something about it that just didn't set well with me. I knew breaking into the warehouse would bring some of the Genocide there, but there were no guarantees that they all would come. That was a problem. Suddenly an idea came to mind—one that just might make all the difference. I turned off the TV and headed down to Riggs's room. As expected, I found him sitting at his laptop working. I sat down in the chair next to him as I asked, "Hey, man. You mind pulling up that footage of the warehouse again?"

"Sure." After a few strokes of the keys, the warehouse appeared on his screen. "You got something on your mind?"

"Yeah, actually I do."

I took a minute to tell him what I was thinking, and as I hoped, he agreed that it was a good idea. "Can you track his phone and find his location?"

"It'll take me a minute, but yeah, I can do it."

"Good deal." I stood up and told him, "I'll get in touch with Shadow and Moose. Make sure they're both good with the change. If they are, Moose can let the others know when he gets back from the hospital."

"Sounds good."

I left his room, and in less than an hour, Shadow, Riggs, and I were in the SUV and heading downtown. Riggs had managed to get Booker's exact location, and since he was holed up at one of the local strip clubs, it wouldn't be hard to get our hands on him. As soon as we pulled up to Satin and Lace, Riggs and I got out and walked inside. We slipped over to a dark corner and started searching for Booker. It didn't take long for Riggs to nod his head towards the stage. "That's him. He's sitting up front ... the one in the maroon shirt."

It took me a second to figure out who he was talking about, but then I saw him. He had a dark complexion and dark hair with a slim, lanky build—nothing like I'd imagined. Riggs and I had thought that he would be there alone, but as luck would have it, he was sitting with three other guys—two who were known to be Genocide members. "I see him."

Knowing we'd need to get him away from them, I called one of the strippers over to us. She was a cute blonde with long, straight hair, pretty blue eyes, and a set of fake tits that would tempt any man. When she approached, I reached for my wallet and pulled out four one-hundred-dollar bills. "What's your name, sweetheart?"

"Chelsey. What can I do for you, handsome?"

As I pointed over at Booker, I asked, "You see that guy, the one with dark hair and maroon polo?"

"The one next to that big guy with curly hair?"

"That's the one." I held out the cash as I told her, "You get him in one of the back rooms alone, and this is yours."

"I just have to get him into a room? Nothing else?"

"That's it. Just be sure to leave the door open when you take him back there."

199

A smile swept over her face as she said, "You got it, baby."

Riggs and I watched as she sauntered over to him. With a sexy look in her eyes, she leaned forward with her boobs just inches from his face as she whispered something in his ear. Booker nodded, then took her hand and stood. His buddies cheered him on as she led him towards the back of the club. We wasted no time following them to one of the private rooms, and just as she was told, Chelsey had left the door open for us. I took my gun out of its holster, and when I pushed the door open, I found Chelsey sitting across Booker's lap, grinding up against him. Clearly startled by our intrusion, Booker knocked Chelsey off of him and tried to scramble to his feet. "Hold it right there, asshole."

Booker glanced at my cut, and panic filled his eyes, making it clear he recognized who we were. Playing dumb, he shouted, "Who the fuck are you?"

Without answering, I reached into my pocket with my free hand and took the cash from my pocket. As I offered it to Chelsey, I said, "You did good, doll."

"Glad to be of service."

She gave me a quick wink, then started towards the door. "Hey, doll ...You got a back door to this place?"

"Sure do. It's right around the corner. You can't miss it."

With that, she slipped out of the room, leaving Riggs and me alone with Booker. His hands were up as he nervously asked, "What do you want?"

"Enough of the fucking questions." I reached for him, tugging him towards the door. "You're coming with us."

When he started to resist, I reared back my fist and slammed it into his stomach, causing him to crouch over and groan. "Motherfucker."

Ignoring him, I jabbed the barrel of my gun into his side and started pulling him towards the door again. When we reached the SUV, Shadow got out and zip-tied Booker's hands behind his back. I shoved him in the back seat and got in next to him, and with Riggs driving, we started towards the Genocide's warehouse. As soon as Booker realized where we were headed, he asked, "What the fuck is going on? What you want, man?"

I was already sick of hearing this dude's mouth, so I reached over and sucker punched him, knocking the motherfucker out. Shadow glanced over his shoulder to the back seat and snickered. "You do realize that's my job, right?"

"Just helping a brother out."

"That you are."

I leaned forward as I asked Riggs, "Did you message Moose?"

"Yeah, he and the others are on their way now."

"Good." I leaned back in my seat. "I'm ready to get this shit done."

"Won't be long now."

Booker was still out cold when we drove around back of the abandoned building next door to his warehouse, making sure the SUV was out of sight. Once we were parked, everyone waited as Riggs used his laptop to disarm the security system at Booker's warehouse. When he was confident that he'd disabled it, we got out of the truck and headed inside. Booker was still pretty dazed when I pulled him out of the truck, so I tossed him over my shoulder and carried him to the front door. Shadow shook his head and said, "Damn, Bone, you got him good."

"He had it coming."

"Yeah, and he's got a lot more coming his way."

Riggs picked the lock on the front door, and I carried Booker upstairs to the office. I dropped him down into one of the chairs and Shadow secured his hands and feet, making sure he couldn't move. I gave him a firm slap on the cheek and said, "Wake up, asshole. It's time to talk."

After he blinked a few times, Booker finally came around. As soon as he realized that he couldn't move, he immediately started tugging against his restraints. No matter how hard he tried, his puny, little ass couldn't begin to break free. "What the fuck?"

"Welcome back." Shadow pulled up a chair and sat down in front of Booker, facing him with a menacing glare. "Word on the street is you and your Genocide boys have taken it upon yourselves to go after Satan's Fury."

"I don't know what the hell you're talking about!"

"Don't waste my time lying, Booker. I'm not in a fucking around mood." Shadow reached into his back pocket and pulled out his knife, using it to trim his cuticles as he spoke, "We did our research. We know about your plan to seek revenge for Lewis's death."

"You're wrong. I got no plans to do nothing."

Shadow clicked his tongue against his teeth before saying, "Strike one."

"I'm serious, man. I—"

Before he could finish his sentence, Shadow took the

knife and rammed it into his thigh, causing Booker to bellow out in pain. "We know Lewis was your cousin. We know you were pissed that we took him and the Disciples down. We know that you started the Genocide in hopes of taking us down. We also know it was you who shot our president."

"I don't know what you're talking about." With that, Shadow took ahold of the knife and gave it a hard turn, and Booker nearly lost his fucking mind. He reared his head back as he hollered out in anguish, and all I could do was smile. That motherfucker had nearly killed Gus, so whatever Shadow had in store for Booker was much deserved. "Fuck! Just fucking stop."

"I'll stop when you start talking."

When Shadow went to turn the knife again, Booker shouted, "You're right! You're right about all of it. It was me. I'm the one who was behind it all, so just kill me and get it over with!"

Shadow yanked the knife from his thigh, then slammed it into the other. With Booker screaming curses, Shadow leaned forward, just inches from his face, and said, "You're not getting off that easy."

"What the fuck do you want from me?"

"I want you to make some calls. You're gonna need to get your members to come here to the warehouse."

"Why? What da hell ya gonna do?"

"That's none of your concern," Shadow growled. "You'll make the calls, or I'll use that knife to fill you full of holes. You get what I'm saying?"

"Yeah, I get it." Booker thought for a moment, then

asked, "And if I get 'em here, what are you gonna do to me?"

"I'm gonna level with you, Booker. No matter how this thing plays out, you're not gonna walk out of here." Shadow crossed his arms as he leaned back in his chair. "But you got a choice. You can either go out fast or I can take my time with you ... make sure you feel pain like you've never felt before. So, what's it gonna be?"

"I'll make the calls."

"Thought so." Shadow pulled the knife from Booker's thigh, then used it to free one of his hands. "Get your phone and start calling. Bring them in three or four at a time."

"How am I supposed to get them here?"

"I'm sure you'll think of something." Shadow's tone turned threatening as he warned, "Don't fuck this up, or there'll be hell to pay."

Booker nodded, then made the first call. As soon as the person answered, Booker said, "Yo, Dreads ... I'm gonna need you to go by and get Nickels and Tiny. Bring 'em over to the warehouse ASAP." There was a brief pause before Booker continued, "I'll explain when you get here."

When he hung up, Shadow asked, "How long will it be before they get here?"

"Fifteen maybe twenty minutes."

Riggs stepped over to Shadow. "I just checked in with Moose. They're in position."

"Good." Shadow turned to me and said, "Now all we have to do is wait."

Just as Booker had said, his men showed twenty

minutes later. From the office, Riggs watched Booker's security feed and used his mic to let us know that they were approaching the front door. "They're about to come in. Big one in the back with two in the front."

"Got it."

With guns in hand, Shadow and I stood on opposite sides of the door with our backs against the wall, staying out of view as we waited for them to enter the building. My heart started to race as the door opened and the three men stepped inside and walked past us as they talked amongst themselves. It was clear that they had no idea we were behind them when they continued towards the office. I glanced over to Shadow, and as soon as he gave me the nod, we both stepped out of hiding. I aimed my gun at the big guy first. I wasn't one who liked shooting a man in the back, but the thought of Gus being laid up in that hospital had me squeezing the trigger. The deafening sound of gunfire echoed through the warehouse as Shadow and I instantly killed two of the three men. When the third started to bolt, I shifted my aim towards him, shooting twice before he dropped to the ground. The scent of burning gunpowder filled my nose as I looked down at the lifeless bodies sprawled out on the floor.

Shadow stepped over to them, giving each of them a nudge with his boot, and once he was certain they were dead, he looked over to me and said, "You radio Moose while I go up and get Booker to make the next round of calls."

"You got it."

As soon as I got word to Moose that the coast was

clear, the brothers rushed into the warehouse and moved the bodies into the car they'd driven here. While they were busy cleaning up the mess and driving the car next door, Shadow and I went upstairs to deal with Booker. Shadow took Booker's phone and put it into Booker's free hand as he said, "Time to make another call."

"I heard gunshots." Panic filled his voice as he said, "What the fuck did you do to them?"

"That's none of your concern. Make the fucking call."

"You killed them, didn't you?"

Shadow got in his face as he roared, "Make the fucking call!"

"Fine ... fine, I'll do it." With his hands trembling, Booker dialed another number, and as soon as the guy answered, Booker said, "Hey, man. I need you to go get Puckett and Leon and bring them over to the warehouse." There was a brief pause before he said, "I don't give a fuck. Get them and get your ass over here."

With a defeated look in his eyes, he hung up the phone and handed it back to Shadow. As he shoved it into his back pocket, Shadow glared down at him and said, "Just remember. You brought this shit on yourself."

"You killed KeShawn in cold blood. Did you really think you'd get away with that shit?"

"He, just like you, thought he could fuck with Fury. That's on him, and tonight is totally on you. Every man you brought into this club of yours is a dead man, and *you* are the man responsible. For every gunshot you hear, just remember that. You did this. You—and only you."

Before Booker could respond, Shadow stormed out of the office. I followed him downstairs, and neither of us spoke as we got into position at the door. We were all ready and waiting when the next group arrived. We followed this same cycle over and over, and like we were killing a line of fucking ants, we picked them off one by one, putting an end to the Genocide.

I'd like to say our work was done, but it wasn't. Not even close. In order to make it look like a gang attack, we had to bring each of the bodies back inside the warehouse, then torch the place along with all the cars. It took a hell of an explosion to ensure that there would be little left of their remains, but Riggs came through, yet again. The place looked like a fucking war zone when we were done, and rightly so. We'd taken out the very army of men who'd tried to rise up against us, and we'd done it together—as brothers. Even though he hadn't been able to fight alongside us, Gus was there in our hearts, urging us on, and for him, we'd do it all again—and again.

16

ALYSSA

I'D LIKE TO SAY THAT EVERYTHING IN MY LIFE WAS GOING great, that I was happy as a lark and things couldn't be better, but if I did, I would be lying. In truth, I was a mess. I was exhausted all the time, barely able to get out of bed in the morning, and even when I was up and going, I felt like I was in a fog. I couldn't eat. I couldn't sleep. My mind was always racing. When I told my mother how I'd been feeling, she convinced me that I was just depressed. She told me over and over that it would pass, but it had been two months since the night I broke it off with Beckett and I was still feeling like an unyielding weight was bearing down on me. No matter how hard I tried, I couldn't seem to shake it. Out of concern for my well-being, my mother came down for another visit. She'd already come two times before, and while it was nice to have the company, it did little to help. But, if anything, my mother was persistent. She was determined to get me back on track.

We'd stayed up late the night before watching some romantic comedy on TV, so I expected her to sleep in.

Unfortunately, that wasn't the case. She was up before eight, and from the racket she was making in the kitchen, I could only assume that she was trying to get me up as well. With a heavy sigh, I tossed the covers back and forced myself out of bed. Dragging myself into the kitchen, I found my dear, sweet mother washing the dishes by hand. I plopped down on one of the stools and groaned, "You do know I have a dishwasher, right?"

"I do." She continued scrubbing away as she said, "There weren't many, so I decided to do them myself."

"Suit yourself." I rested my head down on the counter and asked, "Did you make coffee?"

"I did." Instead of offering to get it for me, she suggested, "Why don't you get up and make yourself a cup?"

"Ugh ... Fine."

With an agonizing groan and acting like an overdramatic zombie, I stood up and shuffled over to the coffee pot. I knew I was being childish and needy, but I felt like I was on my last limb and just wanted to crawl back into bed. Mom glanced over her shoulder, watching silently as I poured myself some coffee and then shuffled back over to my spot at the counter. With an exasperated sigh, she shook her head and fussed, "Alyssa, you're gonna have to snap out of this mood of yours. It's gone on for too long."

"I'm well aware of that, Mother. I'm trying."

"Well, you're not trying hard enough," she scolded. "It's just a break-up. Women go through this kind of thing all the time. You need to pick yourself up and stop behaving like your world is ending."

"I know that's what I should do, but—"

"No buts!" She pointed her finger towards my bedroom. "Go in there, take a shower, put on some makeup, and at least put a little effort into starting your day off right."

"I will. Can I at least finish my coffee first?"

"Yes, you can finish your coffee." She dried her hands with a dish towel, then walked over to me with a troubled expression. "Maybe you should go see a doctor."

"Mom, there's no magic pill that's going to suddenly make me feel better."

"You never know ... You could have a vitamin deficiency or something."

"I doubt it." Going to the doctor wasn't the worst idea. I had several things going on that should've been addressed, but I didn't have the time or the energy to mess with making an appointment and physically taking myself to one. "Besides, with my crazy work schedule, I don't have time to go to the doctor right now."

"Well, if this thing with your depression continues, I'm going to insist that you go." She picked up the TV remote and turned on the small television that Beckett had mounted on the wall next to the refrigerator. The second it came on, the news popped up on the screen. As usual, the local reporter was talking about all the recent gang violence that had erupted throughout the city. It seemed like they'd all decided at once to have this crazy uprising and were causing all kinds of mayhem in the projects. Mom shook her head and sighed. "It's bad enough that I have to worry about your mental state, but with all this going on, I have to worry about your safety too. Hmph ... It's just not right."

"You don't have to worry about my welfare. I'm perfectly safe here."

"Well, I wouldn't have to worry so much if I knew your brother was checking in on you, but you had to go and tell him to—"

"Mom, you know my reasons for telling him to give me my space."

I hadn't told her about that night and what I'd seen. I simply explained that I didn't want to have to depend on Clay all the time, that I needed to figure things out on my own and have a little privacy, but I couldn't do that with him always around. She didn't like it, but I think a part of her understood—or so I thought.

"Well, you could still let him check in on you from time to time. If for no other reason than to make your mother feel better."

"It's not like I don't ever talk to him, Mom. We talk on the phone and—"

"It's not the same and you know it, but I won't push. I'll leave it at that." She leaned forward, peering down at my empty coffee cup. "Looks like it's time for you to hit the shower."

"You're like my own personal drill sergeant."

"*Alyssa.*"

"Fine." I stood up and started out of the room. "I'll go get ready. I'll even put on makeup, but it's not going to make me feel any better."

"Yes, it will!"

I didn't bother arguing. Instead, I went to my room, closed the door, and collapsed on the bed. I lay there for a few minutes, contemplating my life, and after several minutes of drowning in my sorrows, I pulled myself off the bed and went to the bathroom. I turned on the shower, and after I undressed, glanced at myself in the mirror. What a complete disaster. My hair was tangled, there were big dark circles under my eyes, and even though I hadn't been eating much, it looked like I was gaining weight. As I stood there staring at myself, I decided my mother was right. I needed to start taking better care of myself, stop all the moping, and get a little exercise before I swelled up like a balloon. With a newfound resolve, I took a shower, put on a bit of makeup, and even fixed my hair. I had to admit, once I was dressed, I looked pretty decent.

I grabbed my purse and keys, and the second I stepped out of my room, my mother gasped and said, "You look great!"

"Thanks, Mom." I gave her a slight smile and said, "You were right. I do feel a little better."

"I knew you would." She reached over and gave me a hug. "Have a great day at work. I'll make dinner while you're gone."

"That would be great."

"Is there anything else I can do?"

I shook my head. "No, you've already done more than enough."

"Okay. Well, I'm going to spend a little time with Landry and Clay."

"Sounds good." As I walked out the door, I told her, "Tell them both I said hello."

Without giving her a chance to respond with a snarky comment, I closed the door and headed to work. I used the drive over to try and mentally prepare myself for the day ahead. It wasn't easy. I was still feeling tired and wasn't really up for another long day, but I pushed those thoughts out of my head and forced myself to think positively. I tried to focus on the fact that things were going really well with my internship and had even gotten lots of positive feedback from Bisset and the owner on how well I'd been doing. Bisset had even gone so far as to say that I showed real potential of becoming a permanent fixture there, and it wouldn't be long before I was promoted again. That alone was enough to lighten my spirits as I headed into the restaurant. I went to my locker, and I'd just started to put on my apron when Jack walked in. A bright smile crossed his face as he said, "Wow, look at you. You look amazing."

"You saying I don't normally 'look amazing'?" I teased.

"Girl, you know your dazzle has seemed a little on the rough side the past couple of months, but it's understandable. You've been through a lot."

"Well, starting today, I'm going to try a little harder to put that all behind me and begin—"

Before I could finish, Bisset stepped into the locker room and called out to me. "Hey, Alyssa. You got a minute. I need a word."

"Sure." Normally, I would've been concerned about Bisset wanting to talk to me, but something about his tone had me feeling a little curious as I made my way over to him. In case I'd read him wrong, I asked, "Is something wrong?"

"No, not at all." I followed when he stepped away from the doorway and into a private corner. "Antoine and

I were talking, and we both feel that you've earned the opportunity to move up in the line."

Antoine Boucher was the lead chef at the restaurant, and the mere fact that he'd even noticed me was mind-blowing. I couldn't hide my excitement as I said, "Wow, that's incredible. Thanks so much."

"Don't get too excited just yet." His tone grew serious as he continued, "You'll have to prove yourself before we're just going to hand over the promotion."

"And how do I do that?"

"On Sunday afternoon, you will come to the restaurant and present Antoine and me a dish of your own creation. If it is worthy, then we will consider making the move. Understood?"

"Yes, sir. Understood."

"Good." He glanced over the clock and said, "Time to get to work."

"Yes, sir. I'm on my way."

When he left to head towards the kitchen, I rushed back into the locker room and started jumping up and down like a lunatic. Even though he had no idea why I was so excited, Jack started jumping around right along with me. After several seconds, he started laughing and asked, "You gonna tell me what we're celebrating?"

I stopped jumping just long enough to tell him, "It's finally happening. I'm getting my shot at being a real chef! No more cutting potatoes or plating food. I'm finally going to get a chance to show them what I can really do."

"That's awesome, Alyssa." He reached over and gave me a big hug. "I'm really proud of you."

"I can't believe it! I've been waiting for this chance for months."

"I'm sure your dish will knock them off their feet."

"Oh, god. I have no idea what I'm going to cook for them."

"Don't worry. You'll think of something." He nodded his head towards the door. "We better get out there before Bisset comes hunting us down."

I followed him out of the locker room, and I was all smiles as I walked over to my station and started prepping for the day and night ahead. I went over my conversation with Bisset a million times as order after order came in. While I was thrilled about the opportunity, I was a little worried that I didn't have what it took to impress Boucher. He'd been a chef for longer than I'd been alive, so it wouldn't be easy to win him over. With that in mind, I spent the entire day trying to think of the perfect dish to make for them. In fact, I was still thinking about it when my shift was over and I was headed out to the parking lot. I was so lost in my thoughts that I hadn't even noticed someone standing by my car. That realization hit me as soon as I heard a man's voice say, "Well, as I live and breathe. It's Alyssa Hanson. I thought it was you. Man, you're all grown up and looking all kinds of good."

My heart stopped the second I heard his voice. I knew right away it was Lucas Brant, and the thought of being out in a dark parking lot alone with him completely terrified me. In his khaki pants and button-down dress shirt, the brown-haired, blue-eyed ex-football star looked like an everyday, typical guy, but I knew better. Lucas Brant was a wolf in sheep's clothing, and I wanted nothing to do with him. In fact, I wanted to be as far away from him as possible. My breath quickened as I stopped dead in my tracks and said, "I have nothing to say to you, Lucas. You can just go."

"Oh, come on now. We both know that isn't true." My entire body started to tremble when he took a step towards me. "Hell, you followed me all the way down to Memphis just so you could be close to me."

"Are you insane?" I spat. "I don't want to be anywhere near you. I certainly wouldn't have moved here because of you."

"Always did play hard to get." A smirk crossed his face as he took another step closer. "It's one of the things I like most about you."

"You need to go, Lucas. *Now!*"

"Why would I rush off when I've finally got the chance to reunite with one of my old flames?" He continued moving towards me, only stopping when he was right in front of me. I wanted to run, scream for help, but I couldn't move. The fear was holding me prisoner as I listened to him say, "You know I still remember Homecoming night? We had quite the connection."

"We didn't have a connection, Lucas. You raped me."

"Now we both know you wanted it just as much as I did." He started to reach for me, but I quickly stepped back before he had a chance to touch me. His smile widened as he said, "Still playing games, I see."

"Fuck off, Lucas. I didn't want you then, and I certainly don't want you now!"

"Hey, Alyssa?" Jack called from behind me. "Is everything okay?"

"No."

"Should I call the police?"

"If he doesn't leave, then yes. You definitely should." I looked Lucas in the eye and snarled, "Time for you to go."

"What are you gonna tell the cops? You really think they're gonna care that an old friend of yours from high school stopped by?"

"Does it really matter? Either way, they'll file a report."

He gave me a wink before turning to walk away. "I'll be seeing you around, Alyssa Hanson. You can count on that."

Lucas walked over to a bright red Mustang and gave me a quick wave before he got inside. Seconds later, he started the engine and whipped out of the parking lot. I was standing there watching his taillights disappear into traffic when Jack came over to me and asked, "Who was that?"

"That would be my worst nightmare."

When I started to cry, Jack reached out and wrapped his arms around me, hugging me as he whispered, "It's okay. He's gone now."

"I hate him so much."

"He an old boyfriend or something?"

"Or something." As I stepped back, I wiped the tears from my cheeks and said, "I guess you could say that we have history—but not good history."

"Then what is he doing here?"

"Reminding me what a jerk he was." Even though I tried to fight it, the tears kept coming. "I guess he came here tonight because he saw me going into work or something."

"You gonna be okay?"

"Yeah, I don't even know why I'm crying like this." Trying to assure him I was okay, I told him, "I'm just tired and hormonal and stressed."

"I don't know how the girlie bits work and all that, but maybe you should go to the doctor for a checkup or something."

"My girlie bits are fine, Jack. I'm just under a lot of stress."

"I'm sure you are. You've been through a lot, girl. The shooting, the breakup, a new job, and starting a new life in a new city. It's a lot to take on."

I feigned a smile and said, "I'll be fine."

"Well, go home and get you some rest."

"That's an excellent idea."

Jack walked me over to my car and waited for me to get inside. He gave me a quick wave, and then I was on my way. As I started home, I couldn't stop thinking about my conversation with Lucas. It was one thing to see him in a parking lot, but it was another thing entirely to actually have to speak to him. I hated the man with every fiber of my being, and as awful as it might sound, I wished he would die in a fiery car crash so I'd never have to lay my eyes on him again. Unfortunately, that wasn't going to happen, and like it or not, I would be having to face Lucas again—which was something that filled me with dread. I wouldn't have had to worry about it so much if I could talk to Clay or Beckett about it, but no matter how tempted I was to ask them for help, I couldn't do it—not after I'd told them both that I wanted to figure out things on my own. One way or another, I would have to handle Lucas Brant on my own.

The next morning, I got up early, well before my mother. I put on an old sweatshirt and a ballcap, and being careful not to wake my mother, I slipped out of the house. Minutes later, I was on the road driving towards downtown. I had no idea where I was going until I saw the store sign—Guns and Ammo. That's when I knew I had the answer to my problem with Lucas. If he was stupid enough to come see me again, I would be ready.

17

T-BONE

"GODDAMN IT!" GUS SHOUTED AS HE CHUCKED A HAND weight across the room. "I'm sick of this bullshit!"

Patrick, Gus's physical therapist, kept his tone low and calm as he said, "Easy there, Gus. I'm gonna need you to settle down and concentrate so we can get you out of here."

It had been four months since the night that Gus was shot, and after weeks in the hospital and a stint in a rehabilitation facility, he'd made remarkable progress. It seemed the doctors had been right. The bullet had caused minimal damage, and other than a nasty scar, no one would ever have guessed that the man had taken two bullets. He was up and walking, talking like normal, and he'd even gotten most of his memory back, but he was still struggling a little with his fine motor skills. Gus's face grew red as he growled, "Don't see why we still gotta do this shit. I'm fine!"

"I tell you what. When you can write your name in cursive, then we'll consider the job done."

"Cursive? Why the fuck do I gotta be able to do some girly shit like that?"

"I don't know"—Patrick leaned over to him—"maybe so you can sign your name on a check or hold a fork in your hand without dropping food all over yourself."

"Fuck you, Patrick."

"Why don't you take a five-minute break?" Patrick patted him on the shoulder and said, "Cool off a bit and then we'll get back at it."

Before Gus could fire back at him, Patrick turned and walked over to the front desk, leaving Gus sitting alone at the workout table. I could see that he was stewing over there, so I got up and walked over to him. "Having a rough one?"

"Yeah, you could say that." Gus ran his hand over his beard. "I'm tired of spending my days here with Patrick and his fucking torture tactics when I should be at the clubhouse. Fuck, man, I got shit to do."

"You got shit to do right here, Prez." I knew he was frustrated, and rightly so. He'd been busting his ass to recover from his injuries, and while he'd come a long way, he still had his work cut out for him. That wasn't something so easy for Gus to swallow; unfortunately, he didn't have a choice. I tried to be reassuring as I told him, "I know it's not in your nature to take orders from anyone, but Patrick is trying to help."

"Well, Patrick is gonna get my fist down his throat if he isn't careful."

"*Gus.*"

"I know. Damn it, *I know.*" He let out a frustrated sigh. "This whole thing makes me wish I'd handled Booker differently. I should've made that motherfucker suffer instead of just shooting him like I did."

A few days after Gus was released from the hospital, Moose went and picked him up from his house and brought him over to the clubhouse. We'd already given him the rundown of everything that had happened the night we took the Genocide out, and how we'd saved Booker for him. The guy had been in one of Shadow's holding rooms for just over three weeks. He knew his time was coming, and it had to be hell sitting in that room alone, only getting fed once a day as he waited for his end. Hell, the guy actually looked relieved the day Gus stepped into that room. We all knew Gus would kill him. We just didn't know how. He could've tortured him, beat the hell out of him, or wounded him in a way that would've made his death come slow and painful. Instead, Gus turned to Shadow and said, "Give me your Glock."

Shadow nodded, then placed the gun in his president's hand. Gus then stepped over to Booker, placed the barrel at Booker's head and said, "I'll see you in hell."

He pulled the trigger, and the deed was done. Without a word, Gus slowly walked out of the room, and today was the first time he'd talked about it since. I understood his regret. If I were in his shoes, I would want to take all my frustrations out on the piece of shit, but that opportunity had come and gone. I gave Gus a pat on the shoulder as I recalled that night. "He had to sit in that room, and with every gunshot he heard, he knew we'd just killed another one of his men. Trust me when I say, the guy got what was coming to him."

"You're right." He ran his hand over his face with a

huff. "I need to quit whining like a little bitch and get my ass back to work."

"That you do." I stood up and walked over to pick up the weight he'd thrown across the room. I carried it back over to him and said, "I think you'll be needing this."

"Yeah ... Motherfucking stupid shit," he muttered under his breath.

Neither had noticed that Patrick had walked up until he chuckled and said, "Glad to see that you've cooled off."

"Don't start with me, kid," Gus warned. "I'll do the shit you want me to do, but I'm not gonna be happy about it."

"Understood."

"All right then." Knowing they needed to get back to work, I told Gus, "I'll let you boys get to it."

As I started to walk away, Gus called out to me. "Hey, Bone."

"Yeah?"

"Thanks."

Samantha was babysitting Harper, their granddaughter, so I'd volunteered to bring him to therapy today. It wasn't the first time I'd done so and I doubted it would be last. I didn't mind. It meant a lot to me to see the progress he was making. I gave him a nod and said, "Anytime."

I found a chair and sat down, watching quietly as Gus continued his therapy. When he was finally done, I drove him back over to his place. Being typical Samantha, she invited me to stay for dinner—her way of thanking me for taking Gus when she couldn't. No way was I going to turn down a home-cooked meal, so I accepted her offer. Spending time with Gus and Samantha and watching the way they interacted with such love and respect for one another had me thinking about Alyssa. There was a time when we had something a little like theirs, and I won't deny that I missed it. I missed her—more than I cared to admit. There were nights when I'd drive over to her place or the restaurant, hoping to catch a glimpse of her.

I wasn't the only one who was missing her. Clay was struggling with the fact that she was still keeping her distance. They'd had a few quick phone calls here and there, but he hadn't actually seen Alyssa since the night she refused to come to lockdown. Even after the danger had subsided and the lockdown was lifted, he couldn't convince her to come to the clubhouse. I could only assume it was because she knew I would be there.

It had been over four months, and I hadn't gotten so much as a text from her. There were many times when I was tempted to reach out, but I always ended up talking myself out of it. I wasn't the kind of man who pushed himself on a woman, but knowing what we had made it hard to let go. That was one of the reasons why I'd left Gus's place and drove over to the restaurant. It was almost time for her shift to end, so I parked between two trucks that were just a couple of rows down from her car. I turned off my lights and crossed my fingers, hoping that she wouldn't see me. A few minutes later, the back door opened and Alyssa walked out, looking amazing as always. Her hair was pulled up, and she wore a black coat with her purse hanging off her shoulder.

She was approaching her car when I noticed a man get out of his car, and it was clear from Alyssa's expression that she was startled as he walked towards her. The guy's back was to me, so it was difficult to see who he was until she charged past him. Rage washed over me as soon as he turned to follow her and I recognized it was Lucas Brant. Knowing how terrified she was of the guy I opened the door to my truck and was about to get out when Alyssa reached into her pocket and pulled out a handgun. As she pointed it directly at Brant, she shouted, "I'm not playing games with you, Lucas. I've told you to stop coming around here, and I mean it."

"So what ... you're gonna shoot me?"

"Maybe. Maybe not." She took a step towards him, and with determination in her voice, she asked, "Do you really want to take that chance?"

"You're fucking crazy."

"Crazier than you think. Now go, Lucas, and don't come near me again or you'll regret it."

"You'll pay for this shit, Alyssa." Brant turned and started back towards his vehicle. "No one fucks with me and gets away with it."

Relief washed over her face as he got in his car. Wasting no time, Alyssa quickly returned the gun to her coat pocket and rushed to her car, looking completely freaked out. As much as I wanted to go to her and make sure she was okay, I knew I couldn't. I'd made her a promise, and I intended to keep it. But that didn't mean *I* couldn't deal with Lucas. It wasn't the first time he'd come to see her; otherwise, Alyssa wouldn't have had a gun on her. That very thought had me following Brant out of the restaurant parking lot and onto the main street. I wasn't surprised when he pulled up to Mikey's Pub, one of his favorite bars in town. Hell, over the past few months, I'd seen him go in there more times than I could count. He'd have a few drinks and do his best to convince some chick to go home with him, but normally, he'd just end up leaving empty handed, returning to his oblivious wife and baby.

I followed him inside, sat in the back of the bar, and watched as he downed a few shots. Even after all the times I'd kept tabs on the guy, I was still amazed that at one time he'd been a star football player. He was about six-one and weighed about a hundred and eighty pounds, but his build looked more like a guy who never once saw the inside of a gym. Seemed that all the booze and late nights were taking their toll. It wasn't long before he spotted a petite redhead in the back of the bar. Clearly drunk, she was leaning over with her elbow on the table and her chin propped up on her hand. When Brant realized that she was blitzed, he decided to make a play for her. With a shot in hand, he made his way over to her and said, "Hey, beautiful. Can I buy you a drink?"

"Mm-hmm ... thaat'd be ... great," she slurred, barely able to keep her eyes open.

"I tell you what." Brant slipped his arm around her waist and said, "How about I get us a room at the hotel across the street, and you and I can have that drink alone."

She nodded. "Ooo-kaay."

"Great. Let's get out of here."

All smiles, Brant helped the chick to her feet and shuffled her out the door. I waited a couple of minutes, then went back out to my truck. I followed them across the street to a trashy motel, then parked and watched as

Brant rushed inside to get them a room. Moments later, he came back out to his car, and the girl stumbled out, barely able to walk as he latched onto her waist and led her inside the room. The whole scene was enough to make a decent man sick to his stomach. That girl had no idea what was coming. She was too far gone to know that Brant was going to try and take advantage of her. Lucky for her, I was there to make sure nothing happened. I waited a few minutes, giving them a chance to get settled, then I got out of my truck and started towards the room. I was just a few feet away when I heard the girl cry, "Wait ... Stop. What are you doing? No!"

I heard a hard slap, followed by the sound of her crying, and that's all it took. I lifted my foot and slammed it against the door, kicking it open. When I walked in, Brant was on top of the girl, pinning her arms above her head. "Get off her. Now!"

"What the—get the fuck out of here!" Angered by the unexpected forced entry, he shouted, "Can't you see we're in the middle of something?"

"You deaf or something? I said get the fuck off her!"

"Look, man. If this is your girl, I'm sorry." Finally doing as he was told, he slowly eased himself away from her and got off the bed. As he turned to face me, he said, "I don't want any trouble."

"Well, trouble is whatcha got, asshole." I walked over to the girl, and as I helped her up, I asked, "You all right?"

"Uh-huh, I think so."

"Fuck this shit," Brant shouted.

He started for the door but quickly stopped when I

pulled out my gun and aimed it towards him. "Stop right there, Brant. You're not going anywhere."

"Okay, okay." He held up his hands. "I'll stay right here."

I turned my attention back to the girl. "You sure you're okay?"

"Yeah, I'm okay. Thank you for helping me." Tears filled her eyes as she muttered, "I thought he was a good guy, but—"

"I know. Don't worry about it," I interrupted. "I'm gonna need you to go down to the lobby. Wait there until I can get someone to come take you home. Can you do that for me?"

"Yes, I can do that."

"Gonna need you to do me a favor."

"Okay?"

"You never saw me. Got that?"

She nodded. "Yeah, I got it."

"Good. Now get to the lobby." Once she'd made her way out of the room, I turned my attention back to Brant. "You're a real piece of shit, you know that? Bad enough that ya cheat on your wife while she's got a newborn at home, but ya gotta rough up a drunk chick?"

"How do you know I've got a wife and kid at home?"

"I know all about you, Lucas Brant. Grew up in Nashville and were the star quarterback. I also know you got a thing for forcing yourself on women, and that shit don't fly with me."

"Who the fuck are you?"

"I'm a friend of Alyssa Hanson's." His eyes widened with surprise as I continued, "I know what you did to her, how you raped her and stole her innocence, and I also know you didn't leave things there. No, you still keep coming at her, taking more and more from her every time she has to see your stupid face. That shit is about to end."

"I don't know what you're talking about."

I'd had enough. I wasn't going to stand there and listen to his bullshit. I reared back my fist and slammed it right into the side of his head, knocking him out cold. When he collapsed onto the bed, I took my phone out of my back pocket and dialed Hyde's number. As soon as he answered, I said, "Hey, brother. I'm gonna need you to meet me at the Blue Nights motel on Second."

"Now?"

"Yeah. Bring Landry's car, and Hyde?—you need to come packing."

"Got it. I'll be there in twenty."

When he hung up, I dialed Skillet's number. I told him about the girl in the lobby and that I needed him to pick her up and take her home. Once he'd assured me that he'd take care of it, I put my phone back in my pocket and started looking around the room for Brant's car keys. I found them, along with his wallet, on the table next to the bed. After I grabbed them, I went over and lifted Brant off the bed. I tossed him over my shoulder, then carried him out of the motel room and out to the parking lot. I used the keys to open his trunk and flipped him inside. As I stood there waiting for Hyde, I remembered my promise to Gus, assuring him that I wouldn't make a move towards Brant without letting him know. I pulled out my phone and gave him a call. Even though it was late, he answered right away. "Bone?"

"Hey, Gus. Sorry to call so late, but I need to tell you about something."

"Okay, what's going on?"

I took the next few minutes to brief him on what had gone down with Brant. I also told him what I wanted to do about it. When I was done, Gus sighed and said, "Do what ya gotta do, Bone. Just be careful and make sure there's no blowback to the club."

"I'll make sure of it."

"And Hyde's on the way?"

"Yeah, he should be here any minute."

"Good." I could hear the concern in his voice as he said, "You boys be careful."

"You got it. Thanks, Prez."

I hung up the phone and leaned against Brant's car while I waited for Hyde to show. Thankfully, I didn't have to wait long. It had only been fifteen minutes since I'd called him when he came rolling into the parking lot. He pulled up next to me and buzzed down the window. "What the fuck's going on?"

"No time to explain. I need you to follow me over to *the hole*."

I knew Hyde wouldn't be happy when he found out what was going on with Brant and Alyssa. With his temper, I didn't want to take a chance on him losing his shit in the motel parking lot, so that's why I told him to follow me instead. He and all the brothers knew it was the place we went whenever we had to contend with a body. It was an isolated area on the outskirts of town near the Mississippi River. Usually, we'd either bury it or toss it into the river. Tonight, it would be up to Hyde to determine what we'd do with Brant. He gave me a nod, then waited as I got in Brant's car and started towards the hole. It was about a twenty-minute drive, so I wasn't surprised when Hyde jumped out of Landry's car and asked, "You gonna tell me what the fuck is going on?"

"Yeah, but I'm gonna tell you right now—you're not gonna like it."

"Just fucking tell me, Bone."

I took the next few minutes explaining how I'd been keeping an eye on Brant. That in itself came as a surprise to him. He'd been doing the same. Like me, Hyde knew the guy was a piece of shit, but he hadn't gotten to the same point that I had when it came to knowing everything he'd been doing over the past few months. I could tell by his expression that he knew what was coming when I started talking about Alyssa. A mix of anguish and rage crossed his face when I told him about seeing Brant talking to her at the restaurant, and how she'd threatened to shoot him if he came around again. That bit of information had him asking, "Alyssa had a fucking gun?"

"She did." I let out a deep breath. "Seems Brant has been coming around a lot, and she wasn't gonna take any chances."

"*Fuck.* Lyssa never even mentioned anything to me."

"I guess she thought she could handle him on her own."

"That's fucking insane. What the hell was she thinking?"

"She's the only one who can answer that, brother."

After I told him what had gone down with the girl in

the bar and what I'd walked into in that hotel room, I opened the trunk and reached inside to pull out Brant. Once he was on his feet, Brant looked over to Hyde and asked, "What the fuck? Clay? You have something to do with all this?"

"I should've killed you when I had the chance."

Without giving Brant a chance to respond, Hyde started plowing into him. In a matter of seconds, the guy was nothing more than a puddled mess on the ground. Hyde gave him another kick in the side as he growled, "You should've never put your hands on my sister."

I reached down and grabbed Brant by the arm, lifting him to his feet. As he staggered from side to side, he muttered, "I didn't do shit to your sister. I don't know why you aren't getting the fact that the little whore wanted it."

He'd barely gotten the words out of his mouth when Hyde whipped out his gun and aimed it directly at Brant. "You were a piece of shit then, and you're a piece of shit now."

"Hold on, man." Realizing what was coming, he started pleading, "You can't do this. I've got a wife and kid at home. They need me."

"I'm doing them both a fucking favor."

Without saying another word, Hyde squeezed the trigger, putting two bullets into him, and Brant dropped to the ground. We both stood there, silently staring at his lifeless body, and a sense of satisfaction washed over me when I realized he wouldn't be causing Alyssa any more heartache than he already had. After several moments passed, I looked over to Hyde and said, "We need to decide what we're gonna do with him."

"I say throw his ass in the fucking river and be done with it."

"We could do that, but then his wife will report him missing and there'll be a lot of questions."

"All right then, what do you suggest?"

"We could take him and his car out to Frayser. Set it up like a drug deal gone bad. It's not like the guy hasn't been using. I've seen for myself that he's got quite the habit."

"You think it'll work?"

"Yeah, definitely. Just need to wipe the car down, plant him inside with an empty wallet and a quarter of meth at his side. You know the cops. They aren't gonna put a lot of effort into investigating a fucking drug deal."

"Let's make it happen."

We got a tarp from Landry's trunk and used it to cover the front seat. We didn't want him bleeding out in places that might draw undue suspicion. Once we'd gotten Brant positioned in the passenger seat, Hyde followed me to one of the rougher areas of Frayser. While I tended to Brant, Hyde went to track down a quarter of meth. I slid Brant's body over to the driver's side of the car, then removed the tarp. I took his wallet and removed all the cash, and once Hyde returned, he shot him once more, hoping it would be enough to derail the cops. I quickly wiped down the car, then tossed the baggie of meth onto the seat next to Brant's body. I knew with a little bit of investigating, the cops would see that he'd been shot outside of the vehicle, but knowing that dirty drug deals happened here on a nightly basis, I found it highly doubtful that they'd take the time to even check the asshole's wounds.

Once we'd gotten the stage set, Hyde looked over to me and asked, "You think they'll buy it?"

"Yeah, I think we did good."

"Should've done this years ago."

"Can't change the past, brother. At least now you can rest easy knowing he'll never bother Alyssa again. It's finally over."

"Thank fuck for that."

"You mind running me back to my truck?"

"Sure thing, brother." I followed him over to Landry's car, and as soon as we were both settled inside, Hyde looked over to me and said, "Thanks for this, Bone. I owe ya."

"You don't owe me shit, brother. Besides, I didn't do it for you."

"She still hasn't reached out to you?"

"No. About given up on that happening."

"Oh, come on, Bone. Didn't figure you'd give up that easily."

"Don't get me wrong. If she wanted me back, I'd have her in a second, but something tells me that time has come and gone."

"I don't know. I got a feeling that y'all's story is far from over."

18

ALYSSA

"Is there someone you'd like me to call?" the nurse asked with a concerned look in her eyes.

"Is that really necessary?"

"They're prepping you for surgery, Ms. Hanson."

"I know. I heard what the doctor said."

"It's not the time for you to be alone." She walked over and checked the monitor once again. "You need someone at your side. It'll make you feel better. That is, if there is someone to call."

"Yes, there's someone." I could've called my mother, but she was in Nashville and it would've taken her at least two hours to get to the hospital—leaving me with no other option. I had to call Clay. A feeling of dread washed over me at the thought of his reaction. He was going to lose his mind, and I only had myself to blame. It wasn't like I didn't know this day was coming. No, I'd known it for just over four months—since the day Jack finally convinced me to go to the doctor. I'd been feeling so bad. I was still having trouble sleeping and eating, and when

I'd fainted at work, Jack had had enough. Scared that something was terribly wrong, he put me in his car and drove me straight to Convenient Care.

Even then, I thought it was just stress and the fact that I was worrying over the upcoming meal presentation with Boucher and Bisset, but that quickly changed the second the nurse asked me the date of my last period. At that moment, it hit me. I hadn't had a period in months—four to be exact. I don't know how I could've been so stupid to let something like that slip my mind. I guess it just never dawned on me that I could be pregnant. It wasn't like Beckett and I hadn't been careful. We had, but, apparently, not careful enough. I motioned my hand over to the counter. "My phone is in my purse."

"Okay." The little blonde nurse hurried over to grab it, then pulled out my cell. "Do you want to make the call or should I do it?"

"I think you should do it—if you don't mind."

"Sure, sweetie. Whatever you want." She looked down at the screen and asked, "Who is it that I'm calling?"

"My brother ... Clay."

As she dialed his number, I clamped my eyes shut and winced like I was waiting for a bomb to explode. It didn't have to be like this. I could've told them. It wasn't like I didn't have the opportunity. While he'd done his best to respect my wishes about giving me space, he'd still stop by the restaurant or come by the house from time to time to check in. I'd always made sure to have on my coat or my work apron whenever I saw him to conceal my growing belly. At first, I just wanted the time to figure things out. I needed to wrap my head around the fact that I was going to be a mother. I was a wreck. I had a new job, a good relationship with a man that I ruined by pushing him away, and I just didn't know how to fix it. Instead of simply going to Beckett and explaining the situation, I made it all worse by keeping it a secret.

Looking back, I realized now how stupid it all was. Clay and Beckett were good men, and I knew in my heart that they must've had a legitimate reason to go after those guys like they did. Maybe it was the fear of admitting I was wrong to push them away or maybe it was the fact that I was afraid they wouldn't forgive me for doing it. Either way, I doubted they'd ever trust me again. I just prayed that, in time, they'd both find a way to forgive me.

I held my breath as I listened to the nurse say, "Hello, this is Jessica Tandy at Memorial Hospital. Is this Clay Hanson?"

I could hear my brother on the other end of the call say, "Yeah, this is he."

"Well, I'm calling about your sister, Alyssa. She wanted me to let you know that she'll be going into emergency surgery here in the next hour or so. The baby is showing signs of distress, and the doctors don't want to take any chances—"

"Wait ... Baby? Emergency surgery? What the hell are you talking about?" he roared.

"I know this must come as a shock, Mr. Hanson, but it's important for you to remain calm. Your sister's life and—"

"I want to know what the hell is going on!"

"I'll explain everything when you get here. We're in

room five-oh-three." Before Clay could say anything more, Jessica said, "I'll see you soon, Mr. Hanson."

She hung up the phone, and in a matter of seconds, my phone started to ring. Knowing it was Clay, I extended my hand and said, "I'll take that."

I quickly declined the call and put my phone on silent. Jessica looked over at me with her brows furrowed. "I take it that he didn't know you were pregnant?"

"No, he didn't."

"And the father?"

"No, he doesn't know either." I let out a deep sigh. "I've really made a mess of things."

"Well, you don't need to be worrying about that now. You just focus on you and that sweet baby of yours, and everything else will work out."

"You sound pretty sure of yourself."

"That's because I am." She gave me a warm smile. "You aren't the first patient I've had who's kept her pregnancy a secret. It actually happens more than you might think, and every time, things have a way of working out. I have no doubt that the same will hold true for you."

"I certainly hope you're right."

"I am. You'll see." She gave me a light pat on the leg, then said, "I'm going to go check in with the doctor and see how much longer it'll be."

"Okay. Thanks, Jessica."

Once she'd walked out of the room, I ran my hand over my round belly and my chest tightened when I thought about my son being in distress. I had no idea what that meant. I just knew it couldn't be good, especially since they were doing a C-section. I knew it was too soon. He was a month early, and there was a chance his lungs wouldn't be fully developed. There was a time when I wasn't sure I even wanted a baby, but now I couldn't bear the thought of losing him. My eyes filled with tears as I whispered, "Hey there, little guy. I need you to listen to me. I want you to be strong and hold on for your momma. You hear me? I love you and I can't wait to hold you in my arms."

My abdomen tightened with another contraction, taking my breath away. They were coming closer and closer, so I knew it wouldn't be long before they took me to surgery. The pain had just started to subside when there was a light tap on the door followed by the sound of footsteps entering the room. When I glanced up, I found Beckett and Clay standing at the foot of my bed. Neither of them spoke. They just stood there looking like they'd seen a ghost. It had been almost eight months since I'd seen Beckett, and he looked just as good, if not better, than I remembered. I'd often wondered if my feelings for him had changed, but as I lay there gazing at him, I realized I loved him just as much as I had when we were still together.

The tension in the room kept growing until finally Clay cleared his throat and asked, "So, are you going to tell me what the hell is going on with all this?"

"I know you're angry with me, but—"

"Angry doesn't begin to describe what I'm feeling right now, Alyssa." He motioned his hand towards my belly. "You're about to have a fucking kid, and this is the first I've heard of it."

"I was going to tell you, but..."

"Does Mom know?"

"Yes, she was there when I found out, but she wasn't thrilled with the news."

"So, you tell Mom, but you decided to keep the news from me?"

"Can we please not do this right now?" Another contraction hit, causing me to wince in agony. I took a few deep breaths, and when the pain started to subside, I muttered, "Something's wrong with the baby, and they're gonna have to take him early."

"What do you mean by 'something's wrong'?"

"I don't know. His heart rate isn't as strong as it should be." I glanced over at Beckett. He hadn't said a word. Instead, he just stood there staring at me in utter shock. I couldn't blame him. If I was in his shoes, I would be furious with me. "I'm so sorry, Beckett. I'm sorry about everything. I should've told you. I just didn't know how."

"I just don't understand." His voice was filled with hurt as he asked, "I thought we had a good thing. I thought I was good to you ... that I made you happy. What did I do so bad that you'd keep my own kid from me?"

"You were good to me. You both were." Another contraction rippled through me as I groaned, "I was there that night. I followed you...I saw *everything*."

"You were where?" Clay pushed.

"In ... uh ... *Frayser*." I stammered. "On Jackson Street."

Clay's eyes widened in horror when he realized what I was talking about. Before he could say anything more, Jessica and two other nurses came charging into the room. "All right, Ms. Hanson. It's time to get you down to surgery."

Like three little bees, they buzzed around the room, unplugging devices and lifting me over to the hospital bed that they'd use to transport me down for surgery. Once they had everything together, Jessica looked over to Beckett and Clay. "You want to take one of them to the delivery room with us?"

"Beckett ...Will you come?"

He nodded slowly like he was still in shock, then he and Clay followed as the nurses pushed my bed out of the room and into the hallway. We hadn't gotten very far when Jessica looked over to Clay and said, "You can stay in the waiting room. I'll call you as soon as I know something."

"Thank you." Clay knelt down and kissed me on the forehead. "Love ya, Sis."

"I love you, too, Clay."

My heart started to race as they pushed me down a long hallway and through the doors of the delivery room. Everything was happening so fast that I was barely able to make sense of what was going on. As soon as they had me in the room, they started prepping for surgery while they ordered Beckett to put on surgical garb and a mask. The anesthesiologist came over and asked, "How are you feeling?"

"I've been better."

"And your contractions?"

"They're getting pretty intense."

He nodded. "Well, I'm about to make you feel a lot better. Just need you to sit up for me."

"Okay."

With Beckett's help, I sat up and turned with my back

to the anesthesiologist, and it wasn't long before he'd administered my epidural. Once he helped me back down on the bed, he smiled and said, "We'll just need to wait a few minutes for that to take effect, and then we'll be set to start the C-section."

"Okay, thank you."

I watched as the nurses placed a surgical screen above my stomach. Once it was up, I could hear the doctor and nurses moving around and talking, but I couldn't see what they were doing. The whole thing made me extremely nervous, and I was on the verge of losing it when I felt Beckett's mouth at my ear. "It's going to be fine. Just breathe."

"I'm really glad you're here."

"Me too. No other place I'd rather be."

Trying my best not to cry, I whispered. "I need him to be okay."

"It's a boy?"

"Mm-hmm."

"Well, how about that." A sweet smile crossed his face. "A boy. Well, if he's anything like his ol' man, he's a fighter and you've got nothing to worry about."

"I really hope he's like you." I looked over to Beckett as I told him, "I was thinking of calling him Joshua Tucker ... JT, for short. If that's okay?"

"I like it."

"Beckett?"

"Hmm?"

I looked up and back so I could see his face as I whispered, "I really am sorry."

"Don't worry about any of that now. You need to focus on having this baby."

Moments later, the doctor leaned over the barrier and said, "We're about to begin. You might feel a slight pinch, but if you feel anything more, just let us know."

"Okay."

The room fell silent as the doctor began the C-section. Just as he'd warned, I felt a strange pinching and tugging sensation, but no real pain. I tried to listen as the doctor talked back and forth with the nurses, but it was difficult to hear what they were saying. Sensing that I was getting worked up again, Beckett placed his hand on my shoulder and whispered, "It's gonna be okay. Just try to relax."

Suddenly there was a little commotion, and the next thing I knew, the anesthesiologist asked Beckett to move over to the corner of the room. As he took a hold of my IV, he explained, "There's been a slight complication. Everything's fine, but we're gonna have to put you under for a bit."

Before I could ask him what was going on, everything went black. I don't know how long it had been when I woke up in a room with my IV still connected to my arm and no baby at my side. When he saw that I was awake, Beckett came over to me and said, "He's okay. He's down-stairs in the NICU."

"Why? Is something wrong? Did something happen? Is that why they—"

"He's okay. The doctor wasn't happy about his oxygen level, so he sent JT downstairs as a precautionary measure."

"You're sure he's going to be okay?"

"The doctor didn't give me any reason to think otherwise. He believes you and Josh are going to be just fine. He just needs a little time to get his levels up where they need to be." Beckett pulled out his phone and pulled up a picture of our son. "He's beautiful, freckles. Looks just like you."

He brought the phone closer for me to get a better look, and I was in complete awe as I peered down at our son. He had beautiful dark eyes, the tiniest bit of dark hair, and the most precious little fingers and toes. Beckett was right. He was beautiful. Tears filled my eyes as I asked, "When can I see him?"

"The nurse said she'd be back in a couple of hours to take us down to the NICU."

"Okay, good." I studied the picture for a few more moments, then Beckett put the phone back in his pocket. "I know I said it before, but I really am sorry."

"You should've told me, Alyssa. I deserved a chance to explain."

"I know. I was just so confused." I couldn't bear to look him in the eye, so I stared up at the ceiling. "I just couldn't believe that you and Clay would do something like that."

"This isn't the time or the place for this conversation, but I'll tell you this." He inched closer, making sure that none of the nurses could hear him as he whispered, "Those men were the ones responsible for shooting Gus, and they had it in their heads that they were coming after the rest of us. We did what we did to protect our family, Alyssa."

"I didn't know."

"'Cause you didn't ask."

He leaned over and kissed me on the temple. I don't know if it was my raging hormones, the effects of the anesthesia, or the enormity of finally seeing Beckett after so many months, but I was overcome with emotion. I started to cry and soon I was sobbing, making it difficult to say, "There's something else I need to tell you."

"You don't have to say anything, Lyssa. I already know."

"No, I need to say it." His eyes met mine. "I never stopped loving you. Not for one second. Even after what I saw, I still loved you, and I still love you now. I think I always will."

"I love you, too, Alyssa Hanson. I really do."

"Do you think we can figure this whole thing out ... start over or something?"

"No reason to start over. We both made mistakes. We just gotta learn from them and do better next time."

"You make it sound easy."

"Because it is. I want you in my life, and I'm gonna do everything in my power to show you, and our son, just how much you mean to me."

"I do love you."

"And I love you." He leaned forward and pressed his lips to mine, kissing me softly. "I've waited for you my whole life, Alyssa, and trust me when I say, you are worth every second."

19

T-BONE

NATURALLY, IT ALARMED ME WHEN I HEARD ALYSSA WAS IN the hospital, but to say I was in shock after finding out the reason why was putting it mildly. Never once, in all these months, did I suspect that she might be pregnant. It just never crossed my mind. Even now, as I sat there studying the picture of my newborn son, I just couldn't believe it—I, Beckett Walker, was actually a father, and the woman I loved more than anything in this world was his mother. I hated that I'd missed all of her pregnancy—doctor's appointments, ultrasounds, and watching our son grow inside of her, but I couldn't focus on that now. Instead, I needed to concentrate on making up for lost time and being there for Alyssa and JT. I needed to make things right and prove to her that I could be what they both needed—that I could be the one if she'd let me.

Knowing they were all waiting to hear how Alyssa and the baby were doing, I made my way to the waiting room to find my brothers. The second I walked into the room, they all gathered around and listened as I gave them the rundown of everything the doctor had told me. While they were all surrounding me, I took the opportunity to show them the picture of Josh. Blaze was the first to give me hell. "Thank god, he looks like his momma."

"Can't disagree with you there, brother." I chuckled as I said, "I gotta tell ya, I still have no idea how this happened."

"If you don't know that by now then I ain't gonna bother explaining it to ya." Gus teased.

"That's not what I meant, and you know it," I argued. "We were always careful."

"Well, you know they say condoms are only ninety-seven percent effective." Murphy slapped me on the back as he chuckled. "Leave it to you to be in that three percent failure rate."

"Fuck you, Murph."

"Come on, brother. You know I'm just fucking with ya." He reached over and gave me a big hug. "I'm proud for ya. We all are. We got no doubt that you're gonna be a great dad."

"Thanks, brother. Appreciate it."

"We're gonna get going," Blaze announced. "You be sure to let us know if something changes or you guys need anything."

"Will do."

I said my goodbyes, and once the brothers started to clear out, Hyde came over to get a better look of the picture I'd taken of the baby. As he looked down at the screen, he chuckled as he said, "Damn, he's a handsome feller, just like his uncle."

"He looks like his mother."

"Doesn't matter who he looks like. I'll love him the same either way."

"That goes for the both of us."

"You know, I'm having a real hard time wrapping my head around all this. I mean ... damn ... she was pregnant, and she didn't tell us. What the fuck, man? Who does that?" Hyde shook his head. "I gotta tell ya, the whole thing kind of pisses me off. I mean ... I get seeing that drive-by had to fuck her up. Hell, it'd fuck anybody up, but damn, it's embarrassing as fuck that my own sister was pregnant, and I didn't know a goddamn thing about it."

"Trust me when I say, I know exactly how you feel." I took my phone and slipped it into my back pocket. "But we got nobody to blame but ourselves. The fact that she saw anything is on us. We're the ones who fucked up, and because of our mistake, she's spent the last eight months thinking we killed those guys just for shits and giggles. It's no wonder that she was too scared to tell us that she was fucking pregnant."

"You got a point, but still ... She could've given me a chance to explain. I'm her brother."

"You're exactly right. You are her brother—the one person she trusts the most in this world, and you and I both failed her."

I watched as my words sunk in, and sorrow crept across his face. "Damn, you're right. I really fucked up, didn't I?"

"We both did, and now it's up to us to make it up to her ... That is, if she'll let us."

"Well, we'll just have to see that she does."

"That we will." I looked my brother in the eye as I said, "And you need to know, I have every intention of claiming Alyssa as mine. I love her, brother, and no matter what it takes, I'm going to make her and JT happy."

He gave me a pat on the shoulder. "They'd both be lucky to have you."

"We need to get upstairs and check on her. It won't be long before they let her go down to see the baby."

Hyde followed me up to Alyssa's room. When we walked in, she was sitting up on the bed, and I couldn't imagine a more beautiful sight. Her long hair was down, framing her angelic face, and it was clear from her soulful expression that she was deep in thought. I walked over to the edge of the bed and placed my hand on hers. "You okay?"

"Is it strange to miss someone you haven't even met yet?"

"No, freckles. You've spent the last eight months together, so it's perfectly natural for you to be missing him right now." I smiled as I told her, "But don't worry, you'll be seeing him soon."

"I really hope so." Tears filled her eyes as she asked, "They say it's important for the baby to connect with his mother right after birth. What if he doesn't know me? What if he doesn't recognize me as his mother?"

"He will. With a momma like you, there's no way that he couldn't."

She nodded, then brushed a tear from her cheek. "I've been thinking about what you said ... about the shooting and what those men did. I'm really sorry that I assumed the worst. I should've known better. I should've trusted you both and given you a chance to explain. Something, anything—except turning my back on you like I did. I'm really sorry. If I could—"

"Alyssa, this isn't all on you." I looked over at Hyde and said, "We've all had a hand in making a mess of this, but that's over now. Hyde and I are going to do what we can to set things straight, starting with explaining some things about the club."

"I understand why you did what you did that night. They hurt Gus and threatened to hurt more of your brothers. They weren't good men. I know all of that."

Hyde stepped over to her and said, "I'm gonna ask you something, and I want you to be honest with me."

"Okay."

"What was going through your head the day you went and bought that gun?"

Surprise crossed her face. "You know about that?"

"Yeah, we both do." Hyde's expression grew serious and his tone was filled with determination as he said, "You might've turned us away, Sis, but that didn't mean we stopped looking out for you."

"I bought it because of Lucas. He kept coming by my work. He threatened to hurt me again, and I couldn't let that happen."

"What were you going to do?"

Her voice trembled as she said, "I'd kill him before I let him put his hands on me again, Clay. I—"

"I know, Alyssa. You don't have to say any more." Hyde reached over and took her hand. "I understand completely. We had the same thought in mind when we took care of those thugs. Right or wrong, it was a means to an end, but I need you to know, that's a very small part of what goes on in the club. We're not just brothers, we're a family, and we stand by one another through thick and thin."

Alyssa nodded, but I could see that she wasn't completely convinced. "You remember the night we all moved you into your place?"

"Uh-huh."

"That night is what we're about, Alyssa. Being together. Sharing our lives with one another, and we both want you to be a part of that. We want you to see for yourself that what we're saying is true."

"I'd like that." She thought for a moment, then asked, "You were there the night I pulled out my gun after Lucas showed up?"

"I was." Knowing she was going to ask, I said, "Let's just say, you won't have to worry about seeing him again."

"Oh." I could see the wheels turning in her head. I had no idea what she was thinking, especially when that big smile crept over her face. "And here I'd been thinking that he'd run off because I'd scared him with my big, bad gun and ferocious threats."

"Maybe, or maybe it was something else entirely."

"I honestly don't care. I'm just glad that I won't have to deal with him anymore."

We continued talking for several minutes, and while she wasn't on board a hundred percent, I had a feeling that Alyssa was finally starting to understand all the good that the club had brought into our lives. I hoped that in time she'd realize those same benefits were meant for her own life as well, but that would take time. Thankfully, we had plenty of that on our hands. Hyde was busy catching Alyssa up on what had been going on with him and Landry when one of the nurses tapped on the door and stepped inside with a wheelchair. "Hey there, folks. There's a little boy down the hall who wants to see his momma."

"We can see him?"

"You sure can. Well, you and the father can go." She pushed the wheelchair over to the side of the bed. As she started to help Alyssa up and into the chair, she explained, "Since he's in the NICU, there can only be two people in the room, and we'll have to give you an isolation gown to wear, along with gloves, shoe covers, and a mask. I know it's a lot, but we want to keep our babies safe."

"Of course."

"I'm Katie, by the way. I'm the nurse assigned to Joshua, and I'm pleased to tell you that he's been doing really well." A big smile crossed her face as she said, "The little guy didn't care for the oxygen tube in his nose and pulled it out on his own."

"Oh no!"

"It's a good thing. His levels have been great without it."

"That's fantastic news."

"Yes, it is." Her smile faded a bit as she continued, "We just have to get the little man to eat. So far, he hasn't wanted the breast milk you pumped for us. If we can't get him to take it soon, we'll have to administer a feeding tube, but we have some time before going down that road."

Alyssa was practically beaming as we made our way down the hall and into the NICU. The nurse gave us our protective garments to put on, and once we were ready, she led us inside. I have to admit, going into that room with all those tiny babies in their incubators was a little rattling, especially with all the nurses buzzing around to make sure they were all okay. I could tell by the panicked look in her eyes that Alyssa was feeling the same as the nurse brought us to the back of the room. When we reached JT's crib, I was surprised to find it empty. Clearly alarmed by the fact, Alyssa looked over to the nurse and asked, "Where is he? Is something wrong?"

"Umm, no. Actually, he's just fine." She leaned over to the nurse in the next cubicle and said, "Hey, Michele. JT's parents are here."

When the nurse turned around, I could see that she was carrying JT in her arms. As she rushed over to us, she said, "Oh! I'm so sorry. We usually don't have babies his size around here, and I just can't seem to put the little guy down."

"So, he's doing okay?"

"Oh, yes." The nurse bent down and placed JT in Alyssa's arms. "He's doing more than okay."

Tears filled Alyssa's eyes as she looked down at our son and said, "He's perfect."

"Yes, he is." Katie leaned over to me and asked, "Would you like to see if you can get him to nurse?"

I nodded, and Katie carefully helped me to lower my gown. My sutures were still very tender, so she placed a pillow under JT for support. We tried for several minutes to get him to latch on, but he simply wasn't having it. Trying her best to reassure me, Katie smiled. "No worries. He's just going to need some time. How 'bout I go get him a bottle and see if that works any better?"

"Okay. Sounds good."

When Katie turned and walked away, I grabbed one of the empty chairs and moved it over next to Alyssa, and as I sat down, she asked, "What if we can't get him to nurse?"

"Then, he'll take a bottle. Either way will be fine, babe."

"But I wanted him..."

"It'll be fine. *Promise.*"

She nodded, then turned her attention to JT. I watched as she ran the tip of her finger down his tiny nose. "Hey there, handsome. It's your momma. I've been missing you."

He nestled up next her as if he'd done it a million times, and that's all it took. Alyssa's worries about him not knowing her quickly faded, and with a look of complete wonder, she stared down at him as she whispered, "There's someone else here who'd like to meet you, sweet boy. This is your daddy." She winced as she leaned over and positioned JT in my arms. "Your momma didn't tell him she was pregnant with you, so he was kind of surprised to find out about you. But I can tell just by looking at him that he loves you very much."

"That I do." I looked down at my boy, and my heart swelled with emotion. Damn, I'd always thought of myself as a pretty strong, tough guy, but as I sat there with

JT in my arms, it was all I could do to keep myself from crying like a damn schoolgirl. He was just so beautiful, so perfect, and he was mine. For the first time in my life, that empty void in my heart was completely full. That feeling inspired me to say, "Alyssa, I'll leave it all behind. If that's what you want, I'll do it. I'll do whatever you want."

"What are you talking about, Beckett?"

"The club has been my whole life for as long as I can remember, but for you and JT, I'm willing to give it all up. You two are the most important people in my life now, and if—"

"No, Beckett." She reached over and placed the palm of her hand on my cheek. "I would never ask you to give up your brothers or the club. Besides, I want them to be a part of our lives. I want what you and Hyde talked about. You know, for all of us to be a family."

"Are you sure?"

"Yes, I'm sure." Her eyes met mine as she said, "I just want us to be together and for things to be like they were before. Do you think we can do that?"

"Absolutely."

"Well, it's not going to be easy, especially with a baby in the mix, but I want to try. I love you, Beckett, and I've missed you terribly."

"I feel the same, and that's why I think you two should move in with me."

"Wait ... really?" she gasped. "We haven't even been in the same room together for almost six months, and now you want us to move in together?"

"Sure do. The sooner the better." I looked down at JT as I told her, "We've already wasted too much time, and I don't want to miss another second of being with you both."

She thought for a moment, then replied, "Let me think about it."

"What's there to think about?"

"A lot." Alyssa shook her head. "I don't want us to jump into anything just because we had a baby."

"That's not—"

"Beckett," she interrupted. "I'm just asking for a little time to think about it."

"Okay, I get it. Take all the time you need."

We stayed with JT until the nurse came over and told us that visiting hours were over and that we could come back the following morning to see him. Neither of us wanted to leave him, but under the circumstances, we didn't have a choice. Alyssa looked like she was on the verge of tears as I wheeled her out of the NICU and back to her room. With the nurse's help, we got Alyssa back in the bed, and it wasn't long before she drifted off to sleep. Even though I was completely wiped, a storm of thoughts kept whirling around my head, making it impossible to sleep. I just couldn't seem to wrap my head around it all. In one crazy day, my entire world changed. I was a father. I thought the odds of that ever happening had come and gone, but I was wrong. In a blink, I was handed a real chance of having it all.

The next morning, Jessica, the nurse on duty, came down bright and early to take us to see JT. Unlike the day before, he was resting in his little incubator bed, and Alyssa and I were both surprised to see that there was a small tube in his nose. I could hear the concern in Alyssa's voice when she asked, "What's that?"

"It's his feeding tube." Jessica tried to reassure us both by saying, "He's still having a little trouble latching, so his doctor ordered the tube to ensure that he's getting the nutrients he needs. But don't worry, it's not uncommon for preemies to struggle a bit. He'll catch on."

"How long will he need the feeding tube?"

"Just until he can take four to six ounces on his own." Jessica leaned over and picked up JT, then carefully placed him in Alyssa's arms. "He's a tough one. I have no doubt that he'll figure it out."

"So, does that mean no more bottle feeding?"

"Oh, no. We still want to give him every opportunity to try on his own. You can either try nursing him, or I can go grab a bottle if you'd like."

"I just pumped, so a bottle might be best."

"You got it." As she turned to leave, Jessica told her, "I'll be right back."

Alyssa let out a sigh as she looked down at JT. I could see that she was worried. I was too. I felt completely helpless, and that wasn't a feeling I was used to. I was a man who fixed problems, but this wasn't something I knew how to fix. All I could do was try and be supportive and pray that JT would figure out this feeding thing so we could take him home. Alyssa looked over to me as she said, "He's going to be okay, Beckett. I just know it."

"Of course, he is."

"It's hard to think of him being in this place, but at least we know he's getting the best care."

"Yeah, they seem to be on top of it."

Jessica came over and offered Alyssa a small bottle of the breast milk she'd pumped the night before. She leaned down and ran her hand over his tiny head and whispered, "All right, little man. Let's see what ya got."

Alyssa placed the tip of the bottle at JT's mouth, but he quickly turned away. She tried once more, and after the same result, she started to become worried. "He just doesn't want it."

"Maybe Dad should give it a try," Jessica suggested.

"I doubt that'll make any difference," I scoffed.

"Won't know unless we try." Jessica lifted JT from Alyssa's arms and carefully handed him over to me. "Maybe you've got the special touch."

"Mmm, don't know about that." Reluctantly, I took JT in my arms, and as I cradled him close to my chest, I looked down at him and whispered, "All right, mister. Don't make your ol' man look bad."

I placed the tip of the bottle at his mouth, dabbing a little milk on his bottom lip, and to my surprise, he opened up and tried to latch on. He was mostly nipping at it, but it was progress. Jessica chuckled as she said, "Looks like Dad might have the touch after all."

"Look, Beckett. He's actually taking it."

Not wanting to disturb him, I nodded and leaned back in the chair, gently rocking him back and forth as he tried to take his first real go at the bottle. After several minutes, he'd had enough and pushed the bottle out of his mouth. While he hadn't drank much, it was definitely progress. I kept rocking him until he drifted off to sleep. I glanced over at Alyssa and found her staring back at me with wonder in her eyes. "You want to hold him?"

"He's good where he is. Just let him rest a bit." She smiled. "I've been thinking about this whole moving in together thing."

"Oh yeah?"

"Mm-hmm. If we're going to do this, I think we need to set up some ground rules."

"*Ooo-kayyy*... This should be good." I chuckled as I asked, "What kind of ground rules?"

"I'm kind of OCD about things being where they're supposed to be, so no dirty socks and drawers on the floor."

"I can do that."

"If I cook, you do the dishes. If you cook, I'll do them."

"Fair enough."

"I'm not going to be the only one changing dirty diapers."

"What about the gross ones?"

She laughed as she answered, "I think a big, tough guy like you can handle a gross diaper now and then."

"I'll do my best."

"You know it's been a while since we've ... you know, um ... *had sex*." She wiggled her eyebrows. "So, when we're able, I'm gonna need you to make up for lost time."

"Freckles, I'm down for that anytime, anyplace. You just name it."

"Good to know." Alyssa's smile faded as she said, "When it comes to the club stuff, you don't have to tell me everything, but I need to know that you're safe."

"I can do that. Anything else?"

"No, I think that just about covers it."

"Well, I have one rule."

"Okay, what's that?"

"We have to go skinny dipping at least once every summer."

A big smile crossed her face as she replied, "I think I can handle that."

"Then, I guess we're all set."

"All right then. Looks like you got yourself two new roommates."

"No, babe. You're both much more than that. You'll be my ol' lady and future wife, and we'll raise our son together."

"I love you, Beckett."

"Love you more, freckles."

And just like that, my girl was back, and I had a son to boot. As far as I was concerned, life couldn't have been any better.

20

ALYSSA

WHEN BECKETT ASKED ME TO MOVE IN WITH HIM, I HAD MY reservations. We'd been apart for so many months, and even when we were together, it was only late at night when he'd stop by my place after work. I worried that we were fooling ourselves in thinking that we could just slip back into what we had before, but to my pleasant surprise, things were going better than I could've ever expected. After I was released from the hospital, Beckett brought me to his house, and to my utter surprise, all of my things were already there and in place. He'd even started working on a nursery for JT. He'd put together the crib and changing table, and was getting ready to paint. I had no idea how he'd found the time to get it all done, especially with work and all the trips back and forth to the hospital. I think it got his mind off of JT having to stay in the NICU. While his oxygen levels had improved dramatically, he still wasn't eating as much as the doctor would like, so we had no choice but to be patient.

We'd just finished one of our daily visits with JT and

were on our way out of the hospital when we ran into Gus and Samantha. I was surprised to see that Gus was looking really good. In fact, other than the scar, he looked just like he had the last time I'd seen him. Beckett smiled at them both as he said, "Hey, I wasn't expecting to see y'all today."

"We just wanted to come by and see how the baby was doing," Gus replied.

"He's still got a ways to go in the eating department, but we're hoping that he'll be released soon."

"That's good to hear." Gus looked over to me as he asked, "And how about you? How are you making it?"

"I'm hanging in there." I shrugged. "It isn't easy leaving him here, but it helps to know that he's in good hands. The nurses and doctors have been really good to us."

"Any idea how much longer he'll have to stay?" Samantha asked with concern.

"It's hard to tell, but we're thinking it's going to be a few more days." I shook my head. "I really wish it would be sooner, but we've been using this time to get things ready for him. We're almost finished with the nursery, and all that."

"That's great to hear. I'm sure it looks great."

"It does." I glanced over at Beckett as I said, "Beckett has outdone himself."

"Well, I can't wait to see it."

"We won't keep you. Just wanted to check in."

"I appreciate it, brother." A mischievous smile crossed Beckett's face as he asked, "How's that cursive writing going?"

"Don't even start with me, Bone. I can write just fine, thank you."

"I knew you'd get it."

We said our goodbyes, and then, Beckett and I went home to finish up the nursery. Two days later, we got the call that it was finally time to bring our boy home. While we couldn't have been more pleased to have him there with us, it took a little time to get adjusted to the new routine. I'd read all the baby books. I knew as his mother that I should sleep whenever he did, but that simply didn't work for me. I was too busy hovering over him like a worrywart, checking every few minutes to make sure he was not only breathing, but had a dry diaper and a full belly—all while trying to recover from a C-section. I was wearing myself out, and Beckett knew it. He walked in while I was in the nursery rocking JT, then reached down and took the baby from my arms. Confused, I asked, "What are you doing?"

"I'm taking over baby duty. You're going to take a hot bath and get in the bed." He extended his free hand and helped me up. "And before you even think about arguing ... *don't*. You need to sleep, and you know it."

"But—"

"No buts, babe. You're getting some sleep." Beckett leaned down and kissed me on the forehead. "Your hot bath is waiting for you."

"Okay, okay. You win."

"Yeah, I usually do." He teased.

"Hey, don't push it, mister."

"What?" He sat down with a smirk and started rocking JT. "I'm just telling it like it is."

"Mm-hmm. Whatever you say, boss." I was just about to walk out of the nursery when I stopped and glanced over my shoulder. "Hey, Beckett?"

"Yeah?"

"Thank you."

"You got nothing to thank me for, freckles."

"You're wrong." I leaned against the doorframe and yawned. "You moved us into your home and finished the nursery. You've been so good with JT, and—"

"Alyssa, I know what you're doing," he fussed. "Stop procrastinating and get into the tub before the water gets cold."

"Fine." I giggled as I started down the hall. "I'm going."

When I stepped into the bathroom, I was surprised to find candles scattered around the room and the tub filled with hot water and bubbles. I don't know why I was so taken aback. Beckett always seemed to know exactly what I needed. With a smile on my face, I slipped off my sweats and dirty t-shirt, and the second I eased into the soothing water, I could feel the tension in my muscles start to subside. I closed my eyes, and it wasn't long before I was completely relaxed. By the time I was done washing my hair and shaving my legs, I felt like a limp noodle and could barely get out of the tub. After I dried off, I slipped on my pajamas and went into the bedroom. I was just about to crawl into bed when I decided to go check in on Beckett and JT. I started towards the door but quickly stopped when I heard Beckett shout, "To bed, Lyssa!"

"I just wanted to make sure—"

"He's fine, babe. Just fed him and about to give him a

bath." His tone grew firm as he ordered, "Now stop worrying and get some sleep."

I giggled as I turned back towards the bed and shouted, "So bossy!" Doing as I was told, I crawled into bed, and for the first time in days, I slept—really slept.

When I woke up the next morning, I rolled over to find that I was in the bed alone. Worried, I threw the covers back and rushed to the nursery only to find Beckett fast asleep in the rocking chair with JT sleeping soundly on his bare chest. It was a sight that made my heart swell with so much love I thought it might burst. Being careful not to wake them, I tiptoed over to Beckett and slipped my hands under JT, gently lifting him from his daddy's chest and laying him down in his crib. I'd just gotten him settled when I heard Beckett ask, "Did you get some sleep?"

"Yes, thanks to you." I turned and walked over to him, kissing him briefly before I said, "I've got him. Go get in the bed and get some sleep."

"Look who's being bossy now."

"What can I say?" I gave him a wink. "You bring it out in me."

"Mm-hmm." He got up, and in a sleepy haze, he started towards the bedroom. "Landry and Hyde will be here around ten, so make sure you wake me up in a couple of hours."

"Sure thing."

When I heard him rustling the sheets, I checked on JT once more, then headed into the kitchen hoping to clean up a little while I had the chance. I put the dirty dishes in the dishwasher, tossed in a load of clothes in the washing machine, and even managed to get dressed before JT finally woke up. Hoping to get to him before he woke Beckett, I rushed into the nursery and quickly picked him up. "Hey there, buddy."

I changed his diaper before going into the kitchen to make him a bottle. Even though I'd planned on breast-feeding, I didn't want to take a chance on losing all the progress he'd made by moving him from his bottle. The nurses assured me it wouldn't be an issue, but after every-thing we'd been through, I wasn't going to take the chance. JT was fussy, but as soon as I gave him the bottle, he started to settle. I carried him into the living room and sat down in Beckett's oversized recliner.

As I fed him, I looked around the room, and it seemed strange how much it already felt like home to me. Maybe it was because so many of my things were scattered around the house, but I had a feeling there was some-thing more to it—like the fact that Beckett was there. As crazy as it might've sounded, he was my home, and in his arms, I'd found everything I'd always wanted and more.

When JT finished his bottle, I placed him down on my lap with his back against my legs so I could get a better look at him. I was studying his adorable little fingers and toes when Beckett came into the room. He was still his pajama pants with no shirt, and even though he still seemed to be in a sleepy haze, the man was looking all kinds of sexy. It was just another reminder that I couldn't have sex for another six weeks, which wasn't easy considering that it'd been so long since we'd been together. His brows furrowed as he asked, "What happened to you waking me up?"

"It hasn't been two hours yet."

"Actually, it's been three." He kissed my forehead, and then turned his attention to JT. "How's it going, big man?"

"He's been changed and fed, so I'd say he's doing pretty good."

He leaned down and gave me another kiss before asking, "You want some coffee?"

"That would be great."

Beckett nodded, then went into the kitchen. He was just starting to make us a pot of coffee when there was a knock at the door. As soon as he opened it, I could hear Clay say, "Damn, brother. You're looking a little rough around the edges."

"Lack of sleep will do that to a man." As he started back into the kitchen, Beckett continued, "Y'all come on in. I was just making some coffee."

"Where's JT?" Landry asked sounding excited. "I can't wait to see him."

"He's in here with me." As she made her way into the living room, I told her, "He's been waiting to meet you."

Landry rushed over to me, and as she looked down at JT, her eyes filled with emotion. "Oh, Alyssa. He's so precious."

"Thank you." I carefully picked him up and offered him to her. "Would you like to hold him?"

"Are you kidding?" She took him in her arms. "I'd love to."

She carried him over to the sofa and sat down, then cradled JT close to her chest as she stared down at him with the biggest smile. When Clay walked in, he went straight over to Landry and sat down next to her, peering over at JT. "Boy, he's really something, isn't he?"

"Yes," Landry replied. "He makes me want to have a baby."

"I'd be good with that."

Surprise crossed Landry's face as she asked, "Really?"

"Absolutely." Clay ran his hand over JT's little head. "Bet the big guy here would like to have some cousins to play with it."

"I'm sure he would." I smiled as I added, "And I would love to have a couple of nieces and nephews running around."

"Well, it's definitely something to think about." Landry turned her attention to me as she said, "The girls and I were talking, and we'd really like to have a baby shower for you and JT next week. We could do it over at the clubhouse so we'd have enough room for the guys to be there too."

"That's really sweet, but you don't have to do that."

"We want to, and I know the guys would love to meet JT."

It meant so much to me that she'd even thought about having a baby shower for us, especially after the way I'd behaved, but I was still in that overprotective mother mode and wasn't sure that it was a good idea to have him around so many people. Sensing my concern, Clay looked over to me and said, "I'm sure you're worried about JT just getting out of the NICU and all, but Mom's supposed to be coming down this weekend for a few days. Think of it this way...she'd be an extra set of hands while you're opening gifts, or she could take him down to one of the spare rooms and watch him if it gets to be too much and he starts to fuss."

"Umm ... well." I turned to Beckett as I asked, "What do you think?"

"I think it'd be okay." He brought me a cup of coffee as he continued, "But it's completely up to you."

"Come on, Alyssa," Clay pushed. "It'll be fine. Besides, it will be good for you to get out of the house for a bit."

"Okay, I'm in." I smiled as I told them both, "I really appreciate you guys going to the trouble."

"It's no trouble, Alyssa." Landry looked down at JT with a smile. "We'll use just about any excuse to have a gathering, and there couldn't be a better one than for this little guy right here."

Clay and Landry stayed for a cup of coffee and doted on JT for just over an hour, then headed home.

Over the next couple of days, Beckett and I slipped into a manageable routine. In the morning, he'd get up and take care of changing JT and giving him his bottle before he headed into work, and while he was gone, I took over. JT was a good napper, so I was able to get a few things done around the house while he slept. I even had time to get a little cooking done. Being in the kitchen made me miss working at the restaurant but not enough to make me want to go back. I wasn't sure what I was going to do after my maternity leave was over. I was tempted to just stay home with JT, but I'd really worked hard to secure my spot on the line. It was a thought that made me think back on the day I'd presented my dish to Boucher and Bisset. I'd spent hours making the perfect

Coq au vin, which was basically chicken braised with wine, mushrooms, pork, and a drop of brandy. To my surprise, they were both so impressed that they offered me a full-time position on the line. I couldn't have been more proud of myself,

But now, I was really enjoying my time at home with JT. I had a tough decision ahead of me, but thankfully, I had plenty of time to think it over.

When the day came for the shower, I was still feeling a little apprehensive about taking JT out and about, especially when we pulled up to the clubhouse and I saw how many people were there. Thankfully, having my mother with me helped set my mind at ease. A warm smile crossed her face as she said, "It's going to be fine. Let's let everyone meet him, and if he happens to get fussy, I'll take him to one of the spare rooms."

"Okay, sounds good."

As we started walking up to the front door, Beckett looked over to me and asked, "You ready?"

"I think so."

I repositioned JT in his sling carrier, and with him nestled close to my chest, I followed Beckett inside the clubhouse. When we entered the family room, I was surprised to see that the entire room was filled with Beckett's brothers and their ol' ladies. Not only that, it was also beautifully decorated with blue balloons, streamers, and a gorgeous bouquet of flowers resting in the middle of all the food and drinks on the back table. It couldn't have been more perfect. When Landry saw us walk in, she rushed over and asked, "What do you think?"

"It's amazing, Landry. I can't believe y'all did all this."

"We wanted to make today special for both you and JT."

"Well, you did a fabulous job."

We hadn't been talking long when Murphy and Riley came over. They both took a moment to meet JT and congratulate Beckett and me once again on the birth of our son. As soon as they walked away, Shadow and Alex came over, keeping their distance as they met our son for the first time. One by one, each of the brothers and their wives came over to congratulate us, being careful not to bombard us all at once. After everyone had said their hellos, Mom came over and took JT, and once they were settled, Beckett led me over to one of the tables where Landry and Clay were sitting. As I sat down, he asked, "You want me to grab ya some food?"

"Yes, please, and a glass of punch?"

"Sure thing." He leaned down and kissed me before saying, "I'll be right back."

When he walked away, Landry leaned over to me and asked, "How ya making it?"

"Good. Really good." I looked around the room, watching as everyone ate and talked amongst themselves. "I still can't believe you guys did all this."

"I know it's a lot to take in, but this is just one of the many advantages of having such a great family," Landry replied. "We're there for each other. Celebrate the good times and support one another during the bad. It's hard to really understand until moments like these when you can experience it for yourself."

She was right. I hadn't fully understood what Clay and Beckett had been trying to tell me until that very moment. Seeing how they took care of their own and treated one another like family gave me a sense of peace I hadn't expected. I was glad that these men were going to be in our lives and that they would be there to share in the ups and downs of raising our son. I looked back over to Landry as I said, "I think I'm finally starting to get it."

"I knew you would." She gave me a wink as she said, "Welcome to the Fury family, Sis."

EPILOGUE

Six Months Later

I WAS STANDING IN THE LIVING ROOM, GATHERING UP everything we'd need to take with us to the church when Alyssa walked into the room wearing a knee-length black dress that hugged all her curves in just the right places. Damn. The woman looked absolutely incredible, making it impossible for me to keep my focus on the task at hand. When she started walking out of the room, I followed behind her. Once we were in the bedroom, I quickly locked the door behind us and smiled as I went over to the dresser where she was putting on her earrings. I slipped my arms around her waist and pulled her close as I started kissing along the curves of her neck.

"Beckett!" Alyssa fussed. "What are you doing?"

"I'm kissing you."

L. WILDER

"Ummm, I see that." She turned around to face me as she said, "I've got to finish getting ready."

"You still have plenty of time to get ready, babe. This won't take long."

"You're incorrigible."

"What can I say? I just can't help myself." I put one of my hands behind her neck as I pressed my mouth against hers. Her lips parted in surprise as I backed her up against the bedroom wall. I ran my tongue across her open lips before delving deep into her mouth. The kiss was urgent, full of need and uncontrollable want, and all her little whimpers and moans spurred me on even more. She gasped into my mouth when my hands grabbed her ass, pulling her hips closer to mine. A light hiss slipped through her lips when she felt my throbbing cock pressing against her. I lowered my mouth to her shoulder, trailing kisses along the curve of her neck as I whispered, "You're just too damn beautiful."

"Beckett," she breathed as she glanced over at the door.

"Don't worry. Your mother has JT," I assured her between kisses. "And it'll be at least a half hour before we have to leave."

"But I still need to put on my makeup and fix my hair." She placed her hands on my chest, pushing me back as she scolded, "And we're about to take our son to his christening ... *at a church ... with a preacher and bibles and holy water and—*"

"I've been to church, freckles. Know all about it." Smiling, I lowered my mouth to her ear as I whispered, "There's no sin in making love to my wife."

274

A few weeks ago, Alyssa and I had taken JT up to Gatlinburg, and with Landry and Hyde by our side, we said our vows. Alyssa and JT officially took my last name, making it known to everyone around that they were mine.

I began kissing her once again, and it didn't take long for all of her inhibitions to fall away and her desire to take over. She reached for my t-shirt until I pulled it over my head and tossed it to the floor.

I couldn't help but smile as she lifted her arms and waited for me to make my next move. I slipped my hands around her back, quickly unfastening the clasp of her dress before carefully lifting it over her head.

I let my hands roam over her bare skin, only stopping when I reached her full, round breasts. My fingers slipped inside the cups of her bra, pulling her breasts free. She licked her lips in anticipation as I took a step back, my eyes devouring every inch of her as she squirmed from the heat of my stare. A low growl rumbled in my throat as my hands ran up Alyssa's back and unhooked her bra. Her fingers gripped my shoulders when I lowered my head to her nipple and surrounded the sensitive flesh with my lips, nipping and sucking with just enough pressure. Her breath quickened as I moved to her other breast, and I couldn't take it a moment longer. I had to have her.

A rush of anticipation surged through me as I placed my palms on her outer thighs and slowly eased them up to her waist, hooking my thumbs in the band of her lace panties. Goosebumps prickled across her skin as I slowly dragged them down to her ankles. I eagerly watched as she stepped out of them with an inviting look on her face. My hands flew to her waist, and she gasped as I spun her to face the wall and pinned her wrists above her head. With my free hand, I took a hold of her hair, twirled the length around my hand, and gently tugged it as I whispered, "You have no idea what you do to me."

She bit her lip as she looked back at me over her shoulder, leaning slightly forward, just begging my fingertips to trail up the inside of her thigh. My hand slowly slid across her silky skin toward the wet heat, and her breath caught as my fingers drifted against her center, circling her sensitive clit. "Beckett!"

"That's it, baby."

I dropped my free hand to the buckle of my jeans, and Alyssa groaned with need as I continued to torment her with my fingers. Even though I knew the door was locked and her mother was in the nursery with JT, there was an added bit of excitement at the thought of getting caught. I quickly lowered my jeans and freed my throbbing erection before adjusting my grip on her wrists. I took a step towards her, sliding my hard, thick cock between her legs. She moaned passionately as she rocked her hips, gliding me against her center. I lowered myself between us, spreading her thighs, and positioned my cock at her entrance before thrusting inside with one hard, smooth stroke.

A growl escaped my lips as her body clenched down around me, her head falling back as she gasped in pleasure. I moved with slow, deliberate motions and relished the feeling of being buried deep inside her. I reached up, cupping her full breasts in my hands as I started to increase my pace, rolling my hips in a firm, steady rhythm while Alyssa desperately grasped at the wall.

I could feel her entire body start to tremble as I began thrusting into her over and over again. Her breathing became ragged as her climax approached. I lowered my hand between her legs, and a deep moan vibrated through her chest as I used the pad of my thumb to massage her clit. The rhythmic pressure overwhelmed her, sending her over the edge, as she cried, "Don't stop!"

The waves of her orgasm had her body clamping down on my cock like a fucking vise, making it impossible to hold back. I could feel it building inside of me as I continued to drive inside her. Her muffled groans of ecstasy echoed in my ear as I lowered my mouth to her shoulder, lightly biting her as I finally came deep inside of her. "Damn ... Gets better every fucking time."

"That it does." She turned to face me and slipped her arms around my neck. "Totally worth being a few minutes late."

"Glad you agree." I leaned down and kissed her briefly before saying, "You keep tempting me like this, then I'm gonna have to hit the gym."

"Oh, really? And why's that?"

"Only way I'm gonna be able to keep up."

"Yeah, right." She shook her head and started towards the bathroom. "If anyone needs to hit the gym, it's me. You're looking all hot and buff, while I'm still carrying around this extra baby weight."

"You're kidding me, right?" I zipped up my jeans as I walked into the bathroom. "You're fucking hot, and I happen to love every fucking inch of you."

She looked over at me with a bashful smile. "You're too sweet, Beckett."

"Hey, don't say that too loud," I fussed. "I have a reputation to uphold."

"Oh, yeah." She shook her head and laughed. "I forgot about that. I'll be sure to keep it under wraps."

We both got cleaned up and dressed, then gathered up JT along with everything we'd need and headed to the church. When we pulled up, I saw that most of my brothers had already arrived and were waiting for us inside. I was helping Alyssa get JT out of the car when Gus and Moose walked up. Gus was all smiles as he said, "Congratulations on your big day."

"Thanks, Prez." It was good to see that Gus was back to his old self. He was finally done with therapy, and his scars were fading more and more each day. While Moose had done a great job filling in for him, all the brothers were pleased that Gus was back where he belonged—leading Satan's Fury the way he always had. "We appreciate y'all coming out to be with us."

"Wouldn't miss it." Moose and Gus both gave Alyssa and me a hug, then Gus looked over to me and said, "Glad things worked out for you, brother. Nobody deserves it more."

"Thanks, brother. That means a lot coming from you."

"Wouldn't say it if it wasn't true." Gus motioned his hand towards the church. "We best not keep 'em waiting."

"We'll be right in."

When Gus and Moose turned to leave, Alyssa and I

grabbed the rest of JT's things, then headed inside to join the others. I had to admit, seeing all of my brothers sitting in that church wearing their cuts and sporting all their tattoos was a sight to behold. I could only imagine what the preacher was thinking as he stepped up to the pulpit. As we made our way further up the aisle, my brothers each greeted us, giving their congratulations and wishing us well, and as soon as we reached the front, Hyde and Landry came up to join us.

Once we were all in position, the preacher wasted no time getting started with the ceremony. As I listened to him welcome our family and friends, I looked over to Alyssa and JT and couldn't have been more proud. For so long, my brothers were all I had, and I'd always thought they were enough. But now, looking at my wife and son, I realized just what I'd been missing. With them and my brothers at my side, I finally had everything a man could ever want.

The End

ACKNOWLEDGMENTS

I am blessed to have so many wonderful people who are willing to give their time and effort to making my books the best they can be. Without them, I wouldn't't be able to breathe life into my characters and share their stories with you. To the people I've listed below and so many others, I want to say thank you for taking this journey with me. Your support means the world to me, and I truly mean it when I say appreciate everything you do. I love you all!

PA: Natalie Weston
Editing/Proofing: Lisa Cullinan-Editor, Rose Holub-Proofer, Honey Palomino-Proofer
Promoting: Amy Jones, Veronica Ines Garcia, Neringa Neringiukas, Whynter M. Raven
BETAS/Early Readers: Tanya Skaggs, Jo Lynn, Kaci Stewart, and Jessey Elliott
Street Team: All the wonderful members of Wilder's Women (You rock!)

Best Friend and biggest supporter: My mother (Love you to the moon and back.)

A short excerpt of Prospect: Satan's Fury MC-Memphis Book 8 is included in the following pages. Blaze, Shadow, Riggs, Murphy, Gunner, Gus, Rider and Prospect are also included in this Memphis series, and you can find them all on Amazon. They are all free with KU.

Be sure to check out my new series- The Ruthless Sinners.

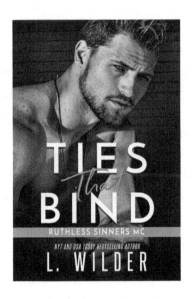

The Blurb:
    Trust.
    Loyalty.
    Family.

These are the ties that bind. As a Ruthless Sinner, I

live by those words--all the brothers do. We're family, our bonds stronger than blood, and as their sergeant at arms, my loyalty has never wavered--until the night they brought *her* to the clubhouse.

The red-headed beauty didn't belong there. It was her brother who'd betrayed us, but there she was, atoning for his sins.

I didn't want to hurt her.

I wanted to protect her, claim her as *my own*, but as secrets started to unfold, I was left with an impossible choice.

The ties that bind often come at a price--some more costly than others.

This is Hawk's story- Book 1 of L. Wilder's new Ruthless Sinners crossover series. Ties That Bind is a standalone MC romance with a group of bikers who will take you on a hell of a ride. They're foul-mouthed, possessive alphas who will do whatever it takes to protect their women. No cheating and a HEA.

You can purchase *Ties That Bind* on Amazon for .99 cents or it's FREE with KU!

VOLUME ONE

PROSPECT EXCERPT

PROLOGUE

I'd always been overly protective, especially when it came to my little sister, Alyssa. She was polar opposite of me. Where I was six-foot-eight and weighed two-ninety, Alyssa was five-foot-six in heels, and thin. Sure, a strong gust of wind might knock her skinny ass to the ground, but don't get me wrong, the girl was far from weak. Lyssa knew what she wanted and was willing to work hard for it, whether it was getting perfect grades or making the cheerleading squad. I respected her for that. Hell, there were times when I was even jealous of the fact. It seemed there was nothing that could stand in Alyssa's way, but when it did, I was there—just like I'd been on the night of Homecoming.

It was after eleven when she came knocking at my door, still wearing her homecoming dress, but now it was wrinkled and hanging off her shoulder. She'd been crying, and a thick line of black mascara had run down her cheek. "I fucked up, Clay ... like really, *really* fucked up."

"What the fuck, Lyssa." I took her by the arm and pulled her into my room, then closed the door behind her. "What the hell happened to you?"

"First, I need you to promise that you won't say anything." She looked up at me with her big, puppy-dog eyes filled with tears and pleaded. "This has to stay between us."

"Why do I get the feeling that I shouldn't agree?"

"Just promise me, Clay," she insisted. "I'm not saying another word until you do."

"Fine. I promise not to say anything," I grumbled. "Now, tell me what the fuck is going on."

She hesitated once again. I didn't understand why until she started, "So, you know tonight was Homecoming, right?"

"Yeah." Homecoming was just another way my sister and I were different. Even though it was my senior year, I couldn't have cared less about it, but it was the *only thing* Lyssa had been focused on for weeks. She was all excited that Lucas Brant, a senior and a varsity football player, had asked her not only to the dance but also to a big party afterwards. She was just a sophomore, so going with a senior was a huge deal—at least it was to her. Having no idea what had made her so upset, I asked, "What about it?"

"Well, the dance and all was fine," Lyssa's breaths became short and strained as she tried to explain, "until everything got all screwed up at the party at Janey Kay's house."

"Why? What happened?"

"It's hard to explain ... Everyone was there. I'd never

seen so many people, and they were all dancing and drinking."

"And what about you? Were you drinking?"

Her eyes dropped to the ground as she answered, "Yeah, I was. I didn't want to be the only one who wasn't joining in, you know?"

"I get it."

"Anyway, I had a couple of beers, but Lucas ... he drank quite a lot." She inhaled a pained breath before adding, "Much more than I realized."

"What the hell is that supposed to mean?"

"It's not *all* his fault, Clay. I should've known what he had in mind when he asked me to go upstairs with him, but I just wasn't thinking." She turned to look out the window and started to sob again. "I'm so stupid."

That familiar rage started to creep over me like a wildfire. "What. Happened!"

"I'm trying to tell you," she fussed.

"No, Lyssa, you're hemmin' and hawin' around. Just tell me what the hell happened!"

"After we got upstairs, he took me into one of the bedrooms, and we started to kiss. It was nice at first, but then I could tell he wanted something more." She turned to face me, and when I saw the anguish in her eyes, it gutted me. I had a feeling I knew exactly what had happened between her and Lucas but didn't want to believe it. I wanted to stop her from saying the words out loud but didn't get that chance. Tears were streaming down her face as she muttered, "I told him that I didn't want anything else to happen, but he didn't listen."

About to come unglued, I asked, "What do you mean 'he didn't listen'?"

"No matter how many times I told him no, he just kept pushing." Lyssa dropped her head into her hands, and I could barely hear her. "I should've never gone upstairs with him. I don't know what I was thinking. I should've known what he wanted, but I was just too stupid to see it."

"Stop that shit right now! None of this was your fault. This was all on him. Every damn bit of it."

"You're wrong! This is just as much my fault as it is his. I never should've gone into that bedroom with him. I know what it means when a guy like Lucas wants to be alone with a girl, especially at a party. I knew there was a good chance that we'd be fooling around, and I think a part of me was actually hoping he'd want me like that." She wiped the tears from her eyes. "All my friends were so jealous that I was going to Homecoming with not only a senior, but with the best-looking senior in school."

"You're fucking kidding me with this shit, right?"

"Lucas could've asked a hundred different girls and not a single one of them would've given a second thought to having sex with him tonight." I couldn't believe my ears when she added, "I should've been happy that someone like him would even choose to be with me."

"Dammit, Lyssa! That asshole fucking raped you!" As I looked down at my sister, so distraught and full of heartache, I found myself thinking about a conversation I'd had with my father. He was truck driver, and it was tough on him being away from home all the time. Knowing he couldn't do it himself, he'd asked me to look after my mother and sister, to protect them in a way that he couldn't. It was up to me to fix this thing, so I didn't resist when the rage rose to the surface and took over as I grabbed my keys off the dresser. I stormed towards the door and told her, "I'm going to fucking kill him."

"Clay, stop!" she pleaded and rushed over to me. "Don't you get it? No one can find out about this. If they do, it'll ruin me!"

"What the hell are you talking about?"

"You know how people can be ... how they twist things around and shift the blame." She ran her hand through her disheveled hair and continued, "No matter how it really played out, everyone will think it was my fault ... that I brought it on myself. I don't think I could handle that."

"So, you're just going to let this asshole get away with raping you?"

"I don't have a choice."

"There's always a choice, sis." I took a minute to consider everything she'd said, and even though I knew there was some truth in it, there was no way in hell I could let Lucas Brant get away with what he'd done to my sister. No matter what she said, there was no way I was going to let this go. I couldn't. I took a step towards her and pulled her into my arms, hugging her tightly as I whispered, "I'm going to take care of this, Lyssa."

"But ..."

"Don't worry. No one will ever know what happened," I assured her. "I'll make sure of it."

I held her a moment longer, then turned and left the room. I heard her calling my name, but I continued out the front door and towards my truck. In a matter of minutes I was on my way to Janey Kay's house, and all I could think about was that dickhead's hands on my little sister while she pleaded with him to stop. The thought sickened me, making me want to rip him apart limb from limb.

When I pulled up, the party was still going strong. The music was blaring as I started up the steps of the two-story colonial home. There were tall white columns along the front porch and an overdone flowered wreath on the front door. As soon as I stepped inside, I couldn't help but grimace at the mess: beer cans and bottles strewn all over the place, tables and chairs turned over, and drunken teenagers wobbling around in an inebriated state as they tried to keep themselves from falling. Several were completely blistered, but I didn't give a fuck about any of them. There was only one person on my mind—Lucas Brant.

When I spotted Michael, one of Brant's friends, walking in my direction, I charged towards him, then grabbed the collar of his t-shirt and twisted it in my fist. "Where's Brant?"

"What the fuck, man?" he scowled.

"Gonna ask one more time." I gave him a hard shove, pinning him up against the wall. "Where the hell is he?"

"Last time I saw him, he was out back by the fire."

I released my hold on him, then turned and stormed through the living room. When I walked out the back door, I spotted Lucas standing by the fire, bullshitting with several of the other guys on the football team. I was filled with so much blinding rage as I headed towards him that everyone else faded from my sight. Without giving him a chance to prepare for my attack, I grabbed him by the shoulder, whipped him around to face me, and then plowed my fist into his jaw. He started to stumble back, so I grabbed the collar of his t-shirt and punched him again and again. With a *thud*, he landed on the ground, and I took the opportunity to pin him down with my knees. Once I was sure he couldn't budge, I started in on him again. A couple of his buddies tried to get me off him, but their efforts were all in vain. Nothing was going to stop me from making Brant pay for putting his fucking hands on my sister. Determined to make a lasting impression, I kept hammering away at him. It wasn't long before Lucas's entire face was bloody, bruised, and swollen, and he was barely conscious. Sensing he was about to blackout, I wrapped my hands around his throat, gripping him tightly as I leaned forward and placed my mouth close to his ear.

My voice was low and ominous as I whispered, "If you breathe a word about what happened tonight between you and Alyssa, I'll end you once and for all. You got that?"

He managed to nod, but I didn't remove my hands from his throat. I couldn't. Every time I tried to let go, I'd see Lyssa's face and the anguish in her eyes as she stood there crying in my room. I knew I should stop. I was reaching the point of no return, but I couldn't pull myself together. The rage was just too much. I kept tightening my grip, slowly squeezing the life out of him. Thankfully, Michael lunged towards me, using all of his weight to push me off Lucas and forcing me to release my grip on him. Before I had a chance to react, several of the others jumped in to help Michael—each of them kicking and punching me wherever they could land a hit. I tried to get back up on my feet, plowing away at each of them like a crazed lunatic, but I couldn't get my footing. There were just too many of them. With one hard blow to the jaw, my head reared back and everything went dark.

Just as I was starting to come around, the faint sounds of police sirens were heading towards Janey's house. I was still sprawled out on the ground by the fire as kids rushed by, scrambling to get the hell out of Dodge before the cops arrived. I knew they'd be there for me, so I tried to get to my feet, but with my head spinning, I only ended up falling on my ass. Just as I was about to try again, Michael appeared in my line of sight with two officers at his side. As he pointed in my direction, I could hear him shouting. "That's him. That's the guy you're looking for." They hardly had time to react before he started in again, "He's the one who attacked Lucas for no fucking reason, and he nearly killed him! Lucas was barely conscious when they took him to the ER."

"Okay, kid. I'm gonna need you to settle down. We've got this," one of the officers warned.

The two cops started towards me, and once they approached, one of them extended his hand. As he helped me to my feet, he asked, "You got a name, son?"

"Clay Hanson."

"All right, Clay. Why don't you tell me what happened here tonight?"

"Nothing," I snapped.

"Now, you and I both know that isn't true." He almost

sounded like he was being sincere when he said, "I can't help you unless you tell me what really went down here tonight."

"Already told ya ... Nothing to tell."

"Have it your way."

Pissed that I refused to answer him, the cop reached behind and pulled out a pair of handcuffs. He turned me around and slapped them over my wrists while reading me my rights. Once he was done, I was led over to the squad car and put inside. Just as he was shutting the door, Michael yelled, "You're going down, Hanson!"

When Michael said those words to me, neither of us had any idea how true they really were. I got off easy when Brant didn't press charges, but my luck ended there. I struggled to get a grip on the anger that erupted when I went after Lucas. I couldn't suppress the rage, the need for vengeance, and all the other intense emotions I was feeling that night. Instead, they lingered on the surface like a parasite, leaving me feeling completely exposed as it waited to rear its ugly head once again.

Unfortunately, I didn't have to wait long for that to happen. Without ever knowing why I'd had the altercation with Lucas, my father's semi-truck was hit by a drunk driver, and he was killed instantly. The injustice of his death seemed to bring out the worst in me, and I started on a downward spiral. I completely lost myself. I wasn't thinking about my mother or sister. Hell, I wasn't thinking of anyone or anything. I just sank deeper into my own madness, finding trouble at every turn: drinking, fighting, and eventually more trouble with the law.

I was fucking up in every way possible, so it shouldn't

have come as a surprise when Viper, my uncle and president of the Ruthless Sinners MC, decided to step in. Knowing I was making a mess of my life, he reached out to his buddy Gus, the president of Satan's Fury, then sent me to Memphis to spend some time with the brothers at their clubhouse. He hoped that I'd find my way with them. Turns out, he was right.

1

CHAPTER 1

"It's not just about knowing the brothers' names and their position in the club. You gotta know *everything* about them," Rider explained. "Their backgrounds ... where they grew up, jobs they've had, past experiences. What their life was like before joining the club ... and after—the good, the bad, and the ugly."

Rider had been chosen by Gus to be my sponsor. It was his job to guide me through prospecting and make sure I knew everything that would be expected of me during the process. Feeling overwhelmed by what he'd just informed me, I turned to him and asked, "I hear what you're saying, but I don't get why it matters so much. I mean, what difference does it make if I know what jobs Blaze had as a kid?"

"It's knowing what your family is all about," Rider answered firmly. "Knowing that Cyrus and T-Bone were here with Gus when he first started up the Memphis chapter and how they helped him find the clubhouse and build our numbers. And knowing that when our brother

Runt was killed, Shadow was the one who stepped up to the plate and saved our asses, earning our vote as the club's new enforcer. It helps you understand where the brothers have been ... where they're going. It gives you some insight to what makes them tick."

"I get that, but how am I supposed to find out all this shit?"

"You listen ... not only to what they say, but what they don't say." Rider looked me directly in the eye. "You'll get it. It's just going to take time."

I hoped Rider was right. I wanted to think that I had what it took to earn my patch, but there were times when I wasn't so sure. If I wanted to be considered family to these men, I had a lot of work to do, and it wasn't going to be easy. There were over thirty members I had to learn about, all the while doing the other crazy bullshit that came along with prospecting. But I wasn't complaining. I'd finally found the life I wanted, and I wasn't going to let anything stand in my way. I gave Rider a slight nod and answered, "I'll do whatever I gotta do."

"I know you will." He lifted his beer. "I'll help where I can."

"I'd appreciate that, brother."

Just as the words left my mouth, Darcy, Rider's ol' lady, came walking into the living room. I could still remember the first time we'd met. I'd only been in Memphis for a few days when the brothers hired her to be the garage's custom painter. There weren't many women who could handle working in a shop full of strong-willed bikers, but she managed it like a pro. Darcy and Rider had grown up in the same small town and had history. It didn't take long for them to pick up where they left off, and they'd been inseparable since. Rider and I were sitting on the sofa when she walked over with a concerned expression on her face. "You know, we could go to the Smoking Gun with Murphy and the others tonight. I can hit one of Brannon's shows another time."

"I'm good with going to Neil's to see him tonight," Rider told her. "With the crowd that'll be at the Smoking Gun, it's not like they'll miss us."

"I know, but I don't want to disappoint Riley."

"I already talked to Murphy. It's all good, babe."

Looking relieved, she smiled and said, "Good. I just wanted to be sure."

"What's the big deal with the Smoking Gun anyway?"

Rider turned to me as he explained, "Riley and the owner of the bar, Grady, are first cousins and best friends, and he's having some big shindig tonight for the playoffs. I'm kind of glad we decided not to go. I wasn't looking forward to fighting that crowd."

"Okay, then I guess it's about time for us to head over to Neil's. Brannon's show starts at eight," Darcy said.

Taking our cue, Rider and I got up and followed her outside to our bikes. I waited as she got settled behind him, then we both fired up our engines and headed downtown. As we made our way towards Neil's bar, I was feeling pretty good about things in my life, and I found myself thinking of the day Viper had come to me about leaving Nashville and staying with Satan's Fury. I couldn't blame him for wanting to get me out of town. I was a ticking time-bomb. Every time something didn't go my way, I'd blow up and do something stupid—get into a fight or be laid-out drunk. When I landed myself in trouble with the law again, my mother freaked out and called Viper for help.

I KNEW the second I walked out of that jailhouse and found him standing in the parking lot he was pissed. I wasn't surprised. I'd fucked up once again, and he was the one who'd pick up the pieces so my mother wouldn't have to.

Once we were inside his truck, Viper turned to me with a fierce expression. "This shit has got to stop, Clay."